1902.59.0508

BOOKS IN THE CROFTVERSE

THE BLUE WOLF SERIES
Blue Curse
Blue Shadow
Blue Howl
Blue Venom
* More to Come *

THE PROF CROFT SERIES
Book of Souls
Demon Moon
Blood Deal
Purge City
Death Mage
Black Luck
Power Game

BLUE HOWL

A Blue Wolf Novel

by
Brad Magnarella

Blue Howl
A Blue Wolf Novel

Copyright © 2018 by Brad Magnarella

www.bradmagnarella.com

All rights reserved. No part of this book may be reproduced in any form by any electronic or mechanical means including photocopying, recording, or information storage and retrieval without permission in writing from the author.

ISBN-13: 978-172661-398-9

Cover art by Ivan Sevic

Wolf symbol by Orina Kafe

Second Edition

Printed in the U.S.A.

For the good people of Old Harbor

1

I stood on a high mountain ridge and scanned the terrain. Beneath an enormous moon, a misty blue landscape of dense forests stretched away to distant ranges, all wild, all mine.

I sniffed the chill air. When the wind shifted, the scent hit my nostrils again. Miles below, something large was moving through a meadow. My vibrating senses sharpened toward the source. I could smell the wet hair and mud-caked hooves, could hear the plodding footfalls, could feel the blood thickening with the coming winter. Above my tightening stomach, my heart beat strong and fast. I reared back my head and released a booming howl.

The hunt was on.

As my call echoed throughout the valley, a haunting chorus came back. My pack. I led the charge down the mountain in powerful bounds. Scree and chunks of earth flew from my clawed feet. Soon trees flashed past. The rest of the pack converged in my wake, forming a mass of panting, hungry predators.

In the valley, I broke into a meadow bisected by a slow, winding river. Our prey, a bull moose, had waded into the water, and now craned its neck. An enormous rack framed its startled face. For an instant, I saw my pack as the moose did: a range of gold eyes glinting through the trees, masses of blue hair and hulking muscles taking shape around them.

The moose turned and thrashed for the far shore. I lowered my head and sped my pace.

Ice-cold water broke around me as I plunged into the river. The wolves at my back barked in excitement. The moose reached the shore and struggled from the water. In three great lunges I was across and burying my teeth into its flank. Blood filled my mouth in an intoxicating rush. The moose let out a hoarse scream and swung its rack around, but the rest of the pack had arrived to pile on.

I released the moose's flank and went for its neck. With a crunching bite and tear, the hunt ended. Wolves leapt away as the massive animal toppled onto its side, the rack coming to a ponderous rest. I warned the excited pack back with snarls before moving in for my meal. The moose's adrenaline-laced flesh filled my stomach and hit my blood like a dose of high-octane fuel.

When I reached the beast's engorged heart, I turned in search of my mate. She should have been beside me, sharing the meal. From a ring five feet away, the wolves peered back at me with eager eyes.

Where is she? I demanded through our connection.

The wolves looked at one another and parted. I turned back to the moose, seized the heart in my teeth, and twisted until the giant mass of muscle came free from the chest. The prize.

I turned to present it to my mate.

Only my mate wasn't a wolf. She stood before the pack, one hand hiding the bare fold between her legs, the other arm shielding her breasts. Her pale frame shivered in the moonlight. She looked from the heart to my face with dark, fearful eyes. A dazed understanding seemed to take hold.

"Jason?" she whispered.

In the corner of my animal mind, something kicked to life.

Daniela?

I sat bolt upright in bed, harsh breaths flaring my nostrils. The dream again, the same damned one I'd been having for the past two weeks. But it wasn't my dream. I was dreaming for the Blue Wolf, only returning to myself at the very end when Daniela appeared.

My bed creaked as I swung my large legs off the side. The digital clock on my nightstand read 3:10 a.m. I ran a taloned hand between my peaked ears and wiped my muzzle.

The dreams had begun with the arrival of fall, when cold air began blowing down from the mountains at night, buffeting our desert compound. That seemed to stir something in the Blue Wolf, ancient memories of hunting the mountain ranges of Waristan, maybe.

That wouldn't explain the moose, though, which probably had more to do with the images I'd been studying—satellite photos of a town in Canada where the Legion team could be sent any day.

Still excited from the dream hunt, and the fear that Daniela had learned my secret, my heart thudded in my chest. Knowing I wasn't going to get any more sleep, I pulled on a pair of camos and left my suite. The building was dead silent as I made my way down the main corridor, but when I stepped into the chill desert night, I caught a familiar scent. At the end of the row of chairs in front of the barracks, I found our program manager bundled in a blanket.

"What are you doing up?" I grunted.

Moonlight winked from Sarah McKinnon's glasses as she turned to face me. If my sudden appearance startled her, it didn't show on her flat expression.

"I woke up and couldn't get back to sleep," she replied in her clipped voice.

"Same here." I pulled a chair from the line and sat angled toward her. Following our return from Mexico about two months before, I had been hoping I would see a more human side of her. We'd been through a lot that mission: me sparing her from a vampire attack, her keeping Director Beam at bay so the rest of the team and I could complete the mission. She had even opened up about a zombie attack that had claimed her parents when she was a girl. But here at the training compound, her walls had gone back up. Our heated disagreements over whether Olaf Kowalski was living or nonliving probably hadn't helped.

She looked at me another moment before returning her gaze to the distant mountains. A large moon stood above them, recalling my dream. *Not my dream,* I reminded myself, forcing it back down.

"Any update on the Canada job?" I asked, knowing she'd been in recent contact with Director Beam. Centurion's computers had picked up a pattern of attacks that summer suggestive of werewolves. We were told to have the Legion team ready, but we'd heard almost nothing since then.

Sarah shook her head. "Centurion reps are still dealing with the mayor of the affected town. He's insisting he can handle the problem locally. It sounds like he's in denial."

Or unable to afford Centurion's price tag, I thought bitterly.

"I have an exercise planned for tomorrow, just in case," I said. "I'd like to run it at night, so why don't we shift the lectures to the morning."

Sarah nodded without comment. I stood and strode several paces from the barracks, my clawed feet digging into sand. The hard-packed layer underneath was still warm from the day's heat. Though I paced in a slow circle, I remained tense. My lupine muscles wanted to chase something, my teeth to rend flesh. I needed to get the dream out of my system.

"Think I'm gonna take a few laps around the perimeter."

"Why are you so concerned about Olaf?" Sarah asked suddenly.

I stopped and turned. I was standing in almost the exact spot where I'd asked Olaf why he had joined us on the final push in El Rosario. When he teared up, I suspected he was more *living* than Centurion was letting on.

Maybe because the question had taken me by surprise, my answer emerged without thought. "Because I can't stand the idea of someone being trapped inside something he's not."

I waited for Sarah to respond, but she only seemed to take in what I'd said.

I fell to my hands and bounded away.

2

The following evening, I called my teammates together in the armory. Except for Takara, dressed in ninja leathers, everyone was outfitted in Centurion's patented digital camos and tactical vests. Olaf plodded up with a large MP88 in his grip and stood beside Takara and Sarah. I waved over the team's tech wiz, Rusty, and our magic-user, Yoofi, who were making last-minute adjustments to their gear. They hurried toward us with apologies and took their places among the others.

"All right," I said. "Tonight's exercise will be a little different. One, we won't be facing off against each other. And two, we'll be using live ammo." I jabbed a thumb toward the mock town that was our battle simulation area. "There are six creatures out there from Yoofi's realm. The second Yoofi sets them free, they'll be coming after us."

"Creatures?" Rusty cut in. "As in big, hungry things?"

"Very much so," Yoofi answered proudly. Instead of a pack, the Congolese priest wore a long brown coat to hold his many flasks and cigars, as well as a wooden idol to Dabu. It was by his god's consent we'd been able to borrow the creatures in the first place. I had consulted Prof Croft to ensure we could bring them into our plane without causing problems. With some well-placed wards—or *lingos*, as Yoofi called them—we were good to go.

"Why don't you brief the team on what they are," I said to Yoofi.

"Yes, the beasts are called *ekalamanga*. That means *death dogs*." He giggled for no apparent reason, which was something I'd gotten used to. "They have two heads and manes like the lions. Dabu uses them as watchdogs in his underworld. Ooh, very mean. You should see the way they look at me when I am down there. Like they want to make a meal of Yoofi."

"And be warned,'" I said. "They're a solid level above the zombie mutts we faced in El Rosario."

"Yes, very clever too," Yoofi added. "They can move without a sound, so you do not hear them coming. And when they work in packs, they are most deadly. Yes, most deadly."

"Sound like werewolves," Rusty muttered, scratching a mutton-chop sideburn.

"Exactly the point," I said. "Instead of silver-laced ammo, though, we'll be packing salt." I gestured toward the magazines I'd had him prepare and array across the tables. "Remember Sarah's lecture on spectral creatures? That's essentially the form the death dogs take up here. With enough salt exposure, they'll disperse back to their realm. Questions?"

"Yeah," Rusty said. "If they're so deadly, how does Dabu handle them."

"With a big staff," Yoofi answered, holding up his. "Many of Dabu's brothers and sisters are very jealous of Dabu. They want the underworld for themselves. Dabu knows this. But he also knows the gods do not want to face the *ekalamanga*, and he keeps thousands down there."

He giggled some more.

"All right, we'll be working in split teams of three," I said. "Yoofi and Sarah, you'll be with me. Takara will lead Olaf and Rusty."

Takara's curtain of black hair glistened as she walked forward, picked up a mag, and slotted it into her M4. As Olaf began loading his MP88, I watched his eyes, but nothing moved inside them.

Rusty joined Takara and Olaf in a sulk. "Team Personality," he muttered.

"The objective is to clear the simulation area of the threat," I said. "Remember what we've been practicing and try not to get bit."

Rusty's helmeted head whipped around to face me. "Why? What'll happen?"

"It'll hurt like hell."

"Ready?" I asked my split team. In my enhanced vision, Sarah and Yoofi seemed to glow. Slivers of light edged their equipment and night vision oculars. Sarah clutched her M4 and nodded while Yoofi moved his bladed staff to one hand to give me an enthusiastic thumbs up.

"Team One ready," I broadcast.

"Team Two ready," came Takara's voice from inside my earpiece.

"All right," I said. "Yoofi's going to set the dogs free in three ... two ... one ..." I pointed at him.

He raised his staff and spoke an incantation. My insides turned squeamish as the obsidian blade warped the surrounding air. When Yoofi spoke a final word, energy pulsed out. It rippled across the mock town to where the death dogs were being held in the town square. I half expected to hear a riot of barking, but the released creatures were eerily silent.

When I cocked an eyebrow at Yoofi, he nodded.

"They're out," I radioed. "Commence exercise."

I led with my MP88's three barrels, one each for the assault rifle, grenade launcher, and flamethrower. Sarah and Yoofi flanked me. Across the mock town I could hear Olaf's plodding footfalls and Rusty's battle rattle. Nothing from Takara, of course. And nothing from the dogs. With the backdraft from Dabu's realm wafting around us—a mixture of fermented alcohol and stale cigar smoke—my nose wasn't picking them up either.

As we advanced down the dusty lane, I scanned the surrounding buildings, my hairs prickling with the anticipation of conflict. I didn't have to wait long. I felt them before I heard them.

"Your six!" I shouted, wheeling.

Two of the death dogs had stalked around behind us and now bore down on Sarah and Yoofi. Tongues lolled from the two-headed beast's slavering mouths. Manes of stringy black hair streamed from their ragged ears. Their rangy builds lent the dogs speed, while their large paws and fang-crammed jaws endowed them with lethality.

I forced myself to remain back, wanting to see how my teammates responded.

Gunfire exploded from Sarah's M4, while the air around Yoofi's blade swirled with fresh magic. Salt rounds stitched a line across one of the dog's twin faces and blew out an eye. With a pained yelp, the dog veered away and disappeared down a side lane.

Yoofi shouted something in Congolese. A spiraling black bolt discharged from his staff and landed in front of the other dog. The dog reared from the explosion of sand and smoke. Sarah sighted on the creature and released another burst. The dog howled with both heads as salt rounds tore open its side. It crumpled to the ground, black smoke billowing through its ribs. The dog was coming apart. Sarah unloaded more rounds until the wind whisked away what remained of the dog's form, leaving a scattering of black ashes.

The entire encounter had lasted mere seconds.

"Well done," I said. But instinct told me the two hadn't arrived alone.

I peered up just as another death dog jumped down from the rooftop above me. I started to bring my MP88 into firing position, then dropped it onto its sling. The wolf in me wanted to brawl.

I shot a fist toward the incoming faces. My knuckles cracked across one set of jaws and then the other, knocking the creature off course. It crashed down beside me and scrambled to its feet. I noticed Sarah and Yoofi watching us, weapons readied, looking for an opening.

"Perimeter security," I growled. "I've got this one."

They turned and monitored the lanes and buildings around me. Across the town, Rusty shouted. Bursts of gunfire followed. It sounded like Team Two had met the enemy as well. I trained my attention on my opponent. Two sets of fiery orange eyes glared at me above muzzles with lips curled back to show their fangs. A lion-like tail flicked between the creature's bony haunches. Every time a drop of saliva struck the ground, steam hissed up.

"C'mon, buddy," I said. "Make your move."

When the dog sprang at my chest, my hands swallowed its front paws and twisted so the dog was beneath me. We landed hard. Slamming a forearm into its right head, I took its other neck in my jaws and bit down. A foul taste of death and ash filled my mouth. The dog choked on a savage bark as I tore out its throat. I did the same to its other head and rose, my heart slamming with the thrill of domination.

Smoke billowed from the dog's wounds, but I could see the creature reconstituting itself. I brought my MP88 around and filled the beast with salt rounds until it came apart for good. When I looked over, I caught Yoofi peering back at me with saucer-round eyes. He looked away quickly.

I swore at myself for going full beast in a team exercise. It wasn't befitting a captain and set a poor example for the others. The Blue Wolf had his place, but I needed to command as Jason Wolfe.

Across the compound, the shouts and gunfire tapered off.

"Two eliminated here," I radioed. "How are you doing?"

"Three eliminated," Takara answered, a note of haughtiness in her voice. Though we had gotten past the hostility that had colored our first weeks together, Takara continued to act like we were in competition. I wasn't sure how much came from the US bombing of Hiroshima, her hometown, and how much from an innate need to win. The second wasn't a bad attribute to have in a teammate—as long as she didn't backslide into insubordination again.

"All right, so one left," I said. "We had brief engagement, but it escaped east. Let's perform a sweep like we practiced. Takara and I will access the rooftops and coordinate movement."

"Wouldn't a drone be easier?" Rusty asked. *"One I could be manning?"*

"We can't always depend on having a drone overhead."

"Yeah, well, no one told me these things were going to have slobber hot enough to boil a damned egg." Rusty was used to working in an office off the armory, managing anything with a circuit board, including the commo equipment and drones. But increasingly I'd been putting him through the same drills and exercises as the others so he could step in if needed.

"Move out," I ordered.

I looked back at Sarah and Yoofi to check their spacing and then scaled the side of the building the last death dog had jumped down from. At two stories, I had a good view of the town. The only structure taller was the three-story municipal building that stood over the square. Across the way, I could see Takara settling onto a rooftop, her M4 in firing position as she scanned the surrounding streets. I searched my sector, but there was no sign of the final death dog.

I was wondering if it had returned to Dabu's realm with the others, when Rusty cried, *"Damn!"* The outburst was followed by the popping of semi-automatic fire. I heard the deeper thudding of Olaf's MP88 join in. The sounds from both weapons ended abruptly.

"Contact?" I asked.

"For a second," Rusty answered. I could all but hear his heart beating through his words. *"Then the thing disappeared in a cloud of smoke."*

I nodded and lowered my MP88. "That's all of them, then."

"No," Olaf said in his Eastern European monotone. *"Rounds did not strike dog."*

"Say again? You didn't hit it?"

"No," Takara replied. *"And neither did Rusty or I."*

I was considering what that meant when Yoofi hollered. I looked down to find the death dog seizing his forearm in one set of jaws and his staff in the other. How in the hell had it crossed the town that fast? I took aim at one of the dog's heads. Before I could squeeze off a shot, the dog vanished in a sudden burst of smoke. Yoofi remained behind, steam rising from the contact.

"You all right?" I called down.

"I think so," he answered through gritted teeth. "But, owie, that hurt!"

"Watch the saliva. Like Rusty observed, it's boiling hot."

"What happened?" Takara radioed.

"The dog showed up over here," I said.

"I thought only one remained."

"It must be jumping back and forth to its realm."

And if its strategy was to use guerrilla tactics, then it was time to adapt.

"Everyone to the town square," I ordered. "Backs to the main building. Cover the square in sectors. Hit anything that drops in. I'll provide overwatch from the roof. Takara, take the rooftop across the square."

We moved into position, Takara and I going from rooftop to rooftop—her flying, me leaping—and covering our teammates until they were breaking into the town square. Rusty and Olaf took up positions at the municipal building's corners, while Yoofi and Sarah stood in front. With a final jump, I landed on a ledge running around the municipal building's upper level, my talons punching into mortar. From there, I scaled my way to the top. A gust of cold air hit my face as I swung my legs over the retaining wall and scanned the streets.

I brought up Yoofi on a secure line. "Are you sure your lingos can keep this thing inside the town?"

"I think so," he answered.

"You think so," I repeated dryly.

I preferred certainty—I didn't want the dog getting out into the larger base—but the creature had pegged me and my teammates as a threat. Something told me it wouldn't try to escape before dealing with us first.

With that thought, black smoke burst around Olaf. He grunted as the death dog appeared and seized his throat with one head and his trigger hand with the other. With a grunt, Olaf staggered backwards.

Takara and I took aim, but the dog disappeared—only to reappear at Sarah's side. As Olaf dropped to the ground, the dog buried its heads into Sarah's left arm. By the time I switched aim, the dog had left Sarah and, in a fresh explosion of smoke, was taking Yoofi to the ground.

It's going down the line, I realized.

The rifle barrel of my MP88 moved past Yoofi and steadied on Rusty.

When I heard Takara pop off a shot, I pictured the round breaking harmlessly through smoke. I took it as a cue to squeeze off my own shot. My target was the space immediately in front of Rusty.

Sure enough, that's where the death dog manifested next. My incendiary round drove into its head and exploded in a flash of salt, fire, and death-dog matter. The creature's broken body wobbled backwards. Takara, who had been denied the decisive shot a moment before, finished it off with a tight burst of gunfire.

When the dog broke apart in a final dispersion of smoke, I keyed my radio. "Mission accomplished."

Time to check the casualties. I dropped from the top of the building and landed in a plume of dust. Takara seemed to pedal air as she descended from her own perch and crossed the square. She came to a running stop in front of Olaf. I went over to Sarah. She had removed her helmet and was rubbing the arm where the dog had bitten down.

"How are you?" I asked.

"Deep contusions, but no bleeding or breaks," she answered as if she were diagnosing someone else.

"My bad. I didn't know they'd be able to appear and disappear."

But Sarah was shaking her head. "No, that was good. We won't always know what we'll be facing in the field."

"You're starting to sound like me. I like that."

Her lips twitched into a semi smile, which I liked even more.

Yoofi limped over, steam rising from his staff. "Ooh, that

makes me remember how much I hate Dabu's dogs," he said. "So mean." He looked from Sarah to Olaf. "Who needs healing magic?"

"I'm good," Rusty said.

Though our tech approached in a swagger, I picked up a sour bite of fear coming off him. To be fair, having a massive two-headed dog intent on ripping out your lungs manifest right in front of you was enough to rattle anyone. "Nice shooting, boss," he said. "I owe you a Bud."

"Heal Sarah," I told Yoofi. "And then see what you have left for Olaf."

Though Olaf remained down, he possessed innate healing abilities, thanks to Centurion's tissue regeneration protocol. I waited until smoke began spilling from Yoofi's staff onto Sarah's arm before heading over to where Takara was still checking out Olaf. I could hear the big man breathing, but it was coming in choppy gasps. I took a knee beside him.

"You all right, buddy?" I asked.

"Crushed windpipe," Takara answered for him. Though she wasn't a doctor, I trusted her assessment. Crushing an opponent's windpipe was among her many aptitudes as a ninjitsu-trained assassin.

Olaf's pale eyes shifted to mine. "Did we do well?" he managed, the words sounding like they'd been stomped on.

Ever the soldier. But who's in control of him?

Rising, I answered loud enough for everyone to hear. "Team Two eliminated three dogs at first contact, and my team eliminated two. My team also maintained good movement, shooting, and communication throughout. Takara?"

"Mine as well," she said. "Even Rusty."

"Thanks for the honorable mention," he muttered.

"And against an opponent that was savvier than expected," I said. "Everyone passed. That's the result of eight weeks of drilling and hard work. I'm proud of you guys. Take the rest of the weekend off. We'll review the video Monday morning."

Rusty's face lit up and he chucked his helmet into the air.

"Las Vegas, here I come!" he whooped.

3

I met Sarah as she was stepping out of the infirmary where we'd taken Olaf earlier. She had shed her tactical vest and pack and was wearing a white lab coat with a stethoscope hung around her neck.

"How's he doing?" I asked. Yoofi had applied healing magic to him—the first time he'd ever done so—but it hadn't taken, possibly because of the unique makeup of Olaf's non-living tissue.

"He's on recovery protocol now. Twenty-four hours bed rest."

"He's not in any pain?"

"Olaf doesn't feel pain."

The wolf in me bristled at the challenge in her tone. "I'm still not convinced."

"He forewent a week of training to be tested," she reminded me. "The EEGs and functional MRIs—"

"Yeah, I know what the report said," I cut in. "You gave me a copy. But it doesn't explain why he was determined to join our final push in El Rosario despite being injured and a potential liability. That would have gone against his training. When I questioned him, he teared up."

"That's going to happen."

"What, tears?"

"Emotional displays. They wouldn't even need a thought to incite them. A random discharge of neural activity could set them off. Without higher brain centers to override—"

"Sure. Olaf's just a ball of emotions."

"I said *random*, not frequent," Sarah replied stiffly.

"So you think the taps just happened to open when I implied he'd wanted to make up for the bombing in Waristan? C'mon, Sarah, that's a huge stretch. I think even you know that."

"It's possible."

"So is hell freezing over."

We were rehashing an old argument, just using different words, but I wanted her to hear the improbability of what she was saying.

She shifted her stance. "No one's doubting what you saw, Captain. I'm prepared to send Olaf back for testing as often as you request it, but I can only base my conclusions on the reports."

"And you trust them?"

"What's the alternative?"

And that was the fundamental problem. While I relied on instincts and subtle cues, even more so since becoming the Blue

Wolf, Sarah depended on intellectual analysis and hard data. She could believe what I was saying, but couldn't accept it as a basis for decision-making.

I grunted. On the topic of Olaf, we were at an impasse.

Sarah looked at me another moment, then stepped past me, her ponytail lashing the collar of her lab coat as she headed toward the compound's main building, where her office was.

I entered the infirmary and made my way to Olaf's room. A rectangle of light grew over him as I opened the door. Sarah had restrained his wrists and ankles to the bed frame with metal cuffs. The restraints were to keep him from disturbing the various monitoring lines and infusion tubes attached to him, but the sight kicked my heart into a claustrophobic gallop. Olaf, who had been staring at the ceiling, rolled his eyes toward me.

"Hey," I said. "How are you doing?"

"I am fine," he answered, his voice still raw from the damage to his throat. Despite what Sarah had said, it sounded painful.

I eyed the bandages over his Adam's apple, where Sarah had had to perform minor surgery. I saw the dog gripping his neck in one of its powerful jaws and shaking him. How necessary had the exercise been? I wondered now. A way to challenge my teammates, as I'd told them? Told myself? Or had I wanted to give the Blue Wolf the fight he'd been craving ever since learning we could be facing werewolves?

I had forgone the use of drones or access to the live surveillance feeds this exercise. Important not to depend on them, yeah, but also a good excuse to hunt, to lead my pack to the kill.

"How are you?" Olaf asked, breaking up the thought.

My eyes had drifted to the monitors over the head of his bed, but now they dropped back to my teammate. I couldn't remember him asking about someone else's status before.

"Why do you ask?"

Olaf stared back at me. His dull eyes could have been implants.

"Were you worried about me and the others?" I prompted.

He blinked once, then continued staring. Still nothing. At last his eyes rolled back toward the ceiling. On the monitors, his abnormally low vital signs hadn't changed at all. I sat with him, trying to come up with a surefire way to test whether he was still human. Before long, I heard someone enter the infirmary. My nose caught Sarah's scent before she spoke.

"Jason?" she called.

I craned my neck toward the door. "In here."

"Director Beam's on the line," she said, entering the room. She looked between me and Olaf with a taut expression, as if bracing for another debate. "He wants to video conference."

"Right now?"

She nodded. I followed her out of the infirmary and into the main building. The LCD panels that curved around one end of the conference room were already on when we entered, casting the space in blue light.

We took a seat at the table. Sarah pulled her small tablet from a pocket and, with a series of efficient taps, established the connection. A moment later, Director Beam's thin, aristocratic face appeared on the center screen, his gel-parted hair glistening beneath an overhead light.

"Good evening," he said with an affable smile.

"Good evening," Sarah answered mechanically, but I only grunted. I hadn't talked to Beam since he tried to abort our mission in El Rosario, which would have condemned a vulnerable population of several thousand to their deaths. The mission was operating at a loss, he'd said. And that's why I couldn't stand the man. He was running the Legion Program like a CFO, everything reduced to dollars and cents. The thought made my temples throb.

"How's the weather out there?" he asked. "I imagine you're starting to see some chilly nights. We're—"

"You wanted to meet?" I interrupted.

His eyes hardened above his fading smile. "Yes, very well. I'm calling about the situation up in Canada. It's now a formal mission under Centurion's jurisdiction. We're sending Legion in."

Despite my dislike of Beam, his announcement sent a healthy surge of adrenaline through me. Everything seemed to sharpen.

"Did the mayor finally relent?" Sarah asked.

"Not exactly. We weren't getting anywhere with him, so as circumstances changed, so did our approach. A New York businessman took his girlfriend up there on a fishing trip. He left her alone one evening to night fish, and when he returned, she was gone. The empty cabin showed signs of a savage forced entry, fitting the pattern of the other attacks."

"How much?" I asked.

The dimple in Beam's chin deepened as he frowned. "I'm sorry?"

"How much is he paying you?" The price tag had to be well over a million.

"The transactional terms aren't your concern," he replied tersely. "What is are the mission info and objectives, which I'm sending over as we speak. We have the opportunity to end a threat that has already claimed seven lives, possibly an eighth. Wasn't that your overriding concern in El Rosario, Captain?" A thin smile touched his lips. "Protecting the innocent?"

"My concern was finishing what we started," I said.

Sarah interjected herself between us. "When do we head up?"

"I have a crew putting the final touches on the flight plan. A personnel carrier will pick you up at 0600 tomorrow to take you to the main base, where a cargo plane will be waiting."

I could see Sarah looking over at me as I checked my watch. That gave us a little over six hours to review the information, brief the team, pack, and prepare our equipment for loading. And that was with one team member in the infirmary and another in Las Vegas.

"You'll be ready, right?" Beam asked.

I met his challenging gaze. "Why wouldn't we be?"

"One other thing," he said. "To avoid a repeat of El Rosario, I've had the engineers isolate your equipment on a subnet that I'll control."

I felt my hackles go up. "What the hell are you talking about?"

"The next time you ignore an order to return home, I will shut down your drones, your computers, your communication equipment, and certain weaponry—basically anything that would enable you to continue the mission. I trust that won't be necessary, but in the spirit of full disclosure, I thought you should know."

I felt my muzzle wrinkle back. "If you cripple us mid-mission, you're gonna have a lot to answer for, *bud*." In the military, I never would have spoken to a superior like that, but this wasn't the military, and the Blue Wolf was reacting as much as Captain Jason Wolfe.

"Obey orders, and you'll have nothing to worry about," Beam

replied. "And if you're thinking about calling Purdy, don't waste your time. He's in full agreement with the decision."

My nostrils flared. We'd see about that.

"Was there anything else?" Sarah asked, once more, it seemed, to put herself between us.

"You'll find everything in the files I'm sending over. I'll sign off so you can start reviewing them. I can't stress enough how important this mission is. These are the very jobs we're after, so—"

"Don't screw it up?" I said bitterly.

"Oh, I know you won't do that. Not with so much on the line."

Beam could have been referring to the mission stakes, but I knew he meant me and my situation. Command Legion for the rest of the year and Centurion would restore my humanity. I had accepted the terms as my best shot to return to Daniela in the shortest amount of time. But I had also included some provisions of my own, including having control on the ground.

Director Beam lording over our equipment went against that.

"I look forward to your reports from the field," he said. "Good luck."

Sarah nodded. Beam's eyes shifted over to me as though expecting some sort of acknowledgment. But if I had to look at that douchebag's face another second, I was going to say something I couldn't take back. I reached over to Sarah's tablet and killed the connection.

"No need to drag it out," I muttered.

"You don't care for him, do you?"

"What gave it away?"

"Rapid breathing, pupil dilation, a deepening of your voice," she replied, completely missing my sarcasm. "And I could feel heat coming off you. At first I thought it was the anticipation of the mission, but then I observed the way you were locking eyes with him on the monitor. Your canines were showing as well. That's a very lupine response to challenge, often seen among competing Alphas."

I wasn't in the mood for a psych eval, especially one that hit so close to home. "Well, how do you feel about Beam having authority over our equipment?" I said, making sure my teeth weren't showing. "If he'd had that power in El Rosario, we'd be talking mission failure."

"We exploited a loophole, and he closed it," Sarah said matter-of-factly. "If you consider it from his position, it makes sense. His mandate is to establish Legion as a profitable arm of Centurion."

"And ours is to protect those we've been sent to help."

"Yes, but—"

"Beam is higher up the chain," I interrupted. "Yeah, I get it. I was in the military too, remember? Doesn't mean I have to like it." I pushed myself up from the table. "All right, we've got a lot to do in only a few hours. If you want to start reviewing the mission info, I'll wake up Takara and Yoofi and call Rusty back to base. We'll have to arrange Olaf's transfer to the main campus. He can be flown up once he's healed. Let's schedule the mission briefing for 0100."

Sarah nodded and we went our separate ways. En route to the barracks, I pulled out my phone and called Reginald Purdy. He'd agreed with my decision to finish the mission in El Rosario, despite Beam's objections. I refused to believe he was cool with Beam taking control of our equipment.

"Captain Wolfe," he answered in his old-time lawyer's voice. "How are you?"

"I'm sorry to be calling so late, but we just got off a call with Director Beam."

"Yes, I understand he has a mission for you. How do you and the rest of the team feel?"

Though Reginald Purdy carried a mysterious air, he had yet to give me a reason to treat him with anything other than respect. "The team has come a long way since El Rosario," I replied. "The extra weeks of training have helped. We're not where I want to be yet, but we're getting there."

"Excellent," he said with what sounded like sincerity. "Now, is there something I can do for you?"

"Did you know Beam has root control over our equipment?"

Purdy chuckled. "I didn't suppose that was going to go over well." A pause followed in which I imagined him touching his folded handkerchief to the corners of his mouth. "Sometimes, Captain, one must cede a battle or two in order to prevail in the larger war. Let me handle things on this end. You just focus on the team and mission."

I interpreted that to mean he would keep Beam out of our way. "I appreciate that."

"Was there anything else, Captain?"

"Any updates from Biogen?"

It had been over three weeks since my last stay in the biogen building, and I had no idea how close or far they were to a cure. The most I'd gotten was that we were still in testing.

"I'll make it a point to speak with the head engineer this weekend," Purdy said. "Perhaps I'll have some favorable news upon your return. Good night, Captain. And good luck with your mission."

I ended the call just as I reached the barracks. Inside, I knocked on Yoofi's and Takara's doors and informed them we were in mission planning and prep. Once I heard them moving, I dialed Rusty. Down the hall, a phone rang. It was coming from Rusty's suite.

"Oh, you've got to be kidding me," I muttered.

A moment later, his voicemail came on. I ended the call and accessed the app to locate him via GPS. Pulsing icons came up, showing everyone's position on the team. Everyone was supposedly on base, including Rusty. I knocked on his door to be sure he hadn't returned. When he didn't answer, I went in. Immediately, his stale scent told me he wasn't there. In a pair of pants he must have changed out of at the last minute, I found his phone and GPS locator.

I thought back to Beam's smartass comment: *You'll be ready, right?*

"Dammit, Rusty," I growled. "Not tonight."

4

I'd only seen the Vegas Strip in movies, and as I looked around at the flashing lights, drunken tourists, and too-obvious call girls, I wasn't impressed. The Strip, never glamorous to begin with, had tumbled since the Crash. Most of the casinos had been taken over by elements even more criminal than the ones running the show before—some of them supernatural, according to Sarah.

Beneath the bright lights and thousand-watt smiles, I could smell strange, dark energies and cold vampiric currents. I wasn't thrilled about Rusty's trips down here, but he insisted it was the only way he knew to relax. As long as he was back before curfew, I let it fly. Of course I thought he possessed enough common sense to bring his phone and locator with him.

I sniffed for him through my cracked-down window as I steered, but there were too many competing odors. In the past, Rusty had mentioned the Paradisio Hotel and Casino. He liked their blackjack tables. Specifically, he liked one of their dealers, a young woman he called "the Russian."

A few blocks later, I was swinging the SUV in front of the Paradisio, a gaudy building lit up in multi-colored lights. I donned my helmet before stepping from the vehicle and swapped my keys with a fleet-footed valet for a ticket. My bulky seven-foot frame drew a few stares, but with the Strip already considered a place where just about anything went, the stares didn't linger.

Ducking through the hotel's front doors, I made my way toward the casino. Amid smells of perfumes, colognes, carpeting, various body odors, and the warm currents from a buffet drifting down from the mezzanine level, I picked out a few threads belonging to Rusty.

Hopefully this'll be quick.

At the blackjack pits, I scanned the tables. I didn't see anyone in a trucker hat with rust-colored mutton chops, but my hearing picked up a woman's voice with a distinctly Russian accent. I honed in on a young dealer with dark hair and pouting lips: Rusty's *girl*.

I walked over and waited until she had finished paying out the chips from the last hand before leaning toward her. "Hey, I'm looking for a friend of mine named Rusty. Has he been here tonight?"

"Oh, him," the Russian said in a thick accent, collecting the cards now. "He left about an hour ago."

"Did he say where he was going?"

"No, but when he drinks so much that he cries, he usually goes to the Pit."

"Where is that?"

"Lower level."

I grunted and headed to the elevators. A poster beside the doors showed a woman in lingerie wearing angel wings and devil horns. The text at the bottom read, THE PIT – FIND SALVATION IN SIN.

My jaw tensed. Not hard to guess what kind of club Rusty had ended up at.

I rode an elevator car down to the lower level and joined a line made up mostly of middle-aged men. Ahead, a large doorman was patting down customers before allowing them inside. Every time the door opened, the eerie glow of black lights and the slow, deep thumps of an electronic beat escaped. I was also getting bourbon-soaked drafts of Rusty.

When I reached the front of the line, the doorman patted me down mechanically. I'd brought two guns, but they were safely stored in a locker in the back of the SUV. My lupine form was usually weapon enough. When the doorman finished, his deadened eyes took in the bulky breathing apparatus that hid my muzzle before moving up to my visor.

"You have to take off your helmet to enter."

I didn't care for his tone. Ditto his scent, which emanated from him in a cold, stale mist. It identified him as a blood slave. Somewhere, probably close by, a vampire controlled him.

I hated vampires.

"I'm not here to cause trouble," I said. "I just want to pick up a friend. Twenty dollars to get in, right?" When I reached for my wallet, the doorman seized my wrist. His grip was solid.

"I said take off your helmet."

A growl grew in my chest, and before I knew it, I had twisted his arm behind his back and slammed his head against the floor. Superhuman strength or not, he was no match for my wolf. Startled voices rose as the men in line behind me shuffled back. Unable to push himself up, the doorman shook and snarled. The vampire who controlled him wasn't used to being manhandled.

"I'm paying you twenty, and I'm going in," I told the doorman.

With my free hand, I picked a twenty from my wallet, and set it beside his head. Shoving myself off him, I went through the door and entered a lounge with a bar at one end. Women in sheer nightgowns and red plastic devil's horns reclined on sofas or drifted beneath the black lights. A techno beat thumped hypnotically. The customers who had entered before me had already made their selections and disappeared. I caught sight of the last man just as a woman led him around the corner and down a corridor.

That's where Rusty's scent was coming from.

The hell are you doing, man? I thought at him in disappointment.

I looked over a shoulder to make sure the doorman wasn't coming, then headed for the corridor myself. I expected the women in the lobby to cut me off. Though most were human, several carried the same cold scent as the doorman. But they only watched as I passed.

I imagined I wasn't like most men who came in here.

Just grab Rusty and get out of here, I told myself.

Doors lined the garish, carpeted corridor, leading to what I guessed were private rooms. The place reeked of perfume and sex. I followed Rusty's inebriated musk to a door midway down the corridor and threw it open.

A plush couch bordered the small room on three sides. Across from me, and sunk between two well-endowed women wearing the barest threads of lingerie, was Rusty. The women had been running their hands over him like a favorite pet, but now they stopped and turned toward me. My teammate, whose eyes were closed, continued to smile dreamily.

"Hey, don't stop now," he murmured. "We were just starting to connect."

"Rusty!" I barked.

He blinked his eyes open and stared at me for a moment as though trying to place me. "Boss?" he asked.

"We need you back home." I pulled him from the couch by an arm. He sagged in my grip like a rag doll before his legs stiffened with enough life to support his weight.

"What about Buffy and ... What was your name?" he asked the other one.

"Let's go," I said, pulling him out the door. The corridor had been empty a moment ago, but now the doorman and three beefy blood slaves filled the end between me and the lounge. They were holding large revolvers. I moved Rusty behind me. I could handle bullets, but absent armor, he couldn't.

It took effort to talk the Blue Wolf down. Man, did he want a fight.

"We're leaving," I announced. "Let us pass, and no one gets hurt."

A woman's laugh sounded, and I turned toward an opening door at the end of the corridor. A tall woman in a black business suit with a stylish pile of white hair stepped from a stairwell going up, probably to an executive office. Her skin was pale, her pretty smile highlighted by slender canines that ended at needle points against her lower lip. When her cold scent reached me, I knew she was the bloodsucker running the show. She released another throaty laugh.

"Something funny?" I growled.

"'Let us pass, and no one gets hurt'? Considering the circumstances, yes, I find that quite funny." Her humorless black eyes flicked past me. I could hear the blood slaves moving forward.

"I paid the cover," I said. "What's the problem?"

"The problem is decorum, Mr....?"

"Wolfe," I said before realizing I'd done so. Her gaze was having a mesmerizing effect. I swore at myself as I dropped my eyes from hers. I'd known that about vampires, dammit.

"Wolfe," she repeated, smiling slyly. "Well, we're a gentleman's club, Mr. Wolfe. And your behavior at the door was hardly becoming of a gentleman. Now, Calvin kindly asked you to remove your helmet. I'm going to request the same."

"Why?" I demanded.

"Because we like to know who visits our club. We have competitors, Mr. Wolfe, and some of them aren't very friendly. Why, just this past summer, one sent a man in here with an incendiary device. When the device went off, it claimed the poor man and six of our girls."

"I'm sorry to hear that," I said. "But like I told you, I just came to pick up a friend." Rusty moaned as I gave him a shake. I was pretty sure he'd passed out on his feet. "And now I have him."

"Then what's the harm of removing your helmet?" the vampire asked.

The harm was that she'd see what I was. If she took an

interest, she could have a minion tail us back to the Centurion campus. With enough persistence, she might even learn about Legion, specifically that it was designed to hunt monsters like her. I couldn't risk compromising the program.

"No point," I said. "You'll never see me again."

"Afraid of what might be *revealed?*" she asked, easing closer. I could hear the blood slaves closing in from behind. Without Rusty, I could have taken them. I *wanted* to take them.

When the vampire stopped two feet away, a new odor exuded from her. Perfume like, but with a biting aftertaste. I held my breath. From Sarah's lectures, I knew I was picking up a powerful pheromone meant to weaken my resolve. Seeing what I was doing, the vampire's face tensed.

"Remove your helmet," she repeated, but without the etiquette of a moment ago. The words emerged like a frigid blast.

When her eyes flicked past me a second time, I shoved Rusty into the room I'd pulled him from. The two girls recoiled as he stumbled between them and landed head first into the couch. Gunfire exploded. Rounds thumped my helmet and drilled the Kevlar shirt I was wearing underneath my coat. Deep bruises opened over my back that immediately began to heal.

Vampire first, I told myself.

She flashed in, her face a terrifying mask of blood lust and death. I met her with a hard kick to the midsection. She flew into the door she'd emerged from, her back arching upon impact, but she bounced off and landed in a nimble tripod stance.

I was on her instantly, my left arm wrapping her upper body and pressing her flat. I hooked a finger into my Centurion belt buckle. When I pulled, a stiletto-like blade slid from the leather and locked into place. The gunfire intensified—and hurt like a mother.

Seeing the blade, the vampire thrashed and tried to twist away. I eyed a spot on her back, just to the left of her upper vertebrae, and drove the blade home. The tip penetrated her heart, shearing off her shriek. Her body locked into something like rigor mortis. Behind me, the shooting stopped.

"I know you can hear me," I told the stunned vampire. "As much as I despise your kind, I was willing to grab my friend, leave, and let you live another day. I was going to be a *gentleman*. But you chose to escalate this. Remember that when you're burning in Hell."

As part of my contract with Centurion, I had agreed to refrain from extreme force outside missions, even against monsters. It was to protect Legion's secrecy.

But the same cold evil I'd felt on the day the vampires had murdered my boyhood friend now oozed from the creature pinned beneath me, making my skin crawl. I pulled my glove from my right hand and extended my talons. The vampire's eyes strained toward them. With two hard hacks, I removed her head.

Rising, I turned toward the former blood slaves. Freed from their vampire mistress, the men began to age, their suspended mortality catching up to them in a horror show of bending and wrinkling. Calvin shriveled into a mummified corpse and fell over. The remaining three staggered from the corridor, decades older, but free.

Screams sounded throughout the club as more former slaves regained their mortality.

I ducked into the room for Rusty. He sat slumped on the

couch, trying to convince the two girls to take up where they'd left off. Only they weren't girls anymore. With their gray hair, sagging bodies, and prune-like faces, they could have been his grandmothers. They blinked at one another in shock while Rusty smiled in dopey oblivion.

"C'mon," I said, seizing his arm.

I carried Rusty from the hotel, and the valet brought the SUV around. Rusty's head lolled as I buckled him into the passenger seat. "Buffy?" he called, looking around blearily. "Bunny?"

I climbed into the front seat and took off. Security cameras at the hotel had captured our ride's make, model, and license plate—not that the vehicle was registered anywhere. Regardless, I didn't know what kind of undead network the vampire belonged to and didn't care to find out.

I accelerated several blocks down the strip, then turned onto a side street. As I glided into the shadow of a broken streetlight, I entered a code on the control panel and selected an option. Outside, a chemical reaction took place, altering the vehicle's color, detailing, and license plate. The sleek black SUV from California that had pulled in front of the hotel was now a beat-up burgundy model from Michigan. As I resumed driving, I looked over at Rusty.

"What the hell's wrong with you?"

He peered around with slitted eyes, his hair and mutton chops a shaggy mess. "What'd I do?"

"I thought you were going to play cards, maybe have a drink or two. But I find you propped up between a pair of prostitutes in that vampire den, drunk as a skunk? And without your phone or GPS? The rule is that you're mission ready at all times, goddammit."

"The Russian was being mean," he whined.

"Who the hell cares?" I roared. "We're leaving for a mission at 0600. We have a briefing scheduled in ten, then we're supposed to pack. You're in charge of weapons and equipment, but because you're in no condition, I'm going to have to pull double duty while you sober up."

He waved a hand. "I can pack that stuff in my sleep."

"What you did was selfish and stupid. You hurt the pack."

His head bobbled around to face me. "The pack?"

"The team—you know what I meant," I snarled. "On top of that, you've got a wife back home."

I couldn't help but think of Daniela and how badly I wanted to make her *my* wife. I'd never been able to understand the reckless behavior of some of the married men I'd served with. Marriage was the most sacred of commitments between two people. You didn't fuck with that.

"I told you," he mumbled. "The thing with the missus is broken."

"So acting like a jackass is your solution? How about being a man and trying to fix it?"

"Harsh words, boss. I'd say fighting words, but there's no way I'm tangling with you."

"And what kind of example are you setting for your kids?"

"My kids are ... are three thousand miles away." I watched Rusty's face crumble as the reality took hold in his mind. He began to sob. "Aw man, I miss them. I miss them so damn much. Little Hodge doesn't deserve to grow up without a daddy. And if he starts taking after his momma..." Rusty cried harder. "You're right. I'm a ... I'm a poor excuse for a man."

Oh, Jesus.

With Rusty's constant joking and comic relief, it was easy to overlook how hard it was being separated from his children. I tempered my voice. "C'mon, man. Hold it together. Listen, after the mission, I'll see about getting everyone some leave. Then you can go home and spend time with Hodge and the rest of your kids. How does that sound?"

After another minute of sobbing, Rusty wiped his face with the sleeve of his flannel shirt. "Sounds good, boss," he managed. "Real good."

And maybe by then Biogen will have a fix that'll let me see Daniela, I thought.

5

I arranged for Sarah to meet us in the infirmary, where she hooked Rusty up to a bag of saline as well as a solution to break down the alcohol in his blood. By the time we reached the conference room, his eyes looked a little clearer, even with a hand propping his head.

"How are you feeling?" I asked him.

"Like a jackass. Sorry about that mess back there."

Yoofi took his cigar from his lips and leaned toward us through the smoke. "Did I miss something?"

"Nothing worth getting into," I said, partly to spare Rusty the embarrassment, but I also didn't want word of the vampire's beheading going up the chain. "Let's focus on the briefing."

"I'll make it up with mission execution," Rusty whispered to me.

Takara, who had been sitting perfectly erect with her eyes closed, glanced over at Rusty's portable IV pole, then oriented herself to the screens. The team was all present, save Olaf, who remained in the infirmary.

Sarah stood from the head of the table and gave her tablet a pair of hard taps. The lights dimmed as the wall-mounted LCD screens came to life. They showed a satellite shot of a small community set in dense forestland along Hudson Bay. It was the same shot I'd been studying for the past couple of weeks. The one I believed had given me the hunting dreams.

"This is Old Harbor, population twelve hundred," Sarah announced. "It's located in the northern part of Canada's Manitoba Province. In July, Centurion's computers flagged a pattern in the area that suggested Prodigium 1 activity. Subsequent findings have placed the case in the high probability category."

"What kind of activity?" Takara asked.

"Disappearances and killings," Sarah replied, tapping the tablet.

Seven headshots appeared over the satellite image with a paragraph of information beneath each one. I read them quickly. These were the victims: four men and three women, all locals, all of them middle aged except for the first victim, a twenty-one-year-old named Connor Tench. I felt a connection to the young man as I eyed his photo, his dark hair cropped to military standards, face browned by the sun. His profile said he'd served in the Canadian Armed Forces. Given his age, he'd probably done time in Waristan.

Red lines connected his and the others' headshots to locations on the map where they were last seen and where their remains had been found. The only clear pattern were the intervals between attacks. They were shortening.

"The attacks appear opportunistic," Sarah continued. "Each victim disappeared at night when he or she was believed to be alone. Their remains turned up later." She tapped her tablet. One of the screens changed to show a wooded crime scene scattered with bone fragments.

Yoofi gave a shudder. "Ooh, I don't like this."

I looked at him sidelong, remembering how his god had turned tail almost every time we'd encountered the enemy in El Rosario. Yoofi insisted he and Dabu had come to an understanding, but I wasn't entirely convinced—especially with Yoofi staring bug eyed at the screen now.

"In most cases, the victim had been deceased for several days," Sarah continued. "Being exposed to the elements and scavengers complicated the forensics, but the Centurion team was able to establish times of deaths. Frankly, the local investigator is more of a game warden. His investigative skills are lacking. He's been calling them bear attacks."

"So how did Centurion settle on werewolves?" I asked. In going to fetch Rusty, I hadn't had a chance to look over the info Beam had sent. The briefing was as much for me as the rest of the team.

"The mode of abduction, for one," Sarah answered. She scrolled through several images until we were looking at a cabin whose front door was hanging askew. The next shot zoomed in on the doorframe, scored with what appeared to be deep claw marks. "Though the marks have animal features, they're too sharp to have been inflicted by a bear," she said, "the only native species that would have produced marks of that size. But they're close matches to those left by other werewolf attacks in Centurion's database."

The image changed again until we were looking at a close-up of a human femur. A deep groove ran down one side. "While many of the remains showed post-mortem signs of gnawing by bears, wolves, coyotes, and the like, the team was able to identify marks left by teeth on an order larger than those belonging to the common scavenger species."

"Damn," Rusty muttered.

"Any trace evidence?" I asked.

"By the time our advanced team arrived, a system of storms had pounded the outdoor crime scenes clean. They found nothing conclusive there or indoors. No eyewitness sightings, either."

"Then what's ruling out a bugbear or other Prod 1?" I pressed.

"Nothing rules them out, but an absence of a history of their kind in the area lowers the probability. Werewolves are another story. An indigenous group in the region, the Woods Cree, have an oral history of encounters with a pack dating back several hundred years. The Masked Wolf People, they called them."

Yoofi repeated the name in fearful wonder.

"The Cree saw them as demigods and left them food offerings after every big hunt. It's unclear whether there were conflicts. The human/werewolf relationship definitely turned adversarial with the arrival of the first Europeans. There are several written accounts of wolf attacks on the settlement." Sarah consulted her tablet. "'The wolves here are unlike the ones back home,' one Scottish account reads. 'They are larger and more intelligent. Deadlier too. Bullets scarce harm them, and Parson Ross swears he saw one running on two legs on full moon last.' When the settlers discovered the werewolves' vulnerability to silver, the attacks tapered off. The surviving wolves were believed to have fled to more remote territory. Over time, locals dismissed the stories as legend, but occasional sightings suggest werewolves persist in the region."

"Why would they be attacking now?" I asked, as much to myself as anyone.

"Shrinking territories, perhaps," Sarah replied. "The area remains remote, but it's become more populated as more Canadians turned to homesteading following the Crash. In addition, much of the province's seasonal water sources dried up early this year due to low snowpack in the mountains. That may have driven the werewolf pack closer to the bay."

"Are we looking at multiple wolves?" I asked.

"That's what the claw-mark evidence suggests. Though the marks are consistent at each scene, the Centurion team noted a discernible size difference *between* scenes, suggestive of a pack. One of our first jobs will be to determine what and how many we're dealing with."

"And then put them down," Takara said.

The red crescents around her irises flashed in a way that told me she was anticipating the hunt and ensuing battle as much as the Blue Wolf. But to Jason Wolfe it was more than taking on a pack to establish dominance. Monsters were preying on the innocent, a fact the faces of the victims had slammed home. Though it burned to admit, Beam had my number there.

"Guess this won't be like El Rosario, then," Rusty said despondently. "At least those victims had a chance of still being alive."

"There might be one," I said, remembering what Beam told us.

"That's correct." Sarah scrolled to a picture of a smiling blonde woman in an evening gown, diamonds sparkling around her neck. Whoever's arm she was holding had been cropped out. "Caitlyn Welch, age twenty-eight."

Rusty perked up for a better look. "Whoa."

"She and her boyfriend, Karl Berglund, arrived in Old Harbor last Friday. They rented a cabin in the woods north of town."

"They were not warned about the attacks?" Yoofi asked.

"Old Harbor's economy depends heavily on guided hunting and fishing," Sarah said. "While the town and guide businesses issue the standard disclaimers about safety, no, they did not warn clients about these attacks."

Might also explain why the mayor declined Centurion's help, I thought. *Didn't want it getting out that they had a man-eater on the loose. Would've hurt business.*

"As I said, local authorities believed they were dealing with a rabid bear, and they've been trying to address the problem with traps and flyovers," Sarah continued. "But the disappearance of Ms. Welch changed the equation. On Wednesday, Mr. Berglund left the cabin after dinner to fish in the bay. He invited Ms. Welch along, but she stayed in. When Berglund returned later that night, he found this." The new picture showed a door to a log cabin completely ripped off. The subsequent series of photos inside the cabin showed smashed lamps and an overturned couch, broken in half. Blood droplets and blond hairs littered the floor.

"Geez Louise," Rusty said.

"Ooh, I don't like this either," Yoofi added.

"Dogs tracked a scent, but they lost it at a river crossing. Another day of searching turned up nothing. Welch's disappearance was just over two days ago." A graph appeared on one screen plotting the shrinking times between the disappearances as well as the killings. "If the pattern holds, the creature or creatures will keep her alive for two more days before killing her, presumably to eat."

"Is that consistent with werewolf behavior?" I asked. I couldn't remember anything in Sarah's lectures or the large binders about a werewolf keeping its victim alive. Werewolves were among the most lethal Prod 1s out there.

"They're isolated, but yes, there are cases of werewolves storing their prey as a food source for later."

I nodded. There was hope then.

"With the mayor declining Centurion's help, the reps approached Mr. Berglund directly. Earlier tonight, he signed a contract to employ Legion's services to recover his girlfriend. The mayor knows we'll be operating in the area, so there should be no conflicts there. We'll be meeting with him, the warden, and Berglund following our arrival."

Sarah adjusted her glasses and turned to me. "Captain?"

I stood and took her place. "We're on a tight timetable, so we won't drill before we leave. We'll review once we're on the ground. Rusty and I will ready the weapons, ammo, and equipment for loading. Takara, I want you to assist Sarah with her prep." Sarah started to say she could manage, but I gave her a subtle head shake. It was an opportunity to start cross-training Takara in the event Sarah ended up in Olaf's position before a mission.

"And me, sir?" Yoofi asked.

"Make sure Dabu's one hundred percent on board. You have

your personal packing list too. Everyone does. Double and triple check them." I would need to take care of Olaf's packs. It was going to be a busy next few hours. I couldn't foresee even a sliver of time to call Daniela.

"Do we have a flight schedule yet?" I asked Sarah.

"It just came. Still departing at 0600."

I turned back to the team. "That means everyone packed and in the armory by 0500. Any questions?"

Clutching his IV pole for support, Rusty wobbled to his feet. "Can I make a pit stop before we get started?"

I looked over the weapons and magazines I had heaped across two of the armory's large tables and checked them against my list. The stringent scent of silver coming off the ammo triggered alarms in my wolf brain, but the entire team, including Yoofi, had met basic proficiency with weapons. The chance of a friendly fire incident or negligent discharge was low.

Back at the ammo bins, I pulled out stacks of magazines of conventional rounds as well as those containing salt. Though the evidence pointed to werewolves, we were still talking probabilities. As El Rosario had taught us, we needed to be ready for anything.

I was rolling out the big containers to pack it all when something crash-landed in Rusty's office.

"Dad-flipping-gummit!" he shouted.

I exhaled hard. Rusty had insisted he'd sobered up enough to handle the computers and commo equipment, but when I arrived at his office doorway, he was looking down at a shattered monitor.

"Darn thing was greasy from when we had fried chicken on Friday," he complained. "Slipped right out of my grip."

"Maybe you should wash your hands after lunch next time." I looked around the office. To Rusty's credit, he'd gotten most of the equipment packed despite being tethered to an IV pole. I would have to double check it all against his list, of course—a fact that still ticked me off.

"Is there a replacement?" I asked.

Rusty nodded toward a closet. "Top shelf."

I lifted down the replacement monitor and slid it into a foam slot in a container that already held several other monitors, hard drives, laptops, and yards of coiled cables and wires.

"All that's left on my end are the drones," Rusty said, closing and securing the container's lid.

"I'll handle those. And the missiles," I added. I didn't want him handling any weapons.

As I pulled one of the hundred-pound drones from storage and carried it into the armory, I eyed its blunt antenna. My shoulders bunched as I remembered Beam all but crowing over having root control over the drones and our other mission-essential equipment.

"Hey, Russ?" I said as I set the drone down.

"What's up?" He arrived beside me, wheeling the container he'd just closed.

"Most of this stuff links to Centurion's servers, right?"

"Yeah, by way of the satellites."

"How hard would it be to circumvent them?"

"Without losing functionality?" He blew out his breath. "I mean, I could probably hack into a private company for the global positioning. Course I'd also have to reconfigure the equipment on our end, which could take awhile. The servers, though? I don't know. What we have is basically the front end. The real functionality is on the back end, and you can't just go in and copy that stuff. Not with their security tighter than a nun's cooch. What's this about?"

"Probably nothing."

I could see in his eyes that, even inebriated, he was reading between the lines. He lowered his voice. "I could, you know, diddle around with it, come up with a plan for just in case."

"Would Centurion know?"

"Naw, I'd just be running models. Nothing that would trigger any alarms."

I would take the responsibility, regardless. There was no way in hell I was going to let Director Beam cripple our team just because the final column on his spreadsheet fell short of a target.

"All right, I'll let you know," I said.

6

Spruce forests glowed and lakes sparkled in the late-morning sun as we flew north over Manitoba. After more than four hours cooped up in a cargo plane, the cold air that leaked into the rattling bush plane felt like freedom. And the terrain below looked so much like the lands in my hunting dream that my heart thudded vigorously. I even caught myself eyeing a river valley in search of large game.

Last night was the first night in weeks I hadn't had the dream, but only because I hadn't slept. Immediately after completing the packing and weighing, I'd had the team report to the armory for outfitting and final inspection. Centurion denied my request to send Olaf separately—too expensive, they said. I had a few choice words prepared, but I held my tongue. Sarah and I made arrangements to fly Olaf in the medical hold of the cargo plane instead. When we arrived at a Centurion base outside Winnipeg, we left Olaf in their care.

I used the short layover to call Daniela from a private sat phone I'd picked up after the El Rosario mission. Centurion didn't need to be listening in on our calls.

"Hey, lovely," I said when she answered. I checked my watch. It was close to eight a.m. in East Texas. "Hope I'm not catching you at a bad time."

"There's never a bad time when it's you."

"That's only because you don't have to put up with me twenty-four seven … yet." When it came to our future, I tried to keep the tone light. I needed it to sound more definite than it was—for both our sakes. "Headed to work?"

"Yeah, just backed out of the driveway. I'm not used to you calling in the morning."

"Well, an assignment came up at the last minute. I'm going to be out for a few days." We'd been talking most nights, in part because I wanted to make sure she was all right after gunning down her ex in self defense. She had good days and bad, but she was in a better place than she'd been two months before. "I didn't want you to worry when you didn't hear from me."

Dani went quiet. Her car engine rumbled through the feed.

"Hello?" I said.

"Sorry. Just remembering this awful dream I had last night."

"Want to talk about it?"

"Not really."

"Might make you feel better."

"You called to tell me you weren't coming back," she blurted. "Not because you couldn't, but because you didn't want to." My body grew warm as I thought about my own dream of hunting with a wolf pack.

"Well, you know that's ridiculous."

"Yeah," she replied, but without enough conviction.

I remembered what Purdy had said about progress on my cure. "I'm being told I could get some leave after this assignment," I said, deciding that Dani needed to hear something hopeful, even if it was flimsy as hell. "We shouldn't make any dinner reservations or anything, but there's a chance." I'd almost said *good chance*, but that would be pushing it.

When Daniela spoke next, I could hear the tears in her eyes. "I know I'm being selfish, but when I had the flu last week, I got so angry you weren't here to take care of me. To bring me Gatorade."

"When I'm back, I'll bring you all the Gatorade you want."

She snorted wetly. "I need to see you."

"That goes both ways."

I noticed Sarah waving to get my attention. It was time to board the bush planes. With the town's proximity to Hudson Bay, they would be easier for getting in and out, and they were less obtrusive than Centurion's attack helos.

"Dani, I love you so much. I *will* see you soon."

"Okay," she said, again in that deflated voice.

"I mean it."

Now, sitting in the bush plane, I replayed the phone call from only an hour before. Above the vast, unfolding wilderness, it already felt disturbingly distant. Shades of Daniela's dream. The thing was, I didn't need to be thinking about Dani's or the Blue Wolf's dreams right now.

I needed to be mission focused.

I pulled my gaze from the rugged landscape and turned to where Yoofi was sitting beside me. His eyes were closed, staff gripped in both hands. Sarah, Takara, and Rusty were riding in the plane behind us. A pair of flanking planes carried Centurion soldiers, and a fifth plane, the rest of our equipment.

"You all right?" I asked Yoofi.

"Dabu does not like being up this high."

"But he's not going anywhere, right?"

Yoofi grinned as he squinted one eye open at me. "No, Mr. Wolfe. I told you he will not run away again. Because if he does, he knows I will swear allegiance to his sister Udu, and he does not want that."

"All right. Were you able to sleep on the flight up?"

"A little, yes."

"Good, 'cause we're going to hit the ground running, and I'm counting on you and Dabu—even more so with Olaf out. You were vital to our success in El Rosario, and you've made leaps and bounds since."

While the other members of Legion ranged from confident to overconfident, Yoofi still got down on himself. Part of my role as his captain was to build him up, not just for his own sake, but the team's. He had shown glimpses of brilliance in the last two months, and I wanted that to become the standard.

Yoofi's smile shone white in his dark face. "I am ready, Mr. Wolfe."

I slapped his knee. "I know you are. Just let me know what's up with Dabu. I don't want any surprises."

"No surprises," he assured me. "It's like Sugar Nice say..."

Sugar Nice was a hip-hop artist Yoofi idolized. I couldn't wait to hear this one.

"...*I got the situation under control, yo, so just sit back and let me run the show, yo.*"

"I'm counting on it."

In another hour, the massive expanse of Hudson Bay appeared beyond a forest of coniferous trees, and our planes descended. We hydroplaned across the water, skiing toward a pier that stood a couple miles from the town. When the pilot secured the plane, I disembarked with Yoofi.

The planes carrying the Centurion soldiers and our supplies had landed ahead of us, closer to shore. While several soldiers took up security positions, others unloaded our containers and carted them toward a cargo van delivered earlier in the day. The second vehicle for our mission, a passenger van, sat nearby. Both had roof mounts for the medium machine guns we'd packed—something that had been missing from the El Rosario mission. Centurion had actually listened.

Rusty came up beside me, shoulders hunched to his ears. "Is it gonna be this cold the whole time, boss?"

Though the late morning sun beyond my visor shone bright from a cloudless sky, the air seeping into my helmet carried a chilly bite. The weather report had shown a strong front surging through later in the day. Having grown up in humid East Texas,

I'd never cared for cold weather, but now the wolf in me savored it. "Just wait till nightfall," I said with a grin.

Rusty swore through his chattering teeth.

With the three barrels of my MP88 pointed toward the wooden planks, I walked down the pier. Away to the south, the main pier for Old Harbor was busy with trawlers and people fishing. I'd been expecting someone official to meet us, but the dirt lot at the end of our own pier was empty save for the vans. When I heard Sarah approaching, I turned toward her.

"I've been in touch with Mayor Grimes," she said. "Our meeting is scheduled for 1300." I checked my watch. That gave us a little over an hour. "In the meantime, we can start setting up our base of operations," she continued. "The lodge is two point four miles from here."

"I read it as two three," I said.

She cocked her head, brow furrowed. "I'm basing that on the GPS and—"

"I'm kidding, Sarah." I wasn't normally a joker, especially at the start of an important mission, but the combination of dense forests, mountainous terrain, brisk weather, and, most crucially, the scent of large game on all sides had the wolf in me feeling exuberant, almost giddy.

"Oh," Sarah replied, not amused.

I chastised myself before turning and waving to Yoofi, Rusty, and Takara.

"We're moving out!"

Fifteen minutes later we were rumbling up a dirt road toward our base, a large timber lodge with an impressive stone chimney. Behind and to the lodge's left, a cache house for storing winter meat stood about twenty feet from the ground. It would make a good overlook position. An advance team from Centurion had already fortified the lodge's windows and doors, and as I eyed the garage attachment, I noticed its brand new steel door.

Fifty meters from the lodge, I had Sarah stop. Rusty, who was following in the cargo van, pulled up behind us. I turned to Takara and Yoofi and activated my earpiece so Rusty could hear me as well.

"Rusty and Sarah, you're on rear guard. Takara, Yoofi, and I are going to secure the cabin." At the pier, I had dismissed the Centurion soldiers to a temporary base twenty minutes away by air. There they'd remain on standby for evacuation and as a quick reaction force.

This was Legion's show now.

"Yes, sir," Rusty answered.

We exited the vans and Takara and Yoofi followed me up the dirt road, weapons readied. Amid the riot of smells gusting in from the Canadian wild, I picked out scents left by Centurion's advance team as well as large animals that had come through. Nothing hackle-raising or fresh, though.

When we'd closed to within ten meters of the lodge, I gave a pair of hand signals. Takara rose into flight and settled on the rooftop while Yoofi and I split to round the sides of the lodge. In the back, near the cache house, stood an outbuilding that smelled of oil. An enormous pile of cut wood leaned beside it. With Takara providing overwatch, Yoofi and I stacked and entered. By the fuel stains on the floor, I guessed it had once held a snowmobile, but save for a smattering of tools and supplies, the building was empty now.

Back outside, I scanned the dense forest around us, then craned my neck until I could see Takara on the roof. She propped her M4 against a shoulder to give a "clear from here" sign.

I turned to Yoofi, who could perceive things the rest of us couldn't. "Anything?"

"Yes, Mr. Wolfe, but I cannot yet say what. There is an energy in the air. I felt it when we first touched down. Something..." He screwed up his eyes as he searched for the right word. "Something *hungry.*"

"Can you be more specific?"

"Hey, boss?" Rusty radioed. *"We've got a vehicle coming up the road."*

I'd heard the distant engine and grinding of tires, but with cabins spread throughout the area, I had blocked it out.

"On our way," I said. "Takara, stay where you are."

Yoofi and I arrived at the Centurion vans just as the vehicle, an enormous black Chevy Suburban, rounded a corner and jounced into view. Beyond the tinted windshield, I made out a bulky silhouette behind the wheel. The Suburban slowed momentarily, as if the driver had taken his foot off the gas, and then sped up again. Our weapons rose into firing positions, and I could feel the warping effect of Yoofi's staff. Sighting on the driver's head, I moved forward so he could see me.

"Stay behind the vans and hold fire unless I tell you otherwise," I said.

The scenario looked disturbingly familiar to the two suicide bombings I'd witnessed at checkpoints in Central Asia. I automatically marked off imaginary lines in the road.

When the Suburban hit the first one, I dropped my muzzle and popped the road with semi-automatic fire. The vehicle's body canted forward as the driver slammed the brakes. The front bumper came to a rest just feet from the second line I'd drawn—the one that would have gotten his engine shot to shit.

I switched my aim as his door opened and a large man jumped out. I pegged him as mid-forties. He was unarmed, but I kept my barrel fixed on him, even as he threw his hands into the air.

"Don't shoot!" he shouted. "Are you with Legion?"

"Who are you?" I shouted back, eyeing his crisp new hunting outfit.

"I'm the one who hired you. Karl Berglund."

Since I hadn't been able to look through the material Beam had sent, I glanced back at Sarah. She consulted her tablet and nodded. It was him, the boyfriend of the missing woman.

I lowered my MP88. "Did you come alone?"

"Yeah, it's just me. I know we were all supposed to meet with the mayor, but, hell, I couldn't wait." Though his voice had an assertive quality, his red-rimmed eyes shifted desperately from one of us to the other. I doubted the man had slept a wink since his girlfriend's disappearance two days earlier.

"I understand, Mr. Berglund."

"It's Karl. Call me Karl."

Turning to the team, I spoke quietly through the commo system. "I'll keep Berglund out here while you clear the lodge. Sarah and I will then sit down with him inside. Takara, remain on overwatch. Once the lodge is clear, I want Rusty to find a secure store for the weapons. Yoofi, give him a hand. Then start getting the computers and surveillance equipment installed."

As the team moved off, I headed down the road to meet Berglund.

"Again, I'm sorry to just show up like this," he said. "But I didn't know how else to reach you."

"How did you find us?"

"Old Harbor is a small community. Word travels fast."

"My name's Captain Wolfe," I said, stretching my right arm forward.

I could tell by his grip that he was used to dominating a shake, but he barely made an impression around my massive hand and Kevlar glove.

He stood back, his eyes searching my bulky helmet. His black hair was dyed, something I picked up by the chemical scent, but it was also at odds with the salty stubble breaking out over the lower half of his face. The red splotches on his cheek and nose, as well as the fermented smell coming off his skin, told me he was a drinker. Throw in his job title, CEO of an aggressive hedge fund, and I marked him as an extreme Type A personality. That could be a problem.

"Thanks for coming," he said. "Every minute we're not doing something is another minute she's out there, you know?"

I followed his gaze into the trees and nodded, thinking about what I'd do if I were in this guy's shoes and it was Daniela who was missing. I needed to remember that while dealing with him.

"Do you really think werewolves have her?" he asked.

"That's where the data's pointing, but it's too early to know for sure."

"*Your* guys seemed pretty fucking sure."

I was wondering how long it would take for his aggression to emerge, and there it was. But I was more irritated at the Centurion reps for giving this guy the hard sell, no doubt saying whatever it had taken to get Berglund to pen his signature and hand over a hefty retainer.

"Base is clear," Sarah radioed into my earpiece.

"Let's head on up," I said to Berglund. "We're going to meet with Sarah, our chief investigator."

Berglund took a couple steps alongside me before seeming to remember something. "Oh, shit, hold on a sec." Hitching up his cammo pants, he jogged back to his vehicle. He pulled out a backpack and rifle case. By the time he returned, he was sweating and out of breath.

"What's that for?" I asked, nodding at the case.

"What do you mean?" he panted. "It's a rifle."

"But why do you need it for our meeting?"

"Didn't your outfit tell you?"

"Tell me what?" I asked, a knot hardening in my gut.

"I'm going to be hunting these things with you guys."

7

I had the phone pressed to my ear so hard that I could hear the electronics buzzing inside the device between ring tones.

Pick up, you piece of...

"I bet I can guess what this is about," Director Beam said when he answered.

My voice was low, barely more than a growl. "There's no way he's coming with us."

"He insisted, Captain. It was part of the agreement."

"That wasn't in the files you sent us."

"It was in the contract, actually."

The son of a bitch had known we weren't going to sit down and read twenty-four pages of legalese. "I don't care," I said. "He's not coming."

"Then the contract is void, and I'll have no choice but to recall you. Is that what you want?"

My boots landed with wall-rattling thuds as I paced a back room in the lodge. Beyond the closed door I could hear Rusty and Yoofi porting equipment, while beyond them, Sarah was beginning the meeting with Berglund.

"Look, it's not ideal," Beam allowed before I could say anything. "But I trust you to figure it out."

"We're an elite team," I snarled. "Not a fantasy camp for out-of-shape cosplayers. The guy couldn't run twenty meters with a ten pound rifle without losing his breath."

Beam chuckled. "Oh, you don't know that."

"It just happened," I shot back. "His girlfriend's missing. I get it. He wants to be involved. But trying to integrate him into our unit without proper training is a formula for a shit show."

"Those were his terms," Beam said with finality.

"Then Centurion should have rescinded the offer."

"With a victim possibly alive and a population under threat? That doesn't sound like the Captain Wolfe I know."

"You don't know me," I growled.

"Listen, the contract doesn't say he has to lead the main thrust or anything. If I remember, the wording was that he would be present and involved in the effort to find and retrieve Ms. Welch. There's wiggle room. Look it over with Sarah. Like I said, I trust you to figure it out."

"Doesn't sound like we have a choice," I said, and ended the call.

I paced the room several more times, trying to cycle down the breaths blasting from my muzzle. The last time a person was forced onto a unit under my command, he ordered an air strike that wiped out the Kabadi's warrior class. Even if Berglund's motives were sincere, there was no way I could include an amateur without putting the rest of the unit in danger.

So my job is to sideline Berglund without losing the contract.

Despite my anger, I was still committed to finding his girlfriend and ending the threat. I wiped my muzzle and secured my helmet back over my head. As I left the room, I almost ran into Rusty, who was wheeling in one of the equipment cases. I placed a boot against it to stop him.

"Remember what we talked about at the armory?" I asked.

His eyes cut to one side, then the other. "You mean stepping around a certain organization?"

"It's not a priority, but any free time you get, I want you working on it." When I heard Yoofi coming in from the garage, I lowered my voice further. I hated keeping members of the team in the dark, but not knowing how Sarah would react, and wanting the others to stay mission focused, it was the choice I was making. "For now, this is between us."

"You got it, boss," Rusty whispered.

I removed my boot from the case and strode into the lodge's living room. Off to the right of where a collection of leather couches and chairs boxed in a massive stone hearth, Sarah was meeting with Berglund at a large table beside the kitchen—or trying to. In the time it took me to reach them, Berglund had interrupted Sarah mid-sentence twice to insert his own loud opinion.

As I'd guessed, the man wasn't a listener.

"How's it going?" I asked, taking a seat at the head of the table.

"We're still on the first step of the mission plan," Sarah responded tightly.

"I was just telling her that all this investigation stuff is a waste of time. Your outfit said you guys could track anything. Hell, that's why I hired you. Forget this investigation bullshit, we need to start here." With a thick finger, he hammered a point on the map Sarah had spread across the table. "The Platt River. That's where we lost the trail a day ago. Your investigator here is talking like she wants to make it two or three more days."

"I never said—" Sarah started before Berglund cut her off again, this time turning to me.

"You're some sort of military badass, right? I mean, surely you understand the concept of time sensitivity?"

I didn't care for the challenge in his voice or for his pointing finger.

"Sarah is trying to lay out the best chance of recovering your girlfriend," I said calmly. "Alive."

When he started to cut in, my wolf voice drowned him out. "You can either listen to what we have to say, and we'll answer your questions when we finish, or you can hunt Ms. Welch and whatever took her yourself. Maybe your little rifle there will get the job done."

"L-little?" he sputtered. "It's a Winchester Model 70."

"Just powerful enough to piss off a Prod 1."

"With silver rounds?" he challenged.

"Do you have some?"

"No, but you do!"

"Exactly," I said.

As Berglund stared at me, I watched the meaning sink in. Silver ammo was rare, even more so in a remote town like Old Harbor. Without us, Berglund would have no access to our armory or ammo.

A blue vein wriggled in his temple. "But the terms—"

"The terms were that you'd be involved," I interrupted. "Not planning the mission." He blinked at me, not accustomed to being challenged. "This isn't a weekend hobby. We do this for a living. The combo of our weapons, technology, training, and knowledge of these monsters surpasses anything out there. We're your best chance, but it has to be our way."

The vein wriggled some more as he looked from me to Sarah and back. After another moment, he gave a hard exhale.

"Fine. You have my attention."

With Berglund where I wanted him, I nodded for Sarah to continue.

"As I was saying, from the evidence at the abduction sites, we have estimated sizes of the creatures in question. We also have a defined area in which they're operating." She hovered her pen over a red circle rendered on the map prior to printing. "With a radius of three point eight miles, that's a little over forty-five square miles. Part of our team will set up a surveillance grid. If anything within the creatures' size range moves through the area, we'll know the instant it happens, and our drones will lock in." Berglund's chest rose as if he was going to interject, but I showed him a finger. "The other half of our team," Sarah continued in a clipped voice, "will begin tracking Ms. Welch and whatever took her."

"Do you have something that beats a dog?" Berglund challenged. "'Cause we tried that."

Testing had shown that my nose as the Blue Wolf was more sensitive than any domesticated dog's. But I was still learning to use the heightened sense to its full potential. "Yes," I replied without elaborating. "Did you bring some of her belongings as instructed?"

Berglund reached into his pack and pulled out a long cotton night shirt as well as a hairbrush. When he handed them to me, I automatically lifted them to the fake breathing apparatus that hid my muzzle, my mind already storing the distinct combination of skin, oil, and a floral perfume.

"You're *smelling* them?" Berglund asked, incredulous.

Sarah cleared her throat. "There are highly calibrated sensors in the helmet."

Nice save, doc, I thought. *And not total BS, either. My big schnoz is technically inside my helmet.*

"Thanks," I said, handing the items back to him.

"You have her scent, let's go," Berglund said as he stuffed the shirt and brush into his pack.

"I need to visit the cabin."

"What for?" he erupted.

"Karl, remember what we talked about."

He exhaled and lowered his shoulders. "What for?" he repeated in a calmer voice.

"Based on the condition of your cabin, chances are good the creature carried Ms. Welch out."

"Yeah? So?"

"That means the creature left a stronger scent trail than your girlfriend's. Where it stepped, branches it brushed against, places it set a hand. Having its scent won't just double our chances of locating Ms. Welch, it will increase them by multiples. But I need it first."

"Yeah, all right. Then we start tracking, right?"

I nodded and turned to Sarah. "Was there anything else?"

"That's it for now," she said thinly.

"Good, where do I ammo up?" Berglund peered around as we all stood from the table.

"I'll take care of that," I said. "Pull your vehicle up to the front. I'll join you in a minute. I want to meet with the team."

"Hey, I'm supposed to be a part of any planning!"

"We'll be speaking in technical terms you won't understand. I'll give you the gist on the ride to the cabin. It'll save time."

In addition to towering over the man, I adjusted my body and voice to establish my dominance. That was the only way this would work—him doing what I told him to, when, where, and how I told him to do it. Sarah walked past him, punched a code into a panel beside the front door, and then opened the door with something like satisfaction.

"I'll join you in a minute," I repeated.

Berglund compressed his lips in frustration, but he lifted his rifle case and pack and plodded out the front door. When Sarah shut it behind him, I summoned Yoofi and Rusty. Wanting Takara to remain on overwatch, I made sure she could hear us through the commo system.

"All right," I said when Yoofi and Rusty arrived and we were all around the table. "Berglund crashing our arrival changes things slightly. I spoke with Director Beam, and apparently Berglund's involvement is stipulated in the contract." Sarah accessed the document on her tablet and began to scroll through it, eyes racing back and forth. "But let me worry about him. Everything else will go ahead like we've outlined. How's the setup going?"

"Computers are up and running," Rusty said. "Just need to

install the surveillance around our base, but that won't take me more than fifteen, twenty minutes. I can have the drone airborne too."

"Yes, and I will install the *lingos*," Yoofi said, referring to his defensive wards.

"Good. When you finish, I want Rusty and Takara to take the cargo van and set up a grid in the hot zone." I pointed to the circle on the map. "There's a copy on your tablets with coordinates." I picked up a scoffing sound from Takara. Standing guard while Rusty worked was well beneath her skill level, but until Olaf arrived, I was having to shift the pieces around.

"I'm going to ride with Berglund to the cabin and see what I can pick up," I said.

Sarah looked up from her tablet. "The scheduled meeting with the mayor is in thirty minutes. Should we postpone?"

"See if he can move it back another thirty and take Yoofi with you."

I felt okay with her leading the interview with Mayor Grimes. Unlike El Rosario, the town wasn't the client. The purpose of the meeting would be to coordinate our actions with the local authorities as well as tease out any additional info that might narrow down the Prod 1 we were dealing with.

"Me?" Yoofi asked in surprised.

"I want everyone out in teams of two," I explained.

Picking up on the fact I would be the exception, Rusty said, "When I finish here, I'll get a drone over to you."

"Sounds good. Questions?" When no one answered, I turned to Sarah. "See if you can get an update on Olaf's status and an estimated TOA. Takara, what's Berglund doing down there?"

"He's on his phone, yelling at someone," she said.

Hopefully not Centurion. I couldn't keep going back and forth with Beam on this.

"Everyone has their assignments," I said. "I'll be in radio contact."

In the back room Rusty had selected as our armory, I loaded my vest with additional mags, frag grenades, and slid a pair of metal stakes into my tactical belt, just in case. I looked over the silver ammo. We had cartridges that would work in an M70, but there was no way I was arming Berglund with them. Instead, I grabbed a box of salt rounds and left the lodge.

He'd never know the difference.

8

As large as Berglund's SUV was, the cab wasn't built for someone my size. By hunkering my head, I was just able to fit into the front seat. Hot air blasted from a dozen vents to stifling effect. Setting my MP88 between my legs, I cracked the window, allowing fresh air to slip in.

Beside me Berglund was shouting into his phone, but not at Centurion. This had to do with "currency exchanges" and "stop trades." He maneuvered the steering wheel with one hand until we were turned around and rumbling away from the lodge.

"Sort it out, Jack. I've gotta go," he said after another minute. He hung up, scrolled through some text messages, swore, then slid the phone into a vest pocket. "Work shit," he explained.

"These are yours." I held up the box of salt rounds and set them in the back seat beside his rifle case. Berglund's face followed the box before returning to the road.

"War injury?"

"Hm?" I grunted.

"The helmet and suit. Were you burned or something?"

"Or something."

I thought he was going to press the issue—he hadn't been shy about asking—but he fell into an uncharacteristic silence.

"My father was military," he said at last. "Marines. He was the one who taught me to shoot. Every year we'd go on a weeklong buck hunt. Big deal for me growing up." His hairy fingers kneaded the steering wheel for a few moments, then he reached into a console for a vial of aspirin. Thumbing off the lid, he shook what sounded like two or three tablets into his mouth.

"Hey, I'm sorry for blowing my stack back there," he said as he crunched them up. "My pressure runs high to begin with, and with everything that's happened ... Look, I can't promise I'll always be on my best behavior, but I hear what you're saying. I know you guys are my best shot. Just bear with my mood swings on this, all right? We're after the same thing."

I nodded. That was pretty much what I'd needed to hear.

"So I'm assuming the meeting was to delegate tasks?" he said.

"It was. Probably something you know a little about as a CEO."

He grunt-laughed as if my remark had caught him off guard and dropped the aspirin container back into the console. "Yeah, you could say that. Getting them to do what you want is another matter." He ran his tongue over his teeth. "That was my partner just now. One of the new guys flubbed an order that set us back two mill in the time it took me to say that."

"Ouch."

"Ouch is right. These aren't exactly high times in finance, especially after the shit show in Lower Manhattan last summer with the big banks. Crackpot mayor claiming they were run by vampires." His cheeks reddened and he swore under his breath. I could see in his eyes that the surrounding forest had faded out, probably replaced by a wall of monitors flashing buy and sell signals.

"Karl, why don't you tell me everything that happened, from the night Ms. Welch disappeared to our arrival."

With two blinks, he returned to the vehicle. "Well, like I told your reps, I left the cabin a little after eight. I had some luminescent lures I wanted to try out. The walleye are more active at night, and I was itching to bag some this trip. I'd packed a pole for Caitlyn, but she wanted to stay in and read." Berglund gave me a rueful look. "She's one of those types who likes the idea of the outdoors more than the cold, damp, and insects of the actual thing. I stayed out till midnight, but the damn walleye weren't biting, so I packed it in. The instant my beams hit the open door of the cabin, I knew something was wrong. I grabbed the rifle. It wasn't until I reached the porch that I saw the door had been torn from the frame. After that, everything slowed down. It was like I was living it through someone else's body."

I nodded, remembering my first intense firefight in the service.

"When I ran inside, my heart was pounding so hard, I thought it was going to break through my chest. I shouted her name over and over. No answer. The couch where Caitlyn was curled up when I left had been ripped in two. The lamp was knocked over. Crap everywhere. I searched the rest of the cabin, but she wasn't there. When I came back to the main room, I started picking out strands of Caitlyn's hair. When I saw droplets of blood, my legs gave out. Couldn't breathe. Thought I was having a heart attack." He snorted dryly. "I probably was."

I felt my own heart pounding as my protective instincts ramped up.

"There's one guy out here who carries a badge, but he handles wildlife issues mostly—fishing and hunting regs, that sort of thing. People out here pretty much police themselves, I've been told. Anyway, when I called the emergency line, he's the one who answered."

"Wabberson," I said.

"Yeah, Shane Wabberson. When Wabberson showed up, he took some video with his phone, including the marks on the doorframe. And then he dropped the bombshell that there had been other attacks on humans in the area. A rabid animal, he said. Bear, probably."

As the SUV hit rougher road, we seemed to bob and weave through the tall conifers on both sides. Though I was listening to Berglund, I kept my senses attuned to our surroundings.

"Wabberson got on the phone and had a pair of local hunters bring their dogs over. The dogs sniffed around the cabin and then picked up a scent outside. We followed it through a couple miles of forest till we hit the Platt River. The water was waist high, cold as shit. The dogs had to swim it, but on the far shore, they lost the trail." He punched the ceiling in frustration.

"We spent the rest of the night going up and down the banks, into the trees. Nothing. I told Wabberson to bring in more help, even offered to pay him, but you know how it is with these fucking government types. Would have to get permission from higher up and that would take a while. In the meantime, he went up in this little bush chopper. While he was searching by air, I contracted a couple extra hunters with dogs to widen the ground search. I was going to find her. But that evening, when we hadn't turned up anything, Wabberson pulled me aside and said the bear had probably dragged her into a den. Without a trail, the chances of finding her were going to be slim to none."

Berglund stopped and wiped his eyes aggressively.

"I lit into him big time. The son of a bitch was giving up on Caitlyn. I sent him packing, told him I never wanted to see his face again. I could have used the chopper, but I was too out of my head to be thinking straight. One of the guys helping with the hunt told me about a group of what he called 'bush crazies' about thirty miles north of here. Former military who had gone off the grid, really backwoods. He couldn't promise anything, but he thought they'd have a better chance of finding Caitlyn than the guides around here. He drew me a map of how to reach them. I headed back to the cabin for my car, and that's when your people found me. They told me we weren't dealing with a rabid bear, but werewolves. Said Legion was the only force in the world that could kill them and recover Caitlyn."

When Berglund looked over at me, his eyes hardened in a way that said, *They better fucking be right*. The wolf in me stiffened at the challenge. I forced my gaze back to the road.

"Have you had any contact with the mayor?"

"Naw, your people said you were going to handle all of that. Besides, what was he going to do? Issue an edict that the werewolves bring her back? But I'll tell you what. When I do get Caitlyn back, I'm going to sue that son of a bitch and this entire town for not saying anything about the attacks. You think I would have brought her up here if I'd known? Left her alone?"

I remembered all the fishing going on at the main pier when we landed. Again, I suspected the town had remained silent so as not to hurt the tail end of the outdoor season. But even if Old Harbor needed the money to get them through the winter, it was no excuse. A beast was hunting humans, and the mayor had known. Berglund had every right to be furious. Hell, the thought made *me* furious.

Ahead, a cabin that rivaled ours in size appeared through the trees. I could already see the missing front door.

"That must be your rental," I said.

"Yeah, I stayed in town last night. The thought of sleeping in the same bed Caitlyn and I had been sharing for the past week, knowing she was still out there ... I couldn't do it." Tires crunched over a gravel drive as Berglund pulled in front of the cabin and killed the engine. "Now what?"

"I'm going to do a walkthrough. I need you to stay outside on guard duty."

I expected another argument, but his chest swelled with importance. "You got it, Captain."

The strong wind that hit me when I stepped out of the vehicle pelted my suit with grains of snow. Dark clouds had moved in, and the temperature was dropping. While Berglund uncased his rifle, I climbed the cabin's front steps with my weapon and moved around the ripped-off door.

The deep claw marks that scored the doorframe were even more impressive than in the photos. They spoke to the Prod 1's strength and violence. I leaned closer, trying to pull in the creature's scent, but all I picked up was wood and the chemical smell of varnish. I peered back at Berglund. He was standing at the rear of his vehicle facing out with his rifle.

Good.

Inside the cabin, a short hallway led onto a main room with a stone fireplace and ribbed walls of timber. Something large had rampaged here. I sniffed over the couch that had been torn apart and made a circuit of the room, noting the scattering of blond strands. I could see the book she had been reading on the floor, a trade paperback by Patricia Briggs.

Drafts of Ms. Welch's scent had reached me outside, but now, suffused with the tang of her blood, it was overwhelming. I could also smell the woman's terror.

As my heart kicked up a notch, I imagined the scene. I all but heard Ms. Welch scream at the creature's sudden appearance. I watched her flail off the couch, maybe going for the iron poker that now lay in the far corner. The creature leapt from the doorway and landed on the couch, breaking it in half. It grabbed her by the hair, its talons raking her scalp.

As I eyed the scatter of red-brown droplets, I hoped that's where the blood had come from. With the scalp's vast network of vessels, even a superficial cut could cause extensive bleeding. The alternative—her being seriously wounded—lowered the chances of finding her alive.

I sniffed to ensure the creature's blood wasn't mixed in with hers, but it was all Ms. Welch's.

I couldn't smell the damn Prod 1 anywhere.

Doesn't make sense. Something that massive doesn't just smash its way in, grab someone, and then take off without leaving a residual scent.

It made me think the dogs had been tracking Ms. Welch's blood and not the creature.

But I was picking up something (*something hungry*, I heard Yoofi saying). An urge that reached into my wolf brain and prodded its most primitive parts. But whatever it was felt feminine, oddly arousing.

My earpiece crackled. *"We're secure here, boss,"* Rusty said. *"Sarah and Yoofi just took off on their assignment; me and Takara are about to do the same. Drone 1 is armed and over home base. Drone 2's headed your way. I've got her coming in low on account of the wind."*

"Thanks, Rusty."

"Hey, that other thing you brought up..."

I considered my conversation with Berglund on the ride over. Though I would still have to manage him, I was more confident now he wouldn't shred the contract. "Just focus on getting the surveillance system up."

"Roger that, boss."

With my MP88 resting against a shoulder, I scanned the room again. If the Prod 1 had left any hairs, I didn't see them. That was strange enough, but what in the hell kind of creature didn't leave a scent? Were we dealing with werewolves, or was this something else altogether?

A gust of wind howled around the cabin. As it settled back down, a rifle cracked and Berglund began to shout. I sprinted outside, my weapon in firing position. Berglund had moved away from his SUV and was taking aim down the road.

When I saw his target, I shouted, "Hold fire!"

The rifle cracked again, and the round found its mark. If

Berglund had been shooting with conventional ammo, we might have had a nasty explosion on our hands. As it was, the incoming drone wobbled and dipped several feet before righting itself and rising above the trees.

"Hold fire!" I repeated.

When Berglund turned toward me, his eyes were large and excited. "The hell is that thing?"

"It's ours," I said.

"Someone just attacked Drone 2," came Rusty's voice.

"Yeah, friendly fire," I radioed back. "What's her status?"

"Looks like she's green on everything except sight. Lens was hit."

I swore under my breath. It was my fault for not giving Berglund a heads-up.

"No worries, boss," Rusty said. *"I'll just shoot her back and swap out the lens. Won't take long."* I could already hear the drone humming off into the distance. *"Finding anything over there?"*

I was about to answer when the wind picked up again. This time it carried a sharp, bestial smell that spoke to the urge I'd felt a moment before. I spun upwind, MP88 in position. Back in the forest, about eighty meters away, a pair of gold eyes glimmered out at me. The creature had been standing on two legs because when it turned to run, it fell to all fours.

And the thing was frigging big.

I squeezed off a series of silver rounds. Bark burst and bullets wanged from trees, but the creature was already out of range. With a roar, I clipped my MP88 to my back and took off after it.

9

"What do you see?" Berglund called behind me. "Wait! Where are you going?"

I plunged into the trees. Within moments, crashing branches buried Berglund's voice. The adrenaline rush of the hunt had taken hold: feet thudding, heart pounding, breath blasting from my muzzle. My gear shook around me as I fell to my hands. It was a running position that would have seemed ridiculous before becoming the Blue Wolf, but now it felt wholly natural, my longer arms coupled with my superhuman strength giving me an extra speed. Trees streaked past. I leapt a small river and scrambled up the far side of its ravine, my senses locked onto the creature.

A female, my wolf mind was telling me. *A powerful female.*

When I cleared a deadfall, I spotted her ahead. For a creature so large, she moved deftly. But I was gaining on her. As if to deny me a shot, she kept the trees between us, her white coat flashing in and out of view.

A werewolf from the Cree stories? I wondered.

We broke into a grassy clearing strewn with boulders. The werewolf raced toward the far side, paws kicking up chunks of earth. I stopped on the near side, pulled off my helmet, and rose to two legs. I had a clear shot. As I sighted on her, I felt something incoming. I turned in time to see the massive werewolf an instant before he slammed into me.

A trap, I thought, as I left my feet. *The she-wolf drew me into a frigging trap.*

My muscles flexed on instinct, twisting my body around so that I landed on all fours, the momentum dragging me into a long skid. I'd dropped my MP88, but the werewolf didn't give it a second glance. He bounded past it, his massive size and deep musk telling me he was an older male.

When I rose to meet him, he reared up in kind. He was a half foot taller than me and at least fifty pounds heavier. Dark markings ringed his fiery gold eyes and lined his wrinkling muzzle. *The Masked Wolf People*, I thought, remembering our briefing. His snarl revealed deadly canines. Muscles bulked and shifted over his arms and legs as we began to circle.

Without warning, the werewolf slashed at my tactical vest, ripping it away. I struck back, but he was already out of reach. In the next instant talons raked my face, nicking into bone.

I staggered away, one hand holding my flayed flesh to my cheek. It would heal with time, but there wasn't any. The werewolf was coming in again. Holding my ground, I met his arrival with a fist to the side of his head. A force that would have shattered a human skull only knocked the werewolf off course. In a flash, he rounded on me. We collided into each other, trading blow for savage blow. His were stronger, though. And his body healed more quickly.

Reeling from his latest attack, I gritted my bloodied teeth.

An excited bark went off to my left. Others soon joined in. In my peripheral vision I caught eyes flashing beyond a tree line darkened by threatening skies. Several of the werewolves were hanging back, waiting. The language of the pack collective was foreign, but I picked up enough to understand I was facing their leader, the Alpha. A fresh charge of energy went through me.

"I'm sending Drone 1 over while I change out the camera on 2," came Rusty's voice into my earpiece. "She's locked onto your position. Should be there in a few seconds."

"Good," I growled. "I have engagement."

"You do? Shit, why didn't you say anything?"

It was a good question. The second I'd seen the she-wolf, I should have broadcast it to the rest of the team. That was basic. Instead, I'd let myself be consumed by her wild scent, by the chase.

As the approaching drone entered my hearing, I suppressed the urge to battle the Alpha for dominance and backed away. I needed to give Rusty a clear shot. The silver in the payload would destroy the Alpha and throw the others into confusion. I'd pick them off as Rusty called in the rest of the team.

"There you are," he said, as Drone 1 appeared over the trees. "Holy crapola, that joker's big!"

The werewolf charged me again. I ducked. Just as the wolf hit me, I thrust with my legs and straightened, flipping the creature. He roared as he sailed overhead and landed with a heavy thud.

"Take your shot!" I shouted.

"Computer's saying you're in the blast radius."

Fuck. As the werewolf thrashed to his feet, I glanced around. "See the boulder at my six?"

"Yeah?"

"Lock on."

The werewolf bounded in on all fours and leapt again, his lethal muzzle straining toward my face. This time I seized his taloned hands and fell onto my back. As his momentum carried him overhead, I drove a boot into his muscled stomach and shoved with all my strength. My force combined with the wolf's velocity sent him in a line drive toward the boulder.

"Now!" I shouted, racing for cover.

Missiles dove from the drone in a series of violent hisses. With earth-rattling booms, they struck the boulder at almost the same moment as the werewolf. I squinted from the heat wave and bits of silver blasting past like a molten sandstorm. The wolves around the clearing flinched back as giant fireballs bloomed from the boulder and dissipated into black clouds. At the boulder's base, the werewolf lay in a heap, smoke pluming from his blood-matted body.

Remarkably, he started to push himself up. He was more human now than wolf, but still massive. A shaky hand grasped the boulder for support. He peered back at me, eyes blood-flecked, mouth hanging open.

"That thing's still alive?" Rusty marveled. *"I hit it with the entire payload."*

But I only half heard him. I was already bounding forward to finish the Alpha. The rest of the pack rushed into the clearing. The two largest ones came between me and their leader. They barked fiercely, warning me back. I might have been able to take one, but not both.

As I slowed to a stop, the other wolves surrounded their Alpha and helped him up. Shielding him, they made for the trees. With final barks of warning, the guard wolves took off after them.

Beyond the retreating pack, the she-wolf stood at the edge of the clearing. As the others rushed past her, she lingered for a moment, the radiant gold eyes set inside her exquisite mask holding my gaze. Then she turned too, her white flanks flexing powerfully.

I recovered my weapon and took off after them. But halfway across the clearing, I became light-headed and stumbled against a boulder. The world spun drunkenly.

"You all right, boss?" Rusty asked. *"From up here, your head looks like a smashed tomato."*

I looked down at the blood spackling the boulder. "Must've caught some silver from the missiles," I grunted, feeling the acid-like burn for the first time. The silver had blown into the deep gashes inflicted by the wolf, preventing the wounds from fully healing. Blood and pus dripped from my cheeks and muzzle and ran down the front of my suit. I was in no condition to pursue the wolves.

Drone 1 shot over the clearing.

"Track them, but don't engage," I told Rusty. "I want to see where they go."

"I'm on them like stink on a skunk," he answered as I checked my watch.

"This is Wolf 1," I radioed the team. "I want everyone to meet back at base at fourteen hundred."

"Is everything all right?" Sarah asked a moment later.

I winced from the pain smoldering over my face. "I made contact with a werewolf pack."

"Our Prod 1s?"

I stared at where the creatures had disappeared. They'd been huge, powerful, deadly—and yet, as crazy as it sounded, something about them didn't line up with what I'd seen at the cabin. Not only that, some deep down part of me wanted to be running with them.

I tore my gaze from the trees. "Yeah, has to be."

10

Sarah, Takara, and Yoofi were outside the lodge when Berglund and I pulled up. I staggered out of his front seat, my vest torn where the werewolf had slashed it, blood leaking from my helmet.

I had stopped at the bottom of the ravine on my return to Berglund and plunged my head into the river. Sucking in my breath, I let the ice-cold water surge around my ragged wounds, washing them out and deadening the pain. But silver remained burned into the tissue because by the time I reached Berglund my face was smoldering inside my helmet and the wounds were closing at a snail's pace—where I could feel them closing at all.

"Ooh, Mr. Wolfe, are you all right?" Yoofi asked, rushing toward me.

"I will be." I handed him my MP88 and watched him stagger beneath its weight.

"I have a bed ready," Sarah called from the porch. I had radioed ahead to give her my status, and now she disappeared into the lodge. I was dying to get out of my helmet and suit, but not in front of Berglund.

I turned to where he was stepping from the Suburban, his rifle already in hand. "I need you on outdoor security again," I said.

"We're going back out there, right?"

"After I brief and prep the team."

"I want to sit in."

"I need you outside," I said firmly.

"Well, what about her?" He pointed past me at Takara. "Can't you stick her back on the roof?"

"Uh-oh…" Yoofi said, backing away.

Red crescents flashed around Takara's irises as she strode down the porch steps. "How about I stick your rifle up your—"

"Takara," I barked, stepping in front of her. "Inside." She glared past me before returning up the steps. I waited until she had entered the lodge before jabbing a finger at Berglund, whose face was breaking out in angry red blotches again. "You're on outdoor security. It's either that or you can go back to town."

"Or I can just cancel the contract."

His eyes hardened with challenge as he squared his shoulders toward me. This was the first time he'd used the contract as leverage. Beneath my torn and agitated flesh, the wolf in me wanted to slam him onto his back and show him my face, my teeth. But there was more than one way to demonstrate dominance. "Do it then," I said, and turned away.

I gestured for Yoofi to enter the lodge ahead of me.

Once inside, he whispered, "So is that it? Are we done here?"

"He's all talk," I said. "How was your meeting with the mayor?"

"Ooh, I did not like him, Mr. Wolfe. His eyes were full of deceit."

"Good to know."

I could hear Sarah in one of the rooms, arranging her medical supplies, but I walked to the room in which Rusty had set up his computer equipment. He was seated in a swivel chair, working the drones with a remote control as his eyes flicked between two monitors.

"You okay, boss?" he asked without looking over.

"Yeah, just caught a little silver. Do you still have the wolves?"

"I think so. They moved off a couple miles, to here." He tapped a monitor to indicate an eruption of stones that formed a sizeable hill. "Must be caves inside or something, because that's where I lost them. I'll tell you what, though. That big wolf was in bad shape."

"Jason?" Sarah called from the room she'd set up as an infirmary.

"Great execution out there," I told Rusty. "We'll meet in a few."

In a bathroom off the room where Sarah was waiting, I unfastened my helmet and pried it off. I looked from the blood sloshing in the upended helmet to the mirror. The Alpha had worked me over pretty good. The superficial cuts had healed, but the deeper gashes continued to bubble and leak fluid.

I set my tactical vest aside and peeled my suit to my waist. Blood had leaked down, matting my blue hair to my muscled torso, but the suit's protective material had done its job. No injuries.

"How did it go with the mayor?" I asked Sarah as I settled onto the bed on my back.

"We'd just begun the interview when you summoned everyone to base, so we didn't get very far. He expressed skepticism that we were looking at anything more than a rabid bear."

"Did his skepticism seem genuine?"

"What do you mean?" she asked, pulling over a rolling table she'd arrayed with medical supplies. "Those were his words."

Reading people still wasn't one of Sarah's strong suits. Fortunately, Yoofi had been there too.

"Never mind," I said. "Does he have a problem with Legion operating in the area?"

"Not as long as we're respecting people's property. Most of the land up here is Crown land, though, owned by the government. The satellite images come with a digitized layer showing public/private boundaries and contact info, should we need to get permission from an owner."

My wounds seethed as Sarah prodded them with a long swab. "Shouldn't be a problem then," I said. "Rusty has a location for the wolves, and it looks pretty remote."

"Why didn't you radio the team when you made contact?" she asked.

"I didn't think to," I answered honestly. "A second after I saw the wolf, she took off. I didn't want to lose her."

"How many were there?"

"Including the Alpha and she-wolf, at least seven."

"Characteristics?"

"Large, powerful. The Alpha was bigger than me, the rest about my size or a little smaller. All of them had white hair, gold eyes, and these dark markings on their faces. Sounds weird to say, but they were good-looking creatures. When Rusty nailed the Alpha with the mini-Stingers, the wolf began turning back into a man. Even bloodied, he had this noble look about him."

"Sounds like the Cree's Masked Wolf People," Sarah said. "According to the legends, they weren't only believed to be demigods, but the first Cree. The Algonquin word for *noble* was frequently used to describe them. Later generations of Cree supposedly lost their wolf features save for the ability to hunt. And you saw the she-wolf at Berglund's cabin?"

"Yeah. Still trying to figure out what drew her there."

"Maybe she thought she had an easy kill."

"Maybe," I echoed. But I was remembering the way she had looked at me across the clearing after the battle. Those striking gold eyes had shown interest, not malice—and certainly not the savagery that was evidenced in Berglund's cabin. I looked over at Sarah, who was now running the swab along the bottom of a Petri dish. She was culturing the wounds.

"What are you looking for?" I asked.

"Cells, bacteria. Our biological database of Prod 1s is still in its infancy, and we have nothing on the werewolves up here."

"That's great, but would you mind taking care of the silver?" I knew she was fulfilling one of her roles, but several of the spots on my face were burning so bad that I was ready to gouge them with a talon.

Sarah capped the Petri dish, labeled it, and set it on the bedside table. She then had me scoot back until my head was hanging off the end of the bed, above a basin. Producing a bottle with a curved nozzle, she began hosing a warm solution into the gashes. "This will dissolve the silver. I didn't want to flush away any valuable cellular material."

"Of course not," I said thinly.

As she moved from one wound to the next, the solution broke down the silver and dribbled into the basin. The effect was immediate. Without the poison, my tissue began fusing in a tingling wave.

"Seven werewolves," Sarah said when she finished. "You're lucky to be alive."

I sat up and dried my face with the towel she handed me. "I'm not so sure it was luck. If the other wolves had attacked, then yeah. But they held back for some reason. They only came in when their Alpha was mortally wounded. That nobility I mentioned earlier—it felt like they were following some kind of code." I blew out my breath. "I don't know, Sarah..."

"You doubt they're the killers?"

"I'm not convinced. The wolves gave off a distinct odor, but I couldn't get a whiff of anything at the cabin. No trace evidence either, and look." I plucked a sharp white hair from my pant leg and held it up. "This belongs to the Alpha, and there's more on my suit."

Sarah took the hair and several others and placed them in a vial. "Though it remains a topic of debate, there are accounts of a werewolf's biomatter disappearing when it changes back to human," she said. "It could explain the absence of hair and scent at the cabin. I'll monitor the sample." She picked up my towel, pink with diluted blood, and stuffed it into a biohazard bag. "I also queried the database before you arrived. When I added the factor of present werewolf activity coupled with a werewolf being sighted at the scene of an attack, the probability that the Prod 1 is a werewolf jumped from seventy-eight to just under ninety percent."

"Any other werewolf packs in the area?"

"No mentions in the research material."

"What was number two in the query?"

"Wraiths, but they're a distant number two. Under thirty percent."

I grunted. That could explain the absence of smell and trace evidence, but it didn't feel like wraiths either. This felt bestial, not spectral. "I respect Centurion's data, but El Rosario taught us some lessons, including that their results don't always paint the whole picture. I'm willing to work off the data until it stops making sense. Can we at least agree on that?"

Sarah adjusted her glasses. "Define 'stops making sense'."

"We'll know it when it happens."

Following a change into a new suit, I had the team meet around the planning table, where I filled them in on the encounter. Halfway through, Berglund began pounding on the front door. Rusty checked the surveillance feed. Berglund wasn't in danger, just pissed off. I ignored him, and he eventually stopped. His engine started moments later, and he left in a hail of gravel.

I ignored that too. He'd be back.

I tapped the hill of stones on the map. "Rusty's tracked the pack to this location."

"Best I can see, they're still there," Rusty chimed in. He was straddling a chair backwards, monitoring the drone feeds on a tablet he'd propped on the chair's backrest.

"The Alpha's badly injured," I went on, "and with silver in his system he's not going to heal anytime soon. The pack will stay with him, which gives us an opportunity to catch them in one place."

"Are we sending the drones in?" Takara asked.

I met Sarah's eyes briefly. "No. I want to talk to them."

Yoofi made a noise of surprise that upset his cloud of cigar smoke. Rusty looked up and blinked several times. "You sure about that, boss? I mean, did you see yourself when you got back here?"

I glowered at him.

Takara's gaze had never left me. "Why?"

Sarah answered before I could. "Because even though Centurion's algorithms list werewolves as high probability, the database is incomplete, and Jason is uncomfortable with the inconsistencies between what he observed of the pack and the scene of Ms. Welch's abduction."

"What she said. And if they're not the Prod 1s we're after, they could have information. They've been here a lot longer than any living human. They know the area and its creatures."

"So we sacrifice the element of surprise," Takara said.

"The chances of surprising the pack were low to begin with. Using the drone's laser feature, Rusty identified an entrance here." I tapped the map. "That's where we'll approach. We should expect the wolves to act defensively—their leader is wounded—but if they become aggressive, we'll take non-lethal shots. I know that's not how we've been training, but it's the default unless I tell you otherwise. Head and heart shots are a last resort. Understood?"

I looked around until everyone conveyed their understanding.

"What about Mr. Berglund?" Yoofi asked timidly. He was the only one besides me who had heard our client threaten to cancel the contract, something I hadn't shared with the rest of the team.

"Where is he, Russ?" I asked.

He consulted his tablet. "He drove down the road a ways, like he was heading to town, but now he's turning around and coming back."

Pretty much what I thought would happen.

"He's not going with us, is he?" Takara asked.

Ten minutes later, our van was jouncing down a dirt road. I manned the roof-mounted machine gun from a console inside the van while Sarah drove. Behind me, Takara had gone into her focusing routine, head and torso erect, eyes closed. Yoofi sipped from a flask, hip-hop music pulsing from his earbuds.

I swiveled the gun around until the console's screen picked up Berglund. He was following in his Suburban, head beams cutting through a thickening snowfall.

He'd apologized for blowing up—it was the stress of everything, he said—but he really wanted to be involved. I told him he could join us as far as a road that would take us to within a mile of our target. Beyond that, it was too dangerous. I gave him a radio and promised to communicate anything important. When he took it, I felt confident we were on the same page again.

"This is it," Sarah said, pulling over.

"How are you positioned?" I asked Rusty.

"Drone 1 is overhead and 2 is at your target," he replied from our base. *"Still no activity."*

"All right, team. Let's go."

I removed the machine gun from its roof mount and swapped it in the van's cargo space for my MP88. As I was closing the door, Berglund hustled up behind me. "Do you want me to guard the vehicles?"

His penitence at the lodge had sounded genuine, but I wondered how long it would last.

"I want you in the van. It was built with supernatural creatures in mind." My gaze dropped to his rifle, still loaded with the salt ammo. "You're to stay inside, doors locked, until we get back. If anything shows up, don't engage. Radio me right away."

"You'll let me know if you find her, right? I mean, immediately?"

I hadn't shared the details of our plan, only that we had located the werewolves and were going in.

"Of course," I said.

"I'm putting a lot of faith in you guys."

And I'm putting my faith in Rusty keeping an eye on you.

Before I could respond, Berglund's phone rang. He pulled it from his pocket. His lower lip curled as he looked at the display. "Aw, shit." He silenced the phone and put it away again. "My wife keeps calling, wanting to know where I am. I was supposed to be back in New York this afternoon."

"Your wife?"

"Sort of complicates things with Caitlyn, but yeah. For now anyway."

He said it so off-handedly that for a moment I could only look at him.

"Hey," he said defensively, "I can't help it that I fell in love with someone else. These things happen. Stick around long enough, and it'll probably happen to you too. You'll see."

And just when I'd begun to sympathize with the man again.

"Let's get you inside the van," I said.

11

Though it was only mid-afternoon, the thick storm clouds cast a grim, dusky shadow over the landscape. Snow continued to fall, and our boots crunched over the thin accumulation. The chemicals in our camos shifted to blend into the changing colors.

When we were within a quarter mile of the rocky hill, the wind strengthened, and I picked up the pack's scent. It carried the Alpha's blood, still fresh. Minutes later, the hill appeared through the trees.

"We've got movement, boss," Rusty radioed. *"Couple of wolves climbing up the hill."*

"Copy that," I whispered. They had heard or smelled our approach and were taking sentry positions.

When we reached a point where the trees began to thin, I signaled for the team to stop and cover me. Sarah and Takara set up behind the spruce trees while the air around Yoofi's staff curdled with energy. I advanced with my weapon until I was in full view of the hill. I couldn't see the wolves concealed among the rocks, but I could feel their eyes on me. I lowered my weapon.

"I've come to help your leader," I called. "I can remove the poison."

I was answered by a pair of rumbling growls. They could smell the silver in my weapon. Leaning to one side, I propped my MP88 against a boulder. I then removed my tactical vest and lay it beside my weapon. When I finished, I pulled the bottle of solution from my pack and held it up.

"Your leader will die without this."

As I spoke, I reached toward the pack collective with my mind and laid my intentions bare. For several moments nothing happened. Finally, a wolf slinked down from behind cover and darted into a cave entrance. Minutes passed. The air around my breathing apparatus plumed vapor as the temperature continued to fall. When the werewolf returned, he climbed soundlessly back up into the rocks. But I sensed another presence beyond the mouth of the cave now. A moment later, he spoke in a low growl.

"Remove your helmet and enter alone."

I glanced back to where my teammates were covering me. Takara had shifted her position, giving her a clear shot at the entrance. I hoped she wouldn't have to take it.

I unfastened my helmet, tossed it beside my other things, and walked toward the cave. The scent of spilled blood wafted up from beneath the layer of snow underfoot. The wolf who had spoken waited for me beyond the entrance. A large beta male. Though I carried myself tall, I avoided eye contact. It wasn't submission, but a non-aggression signal, the lupine in me knowing what to do.

I stopped and held up the bottle of solution for the beta to sniff. He then thrust his thick snout around me to ensure I wasn't concealing anything that could be deadly to their leader. The corners of his mouth were stained pink, I noticed, and his gold eyes had taken on a leaden color.

He backed away and grunted for me to pass. My wolf vision sharpened as I peered into the tunnel. Another beta hulked ten meters further down. I steeled my muscles. If I was walking into an ambush, I was on my own until help arrived.

I watched the second beta carefully. When I was paces from him, he turned and led the way. The first beta followed behind me. The cave twisted and fell into deeper darkness. Ahead, I could hear the Alpha's pants, a ragged cadence that sawed through the thick waves of his scent.

We ducked beneath a jutting rock and entered a large chamber. At the far end, a pair of gold eyes glowed dully. The form taking shape around them didn't belong to a wolf, though, but an older man. He lay sprawled on his side, blood oozing from various wounds over his long, muscled build. Where his tendrils of graying hair ended, his ribs rose and fell in a desperate rhythm.

A woman who looked to be about his age, long white hair wrapping her body, knelt beside him. The shrapnel she had removed from his flesh sat in a bloody pile to one side. I remembered the pink I'd observed around the beta's mouth and the sickness in his eyes. He—and the others, probably—had been trying to lick the remaining silver from their leader's wounds when I'd arrived.

"I've brought something that will purge the poison," I said, opening myself to the collective once more.

The injured werewolf's eyes closed. After a moment, he forced them open again. When no one answered me, I moved toward him. The kneeling woman pivoted, her form morphing into a large wolf's. She planted her front paws and growled at me from deep in her chest. I could feel my own muscles wanting to pull me to all fours, to meet her head on. But I fought the impulse and forced myself to relax. She was only trying to protect her wounded mate.

"How's it going in there, boss?" came Rusty's nervous voice.

The she-wolf's hearing picked up the sound through my earpiece, and she released a sharp bark.

"I'll call if I need anything," I said.

Rusty got the message and went silent.

The wounded Alpha muttered something in a language I didn't understand. The woman's growl trailed off, and she backed away. As I approached, the betas closed in behind me. They were poised to attack the instant I showed aggression. I'd yet to see the she-wolf from earlier, and I caught myself probing the collective for her. I couldn't feel her.

When I arrived above the Alpha, I braced myself.

Much of his backside was torn open, down to his vertebrae. Exposed muscles glistened in my wolf vision. I could see where the wound edges were trying to draw in, but like with my wounds from earlier, the baked-in silver was preventing them from closing.

I wasted no time opening the nozzle and rinsing out the large wound. Where the solution hit silver, it foamed like peroxide. The Alpha drew in his own breath and held it. The elder she-wolf remained nearby, her bright eyes moving between me and her mate. Once more, I bared my thoughts to the collective to reassure them I meant no harm. As the Alpha's large wound healed, his mate eased back. I moved to the other open wounds.

In addition to the werewolf's back, shrapnel had torn into both legs and the side of his head. His left ear was only half attached, but as the solution foamed around it, the tissue began to fuse again.

I was taking a risk by restoring him. We'd yet to definitively rule him and his pack out as the Prod 1s. But besides what my gut was telling me, I couldn't smell Ms. Welch on them or in the area.

It also didn't feel as if I'd walked into a den of mindless killers. The Alpha had waylaid me earlier, yeah, but I had also been aiming my weapon at a member of his pack. There was an order here, something I sensed in the collective as much as I observed in how the wolves had delivered me to the Alpha. An order that didn't fit with a rash of violent killings.

When I squeezed out the last of the solution, I stood back. Many of the smaller wounds had already healed, but the bigger ones needed more time. As the Alpha resumed breathing, his ribs rose and fell in a smoother rhythm.

At last he pushed himself to his hands and feet and began to change. Technically, these weren't werewolves, but shifters, the difference being they could change back and forth voluntarily. He would heal more quickly in his wolf form. Moments later, he was the giant white-haired beast I'd faced in the clearing.

Without warning, he crouched and sprang past me. The betas parted as he landed between them. He took a bounding circuit around the chamber. At the entrance, he craned his neck so that the bold markings around his eyes and muzzle were facing me.

"We will not talk in here," he said.

His mate joined him. Without further explanation, they left the space. I jogged to catch up as the betas fell in behind me. The Alpha and his mate led the way down another passageway that extended deeper into the hill. I understood that they were taking me away from the scent of his blood and the place of his near death. It was a matter of decorum.

We entered another cavern. The Alpha and his mate walked to its far end, turned, and sat on their haunches. I sat facing them, though cross-legged. As my weight settled into my pelvic bones, I was reminded of meetings I'd had with tribal leaders in Central Asia. We would often sit on the floor like this. I had even met with the leader of a resistance group in a cave once.

The wolves' eyes glowed at me through the darkness.

"My name is Captain Wolfe," I said. "My teammates and I are hunting a killer."

"I am Aranck and she is Wawetseka," the male said. "We come from the north, the Far Lands. We know about your killer."

My pulse picked up. "What can you tell me?"

"That it is a matter for the world of men," he replied.

"Do you know something?"

"We have come to retrieve our daughter," Aranck said, ignoring the question. "Once we have her, we will return to our lands."

"Your daughter?" But even as I asked, I could see her in the collective, the same she-wolf who had appeared at Berglund's cabin. "I thought she rejoined you. After our encounter."

"Nadie has fled again."

"Is she involved in the killings?" I asked bluntly.

"No."

"Then what was she doing at the scene of an attack?"

For the first time, Wawetseka spoke. "She is drawn to you, Wolfe."

"Me?"

"She seeks a mate," she said.

My eyes moved between them. Both had been speaking in deep, neutral voices, but now I caught Aranck's muzzle wrinkling into a snarl. I picked up a prickling heat too—some sort of protective energy toward the she-wolf and the future of the pack. The Alpha had veto power in such matters, and he wasn't happy with his daughter's choice of mate: a blue-haired wolfman.

"So Nadie came looking for me?" I asked to be sure I understood them. That would explain her appearance at the cabin as well as her strong, intoxicating scent when I gave chase. The memory set off small charges of arousal in the wolf centers of my brain. I tried to ignore them.

"She followed your scent," Wawetseka confirmed.

"Where is she now?"

"Nadie has gone into the town," she replied. "The one place she knows we will not follow."

"She is *foolish*," Aranck spat, leveling his gaze at me as though I were to blame.

"I'm sorry for aiming my weapon at her earlier," I said. "I thought she was the killer."

"More will aim weapons at her," he growled. "And no one will protect her. She knows the stories of violence against our kind, but she ignores them."

"I need to know everything you can tell me about the killer."

"And we need our daughter back," he said.

I understood that he was offering an exchange. "I can find and bring her to you."

Aranck and Wawetseka looked at one another. I felt something pass between them and us, a binding agreement that I accepted. "What you are hunting cannot be killed," Aranck said at last.

"Does it have a name?"

"Yes, but it is *pastamaw*, a cursed name," he answered. "To speak it is to risk calling it. Only the men from across the water are stupid enough to toy with such things. They do not learn."

I almost asked what he meant by the "men from across the water" when I realized the shifters would have been around to witness the first European settlers. He meant them and their descendants. In my mind I flipped through Sarah's lectures and stacks of Centurion binders, trying to figure out what the settlers could have toyed with.

"Do you know where the killer is taking its victims?"

"It is beyond our senses," Aranck replied.

"Is the killer a spirit?"

"I will say no more until my daughter is safely returned."

Through the collective, I could feel his iron-clad resolve. He hadn't wanted to talk to me. I had healed him, but I had also been the reason he was wounded. That was a wash. But he wanted his daughter back, and he was using information as leverage. That narrowed my options.

Avoiding eye contact, I rose and turned. "I'll go find her now."

The two betas were waiting outside the room. They growled but let me pass.

"Do not be tempted by her, Wolfe," Aranck called after me in a menacing voice. "For I will know."

12

"What did you learn?" Sarah asked as I returned to the team.

"One, that they're shifters, not weres," I said, adjusting my vest. "And two, they're not our killers. They're down here because the daughter left the pack. She's the one I saw at Berglund's cabin. My scent drew her. The Alpha who attacked me was trying to protect her." I left out the part about Nadie seeking me as a mate, telling myself it wasn't relevant. "I was tapped into their collective—everything they said felt true. Do you still have the biomatter?"

Sarah reached into a pocket and pulled out the vial into which she'd placed the Alpha's shed hairs. They were still there.

"The Alpha was in human form when I healed him," I said. "So the lack of bio evidence at the scene isn't because a wolf shifter changed back to human. More proof they're not our Prod 1s."

"So what are we dealing with?" Takara asked impatiently.

"The Alpha would only talk around it. He said its name was cursed and shouldn't be spoken. He also said it couldn't be killed." I turned to Sarah. "Does that mean anything to you?"

She squinted slightly behind her glasses. "A kind of spirit, perhaps. It would explain the absence of evidence and might also account for the variations in claw marks, if its form changes between manifestations."

"Yes, yes, a *hungry* spirit," Yoofi said. "That is very much like what I have been feeling."

"I brought up spirit too," I said. "But the Alpha—Aranck is his name—won't say anything until he gets his daughter back. She's gone into town, but he doesn't want the pack going after her. Too dangerous."

"Staying away from settlements is how they've survived this long," Sarah said.

"I volunteered to bring her back."

"Why is she our problem?" Takara challenged.

"She's not. But if we want more info on what we're hunting, that's the deal."

"While we're in town, I can finish my interview with the mayor," Sarah offered. "He said his wife is the local historian. I'll see if she ever came across a curse. It would probably be a Cree legend."

"Aranck suggested that early settlers around here had invoked it."

Sarah nodded "I can ask about patterns of disappearances and killings too."

"I'll have Berglund give us a lift in." I turned to Takara. "I want you to drive Yoofi back to base. And Yoofi, once you're there, see what you can divine about this hungry feeling you're picking up."

"Yes, Mr. Wolfe."

Takara sighed and, propping her M4 against a shoulder, headed back the way we'd come.

"Did you catch all of that, Rusty?" I asked.

"Sure did. Already sending a drone to town to see if I can spot the she-wolf."

"Good." I had little doubt I'd be able to pick up her scent, but the sooner we located and returned her, the better. Not only was the clock ticking on Ms. Welch, but the creature could strike again. "Let's move."

To Takara's credit, she slowed enough for us to catch up to her and fell into formation. Remembering that Berglund was waiting to hear from us, I activated our channel on the radio.

"Hey, Karl? We're heading back your way. We'll be there in fifteen."

"What happened?" he responded. *"Do you have her?"*

"She wasn't there. I'll fill you in when we arrive."

"But what about the wolves?"

"We're moving right now. I'll tell you everything when we get there."

Feeling a fusillade of questions coming, I killed the connection before he could ask them. I picked up the pace until we were all moving at a fast walk. We were about a quarter mile from the road when Yoofi slowed and turned around. The rest of us came to a stop. I swept my weapon across the trees behind us, but my wolf senses weren't picking up anything.

"What is it?" I said.

"You do not hear the drum?" he asked.

"Drum?"

In the next moment something vibrated deep in my ears. The sensation repeated until it became the slow thumping of a bass drum. I looked around. Where in the hell was it coming from?

"There, Mr. Wolfe!" Yoofi shouted.

I turned toward a drift of white smoke—and something racing toward us. The creature was large and feline with a sleek amber coat and dark spots. *A leopard?* My mind strained for what a leopard would be doing in northern Canada, but it didn't matter right now. The leopard's intentions were clear from its inflamed eyes and pinned-back ears.

"Get behind me!" I called.

Fire belched from the rifle barrel of my MP88. The rounds exploded into the leopard, knocking it to the ground. It tumbled across the snow, trailing smoke where the bullets had torn through. I couldn't see or smell blood, though.

"What in Sam Hill?" Rusty shouted through the feed.

As I watched the leopard struggle to stand, I picked up movement to my right—another flash of spotted amber. I spun, but Takara and Sarah got their shots off first, dropping a second leopard. The creature hadn't made a sound. All I could hear was the incessant drumbeat, growing louder.

Were these the Prod 1s we were hunting?

Yoofi grunted as a spiraling black bolt shot from his staff and nailed the leopard I'd taken down. The creature disappeared in a burst of foul smoke. Yoofi turned and hit the other one as it staggered up, eviscerating it too. The white smoke I'd first noticed was a mist, drifting and expanding from the trees ahead. The drumbeats were coming from somewhere inside.

"What are you seeing, Rusty?"

"A fog bank, like someone set off a smoke bomb or something. And hold on ... Yeah, the wind should be blowing it the other way, but it's coming straight for you, like it's got a mind of its own."

"Move back," I ordered the team. "Takara, watch our six."

With our weapons aimed at the mist, we retreated toward where we had parked the vehicles. Whatever this was, the wolf in me didn't like it. Hell, the human in me didn't like it.

"Any idea what this is?" I asked Sarah.

Before she could answer, Rusty's voice returned. *"You've got something coming. Shit, a whole lot of somethings!"*

As he said it, I picked out forms in the mist. They burst from their concealment in a stampede. If the leopards hadn't made sense, this was even more mind-boggling. It was like someone had thrown open the gates at the Houston Zoo. Elephants were coming at us now, and lions, and hulking silverbacks, their large, muscled arms propelling them in a gallop.

Other creatures filled in the spaces. And they all had murder in their eyes.

Rounds began popping from Sarah's and Takara's weapons. I switched triggers and fired a volley of grenade rounds across the creatures' path. The grenades detonated in a string of thuds, blowing fire and shrapnel into the stampede. Lions and gorillas went flying. Elephants trumpeted and staggered. But like with the leopards, the damage appeared in the form of smoke, not blood or gore.

I fired off another volley and switched back to my rifle. I sighted on two lions breaking into the lead and dropped them with short bursts to the head.

"*Looks like the frigging* Jungle Book *on PCP,*" Rusty cried. "*Want me to take a shot?*"

"Aim for the mist!" I shouted as I released another burst of semi-automatic fire.

The drone's missiles punched into the white bank. Muted explosions flashed pink through the fog and shook the ground. The pressure wave that blew into the emerging animals knocked them around. Sarah, Takara, and I leaned into the force and hammered the downed creatures with more gunfire.

But the only damage that appeared lasting came from Yoofi's staff. He fired one spiraling bolt after another, hitting the creatures and breaking them up. His gritted teeth shone bright in his dark face.

One of the gorillas survived the volley by climbing into the trees and using the thick branches as cover. Now it landed with a thud, all bristling black hair and massive muscles, and bore down on Yoofi. When it screamed, its eyes blazed red above its giant canines.

Knowing bullets would only slow the gorilla, I switched to my flamethrower and hit it with a burst of pressurized napalm. The fire took, blinding the creature with thousand-degree flames. Yoofi, who had been scrambling backwards, set his feet and hit the gorilla with another black bolt. The magic broke apart whatever held the creature together, sending it up in smoke. Its jacket of flames continued to burn in midair for another moment before it disappeared too.

We resumed our retreat, trying to keep a healthy distance from the stampede while also doing our damnedest to slow it. But for every animal we dropped or Yoofi broke apart, another one appeared from the mist. And the incessant drumbeat kept getting louder, closer.

This feels too much like the exercise with Dabu's watchdogs, I thought. Toss in the fact we were facing a menagerie of sub-Saharan animals, and that Yoofi had been the first to detect the drumbeats, and I was starting to get an idea where they were coming from.

"If you've got salt mags, use them!" I shouted to the team.

I found the one I'd stashed in a vest pocket, swapped it with my silver mag, and chambered the first round. The creatures we'd knocked down were getting up, smoke wisping from their wounds. I took aim at an elephant with fierce-looking tusks and squeezed off a shot. The salt round punched through its head in a burst of smoke. Two more shots to the chest broke apart the rest.

"Yoofi, what's going on?" I shouted.

"Don't know! Dabu too angry to talk." He grunted and fired another bolt.

Great, I couldn't wait to hear the explanation. But now wasn't the time. "I've got the middle sector," I called. "Sarah take left, Takara right. Yoofi, hit anything coming at us through the trees. Like those chimps."

He adjusted his aim and released a bolt that swallowed the upper half of a spruce in dense smoke. Limbs crashed to the ground. The chimps' collective screeches withered as he picked off the remaining creatures.

Salt rounds cracked from Sarah's M4, and two gorillas broke

apart. I took out a pride of lions. But I noticed that Takara's weapon had gone quiet. When I glanced back, I saw only trees and snow.

Oh, c'mon. Not El Rosario again.

"Takara," I radioed. "Where the hell are you?"

She surprised me by answering. *"Headed to the van."* Her breaths came hard and short. *"We need more salt ammo."*

She was actually right. I only had the one mag, and I doubted Sarah had packed more than one herself. I took down an incoming rhino before saying, "Okay. Hurry back."

I'd talk to her about communication later. I signaled to Sarah and we widened our sectors so we were accounting for the entire stampede.

Yoofi's scream raised my hackles. Three chimpanzees had dropped from the trees and surrounded him. They weren't cute little chimps, either. These were big and fleshy with jaundiced eyes and bared fangs. One seized Yoofi's staff, but my teammate held on, babbling out an incantation. The other two moved in, fists raised. I picked them off with precise head shots. The one grappling for Yoofi's staff was too close to him for me to chance a third shot.

"Let go of the staff!" I shouted at Yoofi.

"Dabu will not let me!"

Shit.

I returned my fire to my half of the stampede while side-running toward Yoofi. How he was holding his own against the chimp, I had no idea. But as I got closer, I saw energy crackling the length of the staff. He was being aided—or manacled—by Dabu's magic. The chimp screeched and drew back a hand with nails long enough to sever Yoofi's jugulars.

My single shot whispered past Yoofi's helmet and hit the chimp in the chest. Throwing its flabby arms out, the creature stumbled backwards. A follow-up burst of semi-auto fire scattered the chimp into smoke.

"I'm out of ammo," Sarah called.

I checked the count on my display. I was getting low too, and the stampede, though reduced, was getting too close for comfort. I used what remained to take out a phalanx of cheetahs. I was about to tell Sarah to switch back to conventional ammo when a crack sounded behind me.

Takara had returned, now bearing Karl's rifle. She worked the bolt and fired again, but missed her target. Or had she? I squinted past the stampede of animals to where a human figure was emerging from the mist. He was tall, with long braided hair and flowing robes. When the rifle cracked a third time, I watched the figure take the salt round in the chest and continue forward, unperturbed.

He wielded a thick club that he brought down against a leather drum he held beneath his other arm. The strike resounded through the forest as a low, ominous beat—the one we'd been hearing.

"The drum!" I called. "Aim for his drum!"

Takara adjusted her aim and fired again. The drum's covering blew apart, and when the stick descended this time, it made no sound. The animals halted and turned. Without the language of the drum to urge them forward, they raced back toward the mist.

The collective weight of their arrival seemed to collapse the whole thing. The mist spiraled like a whirlpool before shrinking to a point. When it vanished, nothing remained of the drummer or creatures.

The ensuing silence was so immense, it made my eardrums ache. Takara had returned with additional salt mags, but we were all looking at Yoofi. He giggled in embarrassment and hung his head.

"You promised no surprises," I snarled.

"Yes, I know. This is a bad time for problems like this."

"Problems?" Rusty said. *"That was worse than a horrible roll in* Jumanji."

"Who was that guy with the drum?" I demanded.

"His name is Muluku. He is Dabu's brother, god of the rain forest."

"So what's he doing here?" I asked.

"I told you how many of the gods are jealous of Dabu and his underworld? Well, Muluku is one. He does not want to face the *ekalamanga*, though—the death dogs. He tried to surprise Dabu by coming up here and taking my staff."

"What's so special about your staff?" Takara asked.

"It has the power to rule the death dogs. They do not like the staff at all."

I remembered the dogs' reaction to it during the exercise. Twice they'd tried to rip it from Yoofi's grip.

"So now every god and their brother is gunning for your staff?" I asked.

"No, no," Yoofi said, waving a hand. "Muluku surprised Dabu this time, but he will not surprise him again. How Muluku learned about staff, we don't know. But he had one chance, and that chance is gone."

"So no more *Wild Kingdom*?" I asked.

"No, Mr. Wolfe. Muluku wanted his underworld back, but he failed."

"Back?" I turned to face him again. "What do you mean, back?"

"There is always competition for the underworld. In Dea-Dep, the souls are very valuable. Much power in them. Muluku had the underworld once, but Dabu made a bet with Muluku. He bet Muluku that he could not clasp his hands behind his back and tuck his feet inside his hands. When Muluku did this, Dabu tied his hands and feet together with a rubber vine and took his staff." Yoofi started to giggle, but quickly bit it off under the hard stares of Sarah and Takara. "It is a staff like this one, but much bigger, to rule the underworld. When Dabu chose me, he give me a piece of the rock from the blade as a gift."

"You told me you found the staff," I growled. "And now you're saying it's stolen property?"

"No, no, I found the wood for the staff. From a limba tree. Anyway, all the gods steal from each other. When Muluku lost his staff, he went to his sister Kalisia and took her drum so he could rule the rain forest."

I clenched my jaw. Mid mission and we were caught up with bickering gods. "All I want right now is to hear that this *Muluku* and his animals won't be coming back," I said. "Ever."

"Yes, yes, Dabu says not to worry. He will handle everything."

Yeah, where have I heard that before? I thought, but didn't say it.

We had to get to town, find the she-wolf, and then learn the identity of whatever the hell we were actually facing. I glared at Yoofi another moment, then waved for the team to follow.

13

Berglund jumped out of the van when he saw us returning and ran up. "I heard the gunfire. Were you fighting the thing that took Caitlyn?"

"No," Takara said, tossing him his spent rifle.

He bobbled it for a moment, the barrel nearly whacking him in the face, before he finally clamped it in his gloved hands. Takara continued past him and climbed into the driver seat of the van. She wasn't happy about Berglund's earlier comment that she be stuck on the roof, and I guessed she was even less happy about having to chauffeur Yoofi back to the lodge. Yoofi, who hadn't said a word during our return, climbed meekly into the passenger seat with his staff.

I stopped in front of Berglund, whose face was turning blotchy again. He looked wildly between us. I wasn't going to bring up the clusterfuck with Yoofi's gods, so I ignored his question about the shooting. "We have a lead on what might have taken her, but it means a trip to town. Can you give Sarah and me a lift?"

"Town?" He stared at me. "*Town?* Town is the wrong direction, genius. That thing didn't take her to *town*. It took her out there. Into the *wild*." Spittle flew from his lips as he flung out an arm. "What about the werewolves? I thought you were going after them. I thought you were going to hunt them down and kill them. That's what I'm paying you assholes for."

"You're paying us to recover your girlfriend," I snarled. "And that's what we're trying to do."

"Captain Wolfe made contact with the wolf shifters," Sarah said, stepping forward. "We have reason to believe they're not the killers, but they do appear to have information that will aid the mission."

I hadn't planned to bring that up either, but it was out of the bag now.

A sound escaped Berglund that sounded like a cross between a bark and a laugh. "You're fucking kidding me, right?" He rounded on me. "You're telling me you had the wolves in your sights and you, what, you *talked* to them? And now you're running to town on their say so?"

Put that way it sounded crazy, but that was the gist.

"The reps who spoke to you gave you assurances they shouldn't have," I said. "The wolves were a false lead. If we're going to recover Caitlyn, it starts with finding out what took her."

Berglund narrowed his eyes past me, then checked the chamber of his rifle. "Give me some ammo."

"No," I said. "We're wasting time."

"Give me the silver ammo, goddammit. If you're not going to do your job, then I am."

"You're not getting silver ammo."

He threw his rifle to the ground and reached beneath the skirt of his jacket for a pistol he'd holstered to his thigh. Pulling it free, he marched past me.

"They didn't take Caitlyn," I said to his back, "but if you go looking for a fight, they'll rip you apart without thinking twice."

After twenty meters, Berglund stopped and stared into the dark trees. Snow fell silently around him. He stood there for a full minute, and then as if reason had finally taken hold, he turned and walked back toward us. Another case of needing to get an outburst out of his system.

He headed toward his vehicle, but at the last moment he spun, face clenched like a fist, and grabbed the handguard of my MP88. He jerked it while aiming the pistol at my head.

"I'm paying you, now give me your fucking weapon!" he roared.

I seized his pistol, twisted it from his grip, and cracked it across his face. He staggered back, a hand to his bleeding mouth.

"Don't you ever point a weapon at one of us again," I said.

When I took a step forward, he stumbled backwards and fell against the side of his SUV. He slapped himself upright, then ran around to the other side and climbed in. The engine roared. The tires churned up snow, sending the vehicle into a fish-tail. After several meters, the tires caught and the Suburban tore away. Sarah and I stood and watched the dwindling taillights.

"I suppose we're looking at end of mission," she said.

"We'll see what he does," I replied, doubting he'd hack off his nose to spite his face. We were his best chance, and I think somewhere inside all of that Type-A rage he still knew that. "But we should assume that our window to find Welch just got a lot smaller. We'll drop Takara and Yoofi off at base, then head straight to town. Are you seeing anything, Rusty?"

"No lady wolves," he answered.

"Keep looking. And have you been following the action?"

He knew exactly what I was getting at: I was not going to let Beam shut us down.

"Sure have, boss. I'll get on it."

The town of Old Harbor was little more than a rutted intersection. One road headed straight for the piers, where a row of tackle shops and guide posts stood. The other paralleled the shore. Only a few people were out and about, the rest no doubt taking refuge from the weather. I'd half expected to find Berglund here, but I wasn't picking up him or his vehicle.

"Anything?" Sarah asked.

I'd been sniffing the air as we drove in, but had caught no hint of the she-wolf. If we didn't find her in town, I'd go back to where she had split from the pack and pick her scent up there.

"Not yet," I said. "But since we're here, why don't we go ahead and talk to Mayor Grimes, see what he knows." I was also thinking about the sketchy vibe Yoofi had picked up earlier. His intuition was rarely wrong. Though I was still annoyed by the animal battle—a huge waste of time and ammo—I knew it would pay to follow up on his suspicions.

Sarah pulled in front of a small house that served as the mayor's office and we got out. We locked our large weapons in the cargo space and carried holstered sidearms. As we walked up to the front door, I opened my senses. The air smelled of salt water, gutted fish, and the metallic scent of the gathering storm.

At the top of a short flight of steps, I reached over Sarah's head and rapped a knuckle against the door. The young man who answered couldn't have been older than eighteen. His gaunt face was smooth except for a dusting of stubble on his chin. He stared up at me in a way that said, *I've never seen someone so frigging huge in my life, but I'm going to pretend like I'm not scared.*

He swallowed dryly. "Can I help you?"

"I'm Sarah McKinnon—we met earlier. This is Captain Wolfe."

His head bobbled more than nodded at me. "I'm Sean."

"My meeting with your father was cut short and we have more questions," Sarah said. "Can we speak to him?"

"Yeah—I mean, no." He finally pried his gaze from me and blinked at Sarah. "I mean he ain't here. He and Shane are over at the Mustang." I guessed he was referring to Shane Wabberson, the warden.

"Where is that?" Sarah asked.

Someone had been moving around behind the door, loading a wood stove. Now he pulled Sean from the doorway and stood in his place, a larger, more solidly built version of Sean. His older brother, from the looks and smells of him. He was wearing a thermal top pushed over his elbows with bits of wood and bark clinging to the front. His hair was matted, as if he'd recently woken up.

"Just wait a few and he'll be back," he said.

"It's important we talk to him now," I said.

The young man's mouth stretched into a grin that rivaled his dark eyes for recklessness. Unlike his brother, he didn't have to pretend he wasn't scared. There was no fear in him.

"My dad keeps a schedule, and if you're not on it, you wait."

I remembered what Sarah had said about the locals not caring for outside authorities, and I was pretty sure that's what we were dealing with. I pulled out my tablet and accessed the satellite map of Old Harbor. With a tap, lines demarcated properties, complete with business names and owner info. From there, it took all of two seconds to locate the Mustang.

"It's around the corner," I said to Sarah.

"What's so fucking important that he can't take a late lunch in peace?" the older brother asked.

"That's our business," I said.

As Sarah and I descended the steps, I could sense him standing in the doorway behind us, muscles tense, eyes glaring at us. After another moment the door slammed shut. I could hear him chewing out his brother and even caught the sound of a head smack.

"Interesting family," I said to Sarah.

"Sean assists his father in the office. I don't know the story on his brother. There's a photo of him in the file Centurion sent, but no info. His name's Austin. Seems like a hothead."

"You think?"

We walked toward the pier that stretched into Hudson Bay,

the water choppy beneath the dark sky. The falling snow grayed out two fishermen hunched in heavy coats farther down the pier.

The Mustang stood at the end of a line of businesses along the waterfront. Voices whooped above the sound of country music. As we approached, I could smell spilled beer, warm bodies, and the hot, oily drift of fry baskets. I opened the door for Sarah. We stepped into the damp heat of a typical roadhouse, a bar opposite us, pool tables and dart boards to one side, and dining on the other.

As heads turned, the locals' bearded and weather-beaten faces ranged from dull to inquisitive to hostile. Too many of the last for my comfort. I marked them in my mind.

"Over there," Sarah said.

I looked toward a corner booth and recognized Mayor Grimes's clean-shaven face, dark hair pulled into a ponytail. I couldn't see the face of the man across from him, but I guessed it was Shane Wabberson, the warden.

Grimes looked up from a burger and a can of beer as we approached. He had the same eyes as his older son; the recklessness was just better hidden. "Sarah," he said, hesitating an instant before breaking into a smile that also looked a lot like his older son's. He turned to me. I was used to people reacting to my size and the bulky apparatus concealing my head, but he didn't flinch. "And I'm guessing you're Captain Wolfe. How's it going out there? Finding anything?"

"That's why we're here," I said, accepting his handshake. "Do you have a few minutes?"

"No, but I'll make a few," he said.

He came off as friendly on the surface, but I picked up an

edge of aggression. It was written in the thin lines around his eyes. Grimes didn't want us here. More than that, he resented our presence.

"Shane," he said, "would you mind?"

"Not at all." The big, blond-bearded man gathered his plate and beer can and stood.

As he sidled past, I asked, "How are your aerial sweeps going?"

"They're going," he said and continued past me.

Make that two officials who didn't want us here.

Sarah scooted into the booth where Wabberson had been sitting. I squeezed in after her. Not the most discreet meeting place, but the rowdy noises buffered us.

"So what's up?" Grimes asked.

I had a couple of questions for him, but I decided to wait until Sarah had exhausted hers. Mine had a good chance of being meeting-enders.

"You said your wife was Old Harbor's resident historian," Sarah said, "that she's interviewed old Cree?"

"That's right." He looked between us as though trying to guess where this was going.

"Did she ever come across anything about a curse?" Sarah asked.

"A curse?"

"Yes, a legend about a curse."

"Nothing that I'm aware of, but I can sure ask her."

"How about anything in the history having to do with serial killings, mass killings—anything of that nature?"

A light went on in the mayor's eyes and he grinned in a way I was already starting to dislike. "Oh, I get it. You're trying to tie the recent killings with something in Old Harbor's past, aren't you?"

"We're exploring all avenues," Sarah said.

Grimes took a swallow of beer and sucked his teeth in thought. "Can't say that rings a bell either. But like I said, I can ask her. Waste of time, though. Already told you what we're dealing with."

A rabid bear, my ass, I thought.

"Can we talk to her?" Sarah asked.

The mayor's eyes hardened, and he lowered his voice until it verged on menacing. "I've already opened Old Harbor to your organization, and I'm sitting here now willing to talk to you. But my wife is off limits. Do you understand?"

I felt my hackles bristling at the challenge in his words.

"But you'll ask her?" Sarah pressed.

"I already said I would. Twice now."

"Call us as soon as you do," she said. "You have our number."

"Sure, sure. Now if that's all ..." I could see he had no intention of talking to his wife or calling us. He raised a hand, his tongue curled behind his lips in preparation to whistle Wabberson back to the table, but I spoke up first.

"It's not."

Grimes's tongue relaxed into his mouth and he lowered his hand. His chuckle was without humor. "I was wondering if you were going to say anything, friend, or if you were just the hired muscle."

"What do you think is killing people in your town?"

"I've already been over this." When I kept the visor of my helmet trained on him, he sighed. "A bear. A big bear, probably a Kodiak, probably rabid. This is wild country. It happens."

"Not according to Centurion."

He gave a skeptical snort. "So they say."

"Why don't you want our help?" I asked.

"Do you know how much your people were charging?"

"I'm talking about now, with someone else paying."

He looked around and let out a sigh. "It's not me, it's the people. They came up here to be left alone and do for themselves. The only reason I got Shane is to keep the feds off our backs. That's what the people elected me for. So how does it look now with me letting paramilitaries come in and run amok? Listen, I want the killings to stop as much as anyone. Hell, my son Austin was best friends with Connor Tench." He was referring to the first victim, the young man in the military.

"But better us than the Royal Mounted Police, right?"

Grimes blinked at me one too many times. "What are you talking about?"

Earlier I'd believed his reason for playing down the killings and rejecting Centurion's offer was so as not to scare off the fishing and hunting tourists. That might have been part of it, but something in his answers, his body language, the defensive scents emanating from him were telling me that wasn't the whole story. This felt more like self preservation.

"Why would I call in the Mounties for a bear attack?"

"But you don't really believe it was a bear attack," I said.

"Why in the hell would you say something like that?"

"Because it's true." I didn't know that for sure—a lot of people doubted the existence of Prod 1s—but I had him backpedaling. I leaned forward until I was in his face. "What's really killing those people?"

When he narrowed his eyes at me, the recklessness in them began jumping like a live wire. "I don't know what the hell kind of game you're playing, but I can play it right back. You're only here because I gave the okay. I can throw your asses right out of Dodge. How does that sound?"

It sounded like he was hiding something.

Sarah nudged me hard with her leg. "Thank you for your time, Mayor," she said.

"Yeah," I growled. "Thanks."

I got up and led the way back toward the door.

"What was that?" Sarah demanded, catching up.

"Wanted to rattle his cage. See how he'd respond."

"Are you sure you're not trying to get the mission canceled?"

"Just the opposite. I'm trying to..." My voice trailed off, and I held up a hand for silence. Through the noise of the joint, my hearing picked out a man's raspy voice from the direction of the bar.

"...come about the killings," he was saying. "And I, for one, welcome them. There's a killer out there, all right, and it ain't no rabid bear."

I turned enough to scan the bar in my peripheral vision until I spotted the man. He was sitting with his stool turned toward us. Long, knotted gray hair merged into a beard that fell halfway down the chest of a dirty parka. Though there were others around him, none of them were listening.

"Saw the thing with my own pair of eyes," he announced, and threw back a shot of whiskey.

Sarah, who couldn't hear what I could, finally asked, "What is it?"

"Wait for me outside," I said, and made my way toward the old man.

According to the files Centurion had sent us, no one in town had any information on the killings. Made me wonder how hard they had looked. By the time I reached the old man, he had twisted back toward the bar and was waving a hand at the bartender. The hard-bitten woman seemed to make a point of ignoring him. I sidled into a slot beside him.

"Get you a drink?" I asked.

He turned and blinked up at me, his bloodshot eyes swimming into focus. The man smelled horrible, like something shot in the woods and left to die. "Oh, hey, you're one of them."

"Captain Wolfe," I said. "And you're...?"

"Jasper," he said, clasping my offered hand. "Jasper St Croix."

I held up a twenty, and the bartender came over. "Another shot for Jasper," I said.

She looked my helmet over with slanted eyes but took my twenty. She returned with my change and a shot glass sloshing with whiskey. She left both on the bar and moved off, never having said a word.

"What about you?" Jasper asked me. "Why not lose the helmet and wet your whistle?"

A wolfman pounding shots? Yeah, Old Harbor would love that. "I'm good, thanks. Hey, I caught you saying something a minute ago about the thing we're hunting. You saw it?"

He'd brought the shot glass partway up his beard, but now he stopped and set it back on the bar. "Damn right I saw it. Saw it with my own pair of eyes. And it wasn't no bear."

"What was it?"

He looked around, then lowered his voice to a conspiratorial whisper. "A UFO."

"UFO," I repeated.

"This past summer I was out checking my traplines. Nighttime. One in the morning, or thereabouts. I'd just crossed the Platt River when this beam shot down from the sky. I knew right off it was a UFO cause that's what they do—they shoot down beams, usually to take a person. Had one to grab John Foster back in '58."

No wonder no one had been listening to him. When I turned away, he grabbed my arm. "But this time the UFO sent something down instead, cause I heard it." He bared his browned teeth, then opened his mouth wide and let out a screeching roar. I winced from the horrid sound. "Just like that. And that was the same night that boy Connor disappeared."

I hesitated. Maybe Jasper *had* seen something. "And where was this?"

"About a mile northwest of the Platt," he said. "No wait, or was it over by the Black River?" He shook his head as if to rattle his memories around before giving up and throwing back the shot.

"Anything else you can tell me?"

He hacked and drew his sleeve across his mouth before nodding sagely. "You can't take down a UFO with bullets. I had an uncle to try once. Bullets bounced right off on 'count of the magnets they got protecting those ships. Hey, uh, mind spotting me a five for another one."

I filed away what he'd told me about the roar and even the light beam. Maybe there was something to it and maybe there wasn't. Our best lead was still with the wolf shifters, which meant I needed to find the she-wolf and get her back to her pack. Ms. Welch had one day left, tops.

Jasper's fingers dug into my arm. "Hey, you know that gal?"

"Which one?" I asked, following his gaze toward the end of the bar.

"Never seen her before, but she sure's been checking me out." Jasper grinned and waggled his dirty fingers at her.

The attractive young woman standing in the shadows wore her hair in a single dark braid that she'd draped over the front of a shoulder. She was dressed in hunting clothes that looked too large on her and were at odds with her smooth, clean face. She wasn't checking out Jasper.

Her dark eyes were fixed squarely on me.

Seeing I'd spotted her, she smiled and brought a beer mug to her lips. Above the rim, her eyes flashed gold.

I pushed myself from the bar.

I'd just found the she-wolf.

14

I kept my eyes on the she-wolf as I edged my way toward the end of the bar. When I was almost to her, she set her beer down and took a step back. I tensed to give chase, but she was only making room in the long wedge of shadow between the bar and the wall of a back corridor.

She'd been waiting for me.

"Nadie?" I said, arriving in front of her.

But I didn't have to ask. Though she was in human form, the fecund scent of the she-wolf clung to her. The wolf in me began to respond, forcing me to shift my stance. When Nadie smiled, her dark eyes seemed to penetrate my visor. She could sense what I was feeling.

"You're not going to shoot me are you, Captain Wolfe?"

She was referring to our earlier encounter. "How do you know my name?"

Her gaze cut toward the booth where the mayor was sitting. With her preternatural hearing, Nadie had eavesdropped on our conversation, which had started with the mayor addressing me by title and name.

"For what it's worth," she said, "I don't trust him either."

"It's time to go home."

"I just got here."

"Yeah, in someone's stolen clothes. And I'm guessing the money you bought that drink with wasn't yours either. This is a small town. It won't take someone long to see what you're wearing and realize you're a thief."

I was being harsher than I needed to, but my wolf urges were surging like a gunning engine. It was the scent coming off her, the naked way she was appraising me. She was flashing all kinds of signals, mainly that she was mine for the taking. But I belonged to Daniela.

Nadie laughed. "They're too busy looking at my face. Anyway, do you really think I have to buy my own drinks?"

I peered over a shoulder at the men lined up across the bar. All but one or two were watching her with glazed eyes as if nothing else existed. Probably not the first time she'd come here.

"Aranck and the pack want you to return. You're jeopardizing their safety by bringing them this close to town. Hell, you almost got your father killed earlier."

"My father's a tyrant."

I seized her wrist. "Let's go."

Instead of resisting, she stepped closer. "But I haven't gotten what I came for."

I imagined myself looking into Daniela's eyes until my love for her overwhelmed anything the wolf in me was feeling. "Aranck told me why you came," I said, speaking above her left ear. "It's a fool's errand."

She moved closer until our thighs were brushing. "Why?"

"Because I'm engaged," I growled.

"To someone who loves you?"

"Yes."

She raised a dark eyebrow that I imagined morphing into the exquisite markings on her face when she shifted. "*All* of you?"

"Enough of me," I shot back.

I bristled at letting myself be drawn into an exchange, but she'd hit on something touchy. The Blue Wolf was a temporary condition. There was no reason for Daniela to worry about me, fear for me. I didn't want her fearing, period. She'd had enough of that lately.

Nadie smiled as if I'd conceded something.

"C'mon," I said, tugging her harder than I meant to.

Instead of going through the roadhouse and risking problems with the barflies for making off with their eye candy, I pulled Nadie down the back corridor, past the kitchen and bathrooms, and through a door that led outside. We stepped into a yard littered with snow-dusted propane tanks and other detritus that backed up to the lapping shore of the bay.

When I closed the door behind us, Nadie twisted free. I'd become so used to her as a woman that her shifter strength surprised me—and excited my wolf all over again.

"You're going back," I stated.

"What did my father promise for my return?"

Knowing she would sense a lie, I replied, "Information on the recent killings."

"My father isn't the only one with information."

"You know something?"

"I'll give you two choices. We can fight right here—dominate me, and you can take me back to the pack. Or we meet on White Ridge at low sun, alone, no weapons, and I'll tell you what I know."

I looked at her for a long moment before glancing at the pale smudge beyond the ceiling of gray clouds that continued to spew snow. When Nadie saw what I was doing, she laughed.

"That would be in one hour."

"Why not now?" I snarled.

"Because I have things to do."

I wasn't going to fight her, and she knew that. But if I tried to carry her to the van, a fight was exactly what I was going to get. "There's an innocent woman whose life is in danger," I said. "The sooner I know what we're facing, the sooner my team can help her."

"White Ridge. Low sun."

"And you'll tell me what you know?"

"Yes," she said.

I watched to see if she was lying, but she showed none of the normal signs. Then again, she wasn't normal.

"And you'll let me escort you to your pack?"

Her eyes remained steady on mine, as if they were rooted deep in the earth.

When she didn't answer, I asked, "*Where* on White Ridge?"

"Follow your nose, Wolfe."

When she turned, I caught my lupine eyes dropping to her powerful hips as if drawn there by a magnetic force. I pulled my gaze away, but not before she peered at me over a shoulder, eyes smiling beautifully, dangerously. She disappeared around the corner of the roadhouse. I shouldn't have let her go, but my heart was pounding, my head buzzing. I was verging on control loss.

"C'mon, Jason," I muttered. "Get it to-fucking-gether."

I considered having Rusty keep an eye on her, but Berglund was still absent, and I wanted Rusty concentrating on the workaround in the event Beam recalled us. Anyway, the wolf in me knew she'd be at White Ridge. I rounded the roadhouse's other side and found Sarah waiting. When she spotted me, she cleaned the snow from her glasses and put them back on.

"Do you mind telling me what you were doing?"

"I overheard someone at the bar saying he'd seen the Prod 1. The guy turned out to be unreliable, an old drunk. Claimed it was a UFO, but he also described a blue beam of light from the sky and an animal roar on the night of Connor's disappearance. Could be worth looking into."

"I'll query the database for like examples," she said.

"I also found our she-wolf."

Her eyes snapped back to me. "You did? Where is she?"

Though Nadie's scent lingered in the air, she had disappeared from sight. "Gone for now, but we made plans to meet up in an hour. She claims to know something about our killer."

"Do you trust her?"

"She'll keep the appointment, yeah." *And if she doesn't,* I thought, *that scent won't be hard to track. It's burned into all the wrong parts of my brain.* "If you're asking if I think she'll try to hurt me, no, I'm not getting that." Seduction was another question. That was clearly her game.

"Where are we meeting?" Sarah asked.

"White Ridge. But she's insisting I go alone."

Her head tilted. "Why?"

"I'm not sure," I lied. "Maybe because I'm part lupine, like her. But I'll have Rusty overhead. I'll want you and Yoofi stationed where we parked earlier. When I bring Nadie past, I'll have you take up the rear position and provide backup at the hill again." Regardless of what Nadie told me, I was taking her back to Aranck. We didn't need to be on the bad side of a pack of shifters.

"Any word on Olaf?" I asked.

"He'll be delivered this evening at 2000 hours," Sarah replied distractedly. "You don't want Takara on backup too?"

I thought about our meeting with Mayor Grimes.

"I have another job for her," I said.

Back at the lodge, I went in search of Yoofi to see what he'd been able to divine. I found him pacing on the back porch, cigar smoke trailing behind him. He was talking to his wooden idol in Congolese and jabbing it with a finger.

"I am sorry, Mr. Wolfe," he said when he saw me. "This whole time I have been trying to get Dabu's attention. I drink, I smoke, I dance, but Dabu will not speak. He has gone deep into the underworld. He believes his brothers and sisters are planning to take the Dea-Dep and return it to Muluku. Ooh, he is very afraid right now."

I clenched my jaw. "You told me he wouldn't run again."

"I meant run from something up here. Down there is another story."

I didn't have time for this. "Tell him that if he doesn't help you divine what we're facing up here, you'll pledge allegiance to Udu."

"I already tried this, and he doesn't care. His underworld is more important to him right now than Yoofi."

"Then go bigger. Tell him you'll give your staff to Muluku."

"I cannot do that, Mr. Wolfe."

"Why not?"

"Dabu is a very funny god, yes. Makes Yoofi laugh many times. But if I tried to give the staff to Muluku, knowing he would use it to take the underworld back, Dabu would end me. Like that." He looked down at the idol and nodded solemnly. "Dabu just told me that this is true."

"Can you even cast through the staff anymore?"

"Let me see." He raised the blade and then recoiled as a black bolt spiraled out and blasted into the outbuilding we'd cleared earlier. The front face of the building disintegrated in a plume of smoke, imploding the rest of the structure. The wood pile that had been leaning against the building toppled. A flock of crows scattered from the nearby trees.

Yoofi lowered his staff with a frown. "The power feels different, harder to control. I was not aiming for the building."

I winced at both the lingering effect of the magic, which did seem to carry more of an edge than usual, and the sight of the destroyed building. Good thing we hadn't stored any weapons inside.

"Let's head in," I said, opening the door. "We're leaving on another mission soon. You'll be with Sarah. She'll brief you on your assignment." I paused. "Bring the staff, but plan on using your sidearm."

"Yes, Mr. Wolfe."

I found Rusty in the computer room. His trucker hat was askew, eyes bloodshot from staring at the monitors for several hours straight. I stepped inside and closed the door behind me.

"How's it going?" I asked, coming around to his side.

I frowned when I saw he had a game of poker open in a corner of one screen.

"Huh?" He looked over at me, quickly closed the poker window, and resumed typing into a black command box. "Don't worry about that, boss. I play a hand here and there when I get stuck. Idles down the problem-solving part of my brain just long enough so that when I boot her up again, I've got an answer. A few more lines, and I'm pretty sure I'll have us a code that can patch us into a private subnet for GPS. Any word from the ol' director?"

"Sarah's been updating him with situation reports, but we haven't heard back." I looked over at a screen that was monitoring the surveillance grid he'd installed earlier. "Anything showing up?"

"Nothing Proddy," he answered.

"How about Berglund? Any idea of his whereabouts?"

"That's also a negatory." When he glanced over and saw my concerned look, he added, "I can send a drone out for him, if you want. See what he's up to. Still can't believe he whipped out a gun on you."

"No, keep the drones over the grid until we head out again."

"Head out as in your date with the honey?" Rusty's eyebrows bounced up and down.

"How do you know about that?"

"You left your mic open on our channel, and I had eyes on you two outside."

I grunted in annoyance.

"Watch yourself, boss."

"The hell's that supposed to mean?"

"I zoomed in on her pretty good. Man…" He removed his hat and dragged a hand through his shaggy hair before fitting it back over his head. "She's the nicest thing I've seen since the sweetheart they crowned Maysville Pumpkin Queen two years back. And she's making it pretty clear what she wants. There has to be at least a part of you thinking, hell, why not?"

"There isn't," I growled.

"I don't know, boss. Your voice was doing things I've never heard before."

I felt my brows crush down and my irises radiate color. Rusty threw up his hands.

"Whoa, there! I'm just saying be careful is all."

I thought about our conversation on the way back from Vegas when I'd called Rusty out for playing reckless while married. It bothered me how quickly the shoe had moved to the other foot.

"Nothing's going to happen," I said.

"Fine, boss. Jeez, don't look at me like that. I've had nothing but MREs for the past twenty-four, and they're looking for any excuse to blow out the exit chute. In fact, let me take care of that."

He shot from his swivel chair and disappeared into an adjoining bathroom.

I left before the sound effects could begin and headed for the armory. I forced several calming breaths through my muzzle. I'd only lost it because Rusty was right. There *was* a part of me thinking things it shouldn't. My wolf part, granted, but as long as we were hitched to one another, I had to take ownership. There was no reason my mind, my rational captain's mind, couldn't override the most reactionary parts of the Blue Wolf. And then there was Daniela.

I had to keep the importance of the mission forefront as well as my love for my fiancée.

I looked over the stock of arms. Nadie had said no weapons, but that didn't mean I couldn't store a cache nearby. Instead of my bulky MP88, I selected one of the M4 carbines. And since it was starting to feel like anything and its mother could show up out here, I grabbed silver, salt, and conventional ammo mags, along with a similar variety of frag grenades. I stashed them in a duffel bag and was hefting it over a shoulder when Takara spoke from behind me.

"Sarah says you have an assignment for me."

Damn, she moved quietly. I turned to face her. "I do."

"Not another babysitting job, I hope."

"No, this is a better fit for your skill set. Sarah and I met with Mayor Grimes earlier. In a nutshell, I don't trust him. He's hiding something. I think our talk shook him up."

"And you want me to see what he does."

"Exactly. Find out everything you can. Who he talks to, what they're talking about. I'm interested in his wife too. She's a local historian. Might have info on a curse or relevant killings in the past. Grimes put her off limits. Could be out of spite, but it could be something more."

Sarah had needed a little convincing on the ride back to put Takara on him, but I reminded her that there was nothing in the contract preventing us from investigating town officials or their families.

"When do I leave?"

"Sarah and Yoofi are heading out in about thirty. They can drop you off near town."

The red crescents around Takara's irises flashed. "I'd prefer to set out on foot, alone."

I looked at her a moment before nodding. She knew what she was doing. "You'll find info about the town and mayor on your device. And no engagement. This is a stealth exercise."

She turned away.

"One more thing," I said.

She faced me again, this time letting out an impatient sigh.

I lowered my voice. "Your dragon. How is that going?"

Though I had caught glimpses of her dragon nature in the last couple of months, it hadn't come close to manifesting itself fully like in the Chagrath's realm during the El Rosario mission.

"I told you I didn't want to talk about it."

"Look, I'm pretty sure we joined Legion for the same reason. A cure, right?" I had picked up her scent in the Biogen building twice, which suggested they were working on her too. I took her silence now to mean yes. "I'm just wondering how you've managed that part of yourself for so long."

She narrowed her eyes in suspicion. "What do you mean?"

"How have you kept that part of you from, you know, ruling the rest of you?"

For a moment, I thought she was going to shut me down, but her eyes relaxed. "Years of practice. And with these." She held up her palms so I was looking at her hand tattoos.

I had never seen them up close. The blood-red patterns were more complex than I'd realized. The closest things I could compare them to were Tibetan mandalas. But where mandalas were ornate, the markings that stained her palms looked harsh. Takara closed her fingers back over them and lowered her hands.

"Who drew them?" I asked.

"A teacher," she answered. "They control the fire. But to control the mind, I sit in silence."

I thought of all the hours Takara spent in meditation. I'd always assumed the practice was to focus her power, and maybe that was part of it, but she seemed to be telling me it was also to barricade her dragon dimension—something she'd had to have done for the last fifty years, at least.

Was that what it took?

"I can show you sometime," she said.

Her offer surprised me. "Yeah? That might be good."

The problem was I needed control over my wolf *now*.

"Was there anything else?" she asked.

I was about to dismiss her, but she was looking at me with the most openness I'd ever seen on her face. "Look, I know it couldn't have been easy losing your family," I said. "I was only a teenager when I lost my parents, and it wasn't anything like what you went through."

"You know nothing about my family," she snapped, her words

as sharp as her retractable blades. The red crescents flashed around irises that seemed to have gone a deeper, more forbidding shade of black.

"I wasn't suggesting I did."

Takara glared at me, lips compressing as though her dragon fury was going to erupt and consume the entire armory at any moment, but she spun abruptly and left.

I swore at myself. I'd seen an opening to deepen our relationship and gone about it badly. I hoped that hadn't set us back to square one. But more pressing was my meeting with Nadie. I didn't have hand tattoos or years of mental training and practice to lean on. I just had the knowledge of who I had been before becoming the Blue Wolf, and whom I still loved.

That would have to be enough.

15

My nostrils flared as I peered up the snow-blown ridge. I'd had Sarah drop me off downwind from the meeting place, and now I was pacing restlessly, my wolf brain picking through the olfactory threads.

There—Nadie's scent.

I climbed part way up the ridge, past towering spruce and pine trees, until I found a secluded spot for my weapons cache. Choosing a section of ground where a fallen tree had decomposed and softened the earth, I dug out a hole. I peered around to ensure I was alone, then set my duffel bag at the hole's bottom and covered it up.

I completed the climb until I was standing at the top of White

Ridge, so named for the limestone cliffs along one face. Nadie had chosen a spot away from the town, but still close enough that her pack wouldn't risk coming for her. Her scent set off more charges in my wolf mind. I opened my mouth to call for her, but what emerged was the beginning of a howl that I bit off.

Picking up movement to my left, I snapped my head around and found her approaching through the snow in wolf form. Her gold eyes glimmered in the dark markings of her face.

I cleared my throat, but my voice still growled. "I'm here."

She brushed my hip with her shoulder, then circled back. "I can see that."

"Now tell me what you know. That was the deal."

When she rose and reached toward my head, I drew away. "What are you doing?"

"I'm not going to talk to a helmet."

"What's the difference?"

"You sound caged."

I had never liked wearing the thing, and as we stood there, snow falling through the growing dusk, wind blowing through the trees, I did want to be free of it. Not seeing the harm, I undid the hasps that connected the helmet to my suit and lifted it off my head. The cold hit my face in an invigorating rush. Nadie's scent rushed in too, and I took a step back.

She smiled. "Better?"

"What do you know about the creature we're hunting?" I asked.

I was skeptical she knew anything, that claiming to have info was a ploy to get me alone. But it would have been irresponsible not to follow up, especially if her father proved a dead end.

Nadie surprised me when she said, "What you hunt is a man-eater. It's always hungry. This is why it holds its prey captive. It will not consume them until the hunger becomes unbearable. But the abatement doesn't last. No, the more it kills and consumes, the hungrier it grows."

That fit with the shortening windows between abductions and killings. It also fit with what Yoofi had sensed upon our arrival: something hungry. None of that bode well for Ms. Welch.

"How do we find it?"

"Remove your suit first."

"This isn't strip Q&A," I growled.

"And you aren't naked underneath that."

She was right, of course. If anything, my layer of blue hair had been thickening for the past week with the cooling weather. But I didn't like giving her this kind of control. "No more games. I asked you a question."

Her eyes moved up and down my suit.

"Not going to answer me?" I said. "Then it's time to go back to your pack."

I shot out a hand for her scruff. She recoiled just as quickly, leaving me to swipe through air. She pranced around me, gold eyes glimmering with mischief. When I lunged for her, she sprang to one side, and I ended up on hands and feet too. She put a tree between us and peeked out from behind it. Her scent had sharpened with excitement. This was a big turn-on for her. She wanted me to chase her. And the wolf in me wanted to give chase.

Daniela, I told myself.

I rose back to two legs. "We had a deal."

"It's just an artificial layer of fabric," she said.

We were wasting time. With an annoyed grunt, I removed my boots and dug my clawed toes into the snow and soil as I undid the fasteners on my digital uniform. My pores opened to the chill Canadian air as the suit came away, and for the first time in what felt like forever my entire body breathed.

I watched Nadie's eyes change as she looked me over. She liked the massive, muscled form in front of her.

"How do we find it?" I repeated.

She stepped from behind the tree, heat rising from her body in drifts of steam. "It cannot be tracked like an animal. It *is* hunger, absorbing everything around it, including the scent of its victims. You must see it to pursue it. And the only sure way to see it is to call its name."

"What's its name?"

"It comes from the ancient language. I will not speak it because it's a cursed name, especially for the Cree, but I can tell you its meaning. Then you can find it yourself. There are ceremonies for calling it, but none for killing it."

If I'd learned anything from Sarah's lectures it was that every Prod 1 had a weakness. Aranck's pack might not know how to kill this one, but we would find a way, even if it meant consulting Professor Croft. With that info, we could call it up and then put it down permanently.

"What does its name mean?" I pressed.

"I'll tell you after the hunt."

"What hunt?"

Smiling, she turned from me and closed her eyes to the wind and snow. "Can't you smell it?"

All I smelled right now was her. Between that and the pitched battle in my head to keep my wolf from breaking out of its pen, I wasn't attuned to much else. But now I picked up a scent, the same one as in my recurring dream—the scent of something large and plodding.

Hunger stirred in the pit of my stomach.

"There's no time to hunt," I said, swallowing and turning from her.

Nadie moved in a circle around me, brushing against my hips again. "I feel your hunger, Captain Wolfe. Your body is telling you to feed. You're still not fully recovered. You need strength."

Ever since the battle with Aranck, and being poisoned by silver, I hadn't been one hundred percent. Even after healing, it seemed like a part of my core had been hollowed out—the part where my stomach happened to sit.

It shook with another hungry growl.

"See there?" Nadie nudged me with her head. "Come."

She pranced down the ridge a few paces, then stopped and reared her head to the sky. The howl that broke through the fog of her breath resounded beautifully. As it echoed off, members of her pack began to answer from miles away. But the call wasn't meant for them.

She peered at me over a shoulder, then took off in powerful bounds. I responded with a booming howl. The wolf was out. The bonding spell that enabled me to walk like a man but run like a lupine took over. I fell to all fours and followed Nadie, her scent mingling with that of our prey and the wild, snow-covered land around us in an intoxicating rush.

I caught up to Nadie and passed her. She gave the hunt over to me, keeping pace at my flank. Our calls had alerted our quarry.

As we broke into a meadow, I spotted the moose galloping from the river where it had been drinking, its large body glistening as it made for the tree line.

This is crazy, I thought.

But the wolf in me was too absorbed in the head-pounding thrill of the hunt to care what its human companion thought.

I charged across the meadow and caught the moose just as it reached the first trees. It was the dream all over again: The churning muscles of the beast's flank inside my rending jaws. Its legs kicking beneath me. Nadie landing on its back. The moose heaving its rack around to get her off him. And then me going for its throat, my mouth filling with the metallic taste of its blood.

With a growl, I snapped my head to one side and tore out the moose's throat. The beast fell heavily. No sooner than it hit the ground, Nadie and I commenced to feed. Our words from earlier gave over to grunts and the sounds of ripping flesh.

Nadie had been right. Every chunk of the animal I took down was like refilling a reservoir. Soon my body was throbbing with strength and energy. When I reached the heart, I broke through the thick vessels anchoring it and took it in my jaws. Instead of gobbling it down like I'd done everything else, I found myself presenting the gourd of muscle to Nadie.

It was her kill too.

Take it, she said. *You need your strength.*

She hadn't spoken the words aloud. They reached me through a collective consciousness, but not that of her pack. This was a splinter connection, exclusive to us.

Take it, she repeated, her head buried deep in the moose's stomach.

We share, I said.

She lifted her head, muzzle dark with blood, and stepped toward me. Images crashed through my mind—mating, shifter children, growing our own pack. They should have sent me running. Instead, I held the heart toward her. Our lips touched as her teeth cleaved neatly through the muscle.

I took my half down and then closed my eyes as a massive dose of moose adrenaline ran through me like electricity. When I opened them again, everything was crisper, clearer.

I left the moose carcass and walked several paces to a large circle of bare ground beneath a spruce. I lay down to let the meal settle, satisfied in a way I'd never quite been satisfied before. While I'd gorged, Nadie had been more selective. Beyond my outstretched legs, she continued to feed, her white coat luminescent amid the falling snow.

When I caught myself admiring her, my Jason mind struggled awake. What in the hell was I doing? There was a Prod 1 out there. There was a wolf pack waiting for me to return their daughter. There was a mission we needed to finish. There was a woman waiting for me back home.

I tried to rally myself, to get up and take back control, but to my wolf, this was the most natural thing in the world. Loaded with food, his intention to remain here with Nadie sat on my will like an immovable load. No matter how hard I tried to call it up, Daniela remained a murky presence in my memory. At last, the she-wolf stood back from the kill, licked her muzzle, and came over.

"Feeling better?" she asked. Beneath her teasing voice was a tender concern for my well-being.

"Much," I admitted.

She settled beside me, head against my chest. Her weight and warmth felt good.

I remembered Daniela's dream—*You called to tell me you weren't coming back. Not because you couldn't, but because you didn't want to.* But it felt so damned distant.

"That's because this is who you are," Nadie said. "This is where you belong."

I thought she was responding to my memory, but it was to my comment. I gazed across the meadow to the trees and the white cliffs standing above them. As long as I remained the Blue Wolf, nothing less than the wilderness would suffice for a home. Nothing less than a hunt and kill would fully sate my appetite. Along the same lines, no one besides another shifter would understand me so completely. It was delusion to think otherwise.

You're not going to remain *the Blue Wolf,* my Jason mind insisted.

But when Nadie started to lick the blood from around my mouth, I let her. In wolf language, it wasn't sexual. She was grooming me. When she finished, I reciprocated until we were both clean. But that was where it had to end. With Herculean effort, I pushed myself to my feet.

"About the meaning of that name," I said.

As Nadie rose in front of me, a shadow seemed to pass across her markings. "I fear for you."

"The creature has taken someone who needs our help."

For several moments she didn't say anything. Vapor snaked from her moist nostrils as her gold eyes searched mine. She wasn't playing games now. Her concern was palpable. I touched her cheek.

"I'll be all right," I said. "Our team is trained to handle these kinds of—"

Bark sprayed across my face at the same moment I heard the crack of the rifle. I pulled Nadie to the ground, my heart slamming. The shot had come from behind me, downwind from our position. I opened my nostrils anyway and picked up the stringent scent of silver.

Nadie's muzzle wrinkled from her teeth, telling me she could smell it too.

There's cover over there, I said through our budding connection, nudging her toward a gully. We made our way over, staying low to the ground. Two more shots cracked off, but they were high.

Who's shooting? Nadie asked when we arrived.

Don't know, I replied. But that they were armed with silver told me they knew what they were doing. Maybe Centurion's assessment had gotten around and some hunters had decided to go looking for werewolves themselves. The shots hadn't reported like hunting rifles, though. We were talking military grade, the last two sounding an awful lot like shots from an AR-10.

There are four, Nadie said. *Maybe a fifth, but it's hard to tell.*

How do you know?

I hear their breaths, plus two are moving.

I focused until I could hear movement too. Slow, silent, trained.

Where are the other two? I asked.

Instead of answering, a crude image filled our collective mind. It showed the meadow and our position in it. On the far side, about two hundred meters away, two had taken up positions, probably the ones who had fired the first shots. The two in motion were coming around the sides of the meadow, trying to box us in. An opening remained to the south.

Go, I told her.

You can't stay. They have silver.

Then I need to disarm them. Otherwise, they'll keep hunting us.

Then I'm staying too.

If not for the silver, I would have liked our odds.

Listen, I said, *when I was climbing the ridge to meet you, I buried a bag of weapons.*

I know. I watched you.

And here I thought I'd been covert. *I need you to get it,* I said. I looked toward the south end of the meadow and zeroed in on a thick stand of trees. *I'll join you over there.*

What are you going to be doing?

Finding out who we're up against.

Be careful, she said.

You too.

She took off, staying low to the ground. I expected shots, but by the time the hunters would have sighted on her, she was already behind cover and gone. I brought a finger to my earpiece and realized it wasn't there. I swore under my breath. It must have fallen out somewhere between removing my helmet and racing down here. With both drones over the search grid, my teammates had no damned idea where I was or what was happening.

I considered breaking south after Nadie, but I meant what I'd told her. A group of determined hunters armed with silver ammo would only complicate the mission. I wondered how they'd even found us, before remembering the booming howl I'd released prior to the hunt.

Good one, I thought bitterly.

With Nadie gone and the memory of the hunt dimming, I could feel my control returning. And I wasn't happy with where the Blue Wolf had taken things. But the question now was how to handle the hunters. I couldn't blame them for wanting to end the threat. They were just mistaken about what that threat was—and now I was in their firing lane.

The two coming around the sides of the meadow had stopped. I could see slivers of one of them peering from behind a tree through night-vision goggles. I had ID'd his weapon correctly. He was bearing a heavy AR-10. His equipment coupled with his stance told me former military. The same was probably true of the rest of them. They were positioned in a quadrangle so they all had lines of sight on one another. I would be hard pressed to reach one without the other three seeing.

I eyed the man's fur trapper hat, checked wool coat, and multicam pants. A thick beard bulked under a mask covering the lower half of his face. Looked like he'd spent time in the bush.

I stopped suddenly, remembering something.

Earlier in the day, Berglund had told me that right before the Centurion reps reached him he was about to hire a group of "bush crazies" to help with the hunt—former military who had bugged out and set up camp north of Old Harbor. Someone had even drawn Berglund a map.

Son of a bitch went out and hired a second team.

From the time Berglund stormed off until now would have given him enough time to get to their camp and back. I guessed that the hunters had been en route to the hill where the wolf shifter pack was waiting for Nadie and then diverted to the meadow when they heard us howling.

Dammit.

There would be no reasoning with these guys. The best option was going to be to call in the quick reaction force and have them detain the hunters for working in an area under Centurion's jurisdiction. It was bogus, but it would keep anyone—including the hunters—from getting hurt until Nadie and the pack were safely away and we had completed the mission.

Through my connection with Nadie, I sensed that she'd recovered the weapons cache and was heading toward our rendezvous point.

I took off low to meet her. Two shots cracked from the hunter I'd spotted, but I'd already put trees between us. I splashed through a bog, stirring up its thick, muddy smells. By the time I reached the rendezvous point, Nadie was returning with the bag in her mouth.

"Thanks," I whispered, taking the bag from her and opening it.

"Professional hunters, huh?" She had picked up my earlier thoughts through our collective.

"Yeah, I'm going to let someone else deal with them."

A couple of miles away, Sarah and Yoofi were waiting in the van. I planned to radio the QRF from there, give them the hunters' location, and then take Nadie back to her pack. I'd have her tell me the meaning of the creature's name on the way. If Aranck had any more information, great, but I wanted all of them out of here. I noticed Nadie backing away from me.

"I can't return to them," she said.

"It's not up for debate. We had an agreement."

"That was before the hunt."

"What about the hunt?" I slotted a conventional ammo mag into the M4 and checked the sight. At the same time, I was keeping my senses attuned to the hunters. They were holding position.

"It completed our bonding," Nadie said. "That only happens with two who are meant to mate." Her eyes flashed up at me through the falling snow. "I've already broken off from my pack."

"A little premature," I grunted. "I never agreed to anything."

"But you did, you have. It was why you offered me the heart."

I was in problem-solving mode, which seemed to keep the wolf down. When Nadie tried to brush her body against my hip again, I stepped away, and held out a hand for her to stop. My ears cocked to the south. I was picking up a sound.

"Boar," she said. "I smelled them coming back."

I was picking up the musky scent too, but something wasn't right. The smell was too stagnant.

"Down!" I shouted as two cracks sounded.

A bullet nicked past my shoulder, but the other entered Nadie's side and blew out in an explosion of blood and hair. The pain tore through our collective like a row of talons. Nadie fell onto her side, eyes large with shock. I scooped her up and dashed behind cover. More shots cracked in our wake. By the time I set her down, she had reverted to her human form, her dark hair wrapping her body. She was pale and panting. I could smell the silver coiling up from her wound.

I bared my teeth, fury roaring through my head.

"Got one," a man said in a deep, muffled voice. "The other one's pinned."

His walkie-talkie crackled in answer. *"We're coming in."*

Absorbing as much of Nadie's pain as I could bear, I reared back my head and released a ragged howl.

16

Shots popped off, hitting the trees that concealed me. It was the hunter who had dropped Nadie. I brought the barrel of my M4 around the side of a large tree and squeezed off an answering burst.

"Holy shit!" the hunter shouted.

"Was that you?" another hunter radioed.

"No, one of them's armed. Need backup, now!"

I released another burst to keep him pinned and sprinted in the fusillade's wake. I reached his position within seconds, just as he was peering out. My talons met his lower jaw in a hard, arcing chop. He grunted as the rest of my mass plowed into him. We came to a violent rest against the ground, me on top. The hunter had managed to maintain a grip on his weapon, but it was trapped under my knee. I doubted he even knew he still had it.

The man stared at me in shocked horror. Blood bubbled from a bearded mouth that had been knocked almost beneath his left ear. I could smell the boar musk he'd sprayed to disguise his scent. With the other hunters securing the north end of the meadow, he'd worked his way in from the south. I gave him marks for tactics, but with the image of Nadie's vulnerable, blood-soaked body pounding through my head, I felt no mercy.

I buried my muzzle into his neck and emerged with his throat.

I rose, panting, and spit out the gritty taste of him. I had enough wherewithal to disarm his weapon and stick the mag in my duffel bag. I took some spare mags and a sidearm off him as well.

His walkie-talkie crackled. *"Resal, do you copy?"* A pause. *"Res?"*

There was panic in the voice. The hunters might have been military trained, but they'd never faced something like me. I attuned my hearing to their approach. It sounded like bounding overwatch—the two hunters who had been positioned at the far end of the meadow were coming in, past the two who had taken positions at the sides of the meadow.

I pulled a handful of frag grenades from the bag and moved to the meadow's edge. Moments later, I picked up what I'd been listening for: a whispered exchange off to the west as the hunter in motion drew even with the hunter on overwatch. I armed the grenade and hurled it high. I watched its arcing trajectory, then armed a second grenade and heaved it at where the hunter had been on overwatch on the east side of the meadow. By the time that grenade was away, the first one was dropping through spruce branches.

It detonated with a violent boom.

The second grenade tumbled down and went off. Having thrown that one blindly, I cocked my ears toward the aftermath. One of the hunters had been dropped. I could hear him gasping in pain. The other was running. I armed a third grenade and hurled it toward his flight path.

I then took off toward the west side of the meadow where I'd thrown the first grenade. One of the hunters was screaming, the sound punctuated by the boom of the third grenade.

I slowed as I drew near. I found the other hunter, the silent one, facedown in the snow, not breathing. I was half surprised to see it was a woman, her hair cropped short. I disarmed her, then stepped over her body and around a tree, toward the screamer. He lay propped on one arm, squeezing his right knee with the other hand. The lower leg was nearly severed. I looked around, but his weapon was nowhere in sight—probably blown away when he'd been hit.

The soldier in me considered treating him, but the wolf acted first, finishing him with a head shot.

From the edge of the meadow, I peered across the snow-covered expanse to the opposite line of trees. I couldn't see the other hunters. I squeezed off a suppressive burst then sprinted into the open, watchful for the least movement. When I reached cover, shots began to crack. They were coming from the far side of a deadfall. It had to be the hunter who had been gasping earlier, but he was firing blindly. I eased around the deadfall until I had a clear shot.

I put him down for good.

One left, I thought with a growl.

Then I had to get Nadie help. I could feel her presence thinning in our connection.

I moved in the direction I'd heard the final hunter running before I'd heaved the grenade. Soon I arrived at the place where the grenade had detonated. Bark and splintered branches littered the snow. My gaze stopped at a spray of blood. I locked in on the scent, but I didn't have to. A bright trail dribbled off to the south.

I followed it at a loping run, heart pounding with the hunt once more.

I caught up to the hunter shortly. He was staggering like a drunk and aiming for a ravine. Even though he was still carrying his AR-10, I walked behind him for several paces, matching his steps so he wouldn't hear me. I listened to his wheezes and broken pants, a part of me glorying in the control I held over this man's final moments. This man who had attacked my pack.

I lengthened my next stride so that my foot came down on a fallen branch.

He flinched at the sound of cracking wood. By the time he brought his weapon around, my talons were slashing toward his neck. I relieved him of his rifle as he thudded to the ground.

I stood for a moment to make sure that had been all of them.

But as I was about to return to Nadie, the wind shifted, carrying with it a familiar smell.

You son of a bitch.

I took off through the trees, rage crackling inside my chest. At the north end of the meadow, the land fell to a double-track road.

I spotted the vehicles the men had arrived in, a pair of pickups with studded snow tires. Behind them was a third vehicle. A black Chevy Suburban.

The hunters had no doubt ordered Berglund to stay inside his vehicle, but the gunfire and explosions had drawn him out. He was pacing the side of the road now, sweeping the trees with a rifle. Though the snow gave off a dull luminosity, Berglund lacked any kind of night vision.

I descended quietly and came around behind him.

"Your hunters are dead," I snarled.

When he wheeled, I jabbed the knuckles of two fingers into his eyes to temporarily blind him. I caught his rifle barrel in my other hand and wrenched the weapon away. With a cry, he staggered back, pawing for the pistol holstered to his thigh. I let him draw it, then smashed it from his grip with a backhand. Something snapped in his wrist. He pulled it to his chest.

"Their deaths are on you," I finished. "You stupid, stupid man."

Pinned to his vehicle, Berglund tried to squint up at me. I was without my helmet, but I would have been a blurry shadow through his tears. The stink of fear and alcohol poured from his body. He must have been drinking the whole way to and from the hunter's encampment.

"Don't kill me," he slurred.

"Why not?"

His head tilted as my voice registered.

"Captain Wolfe? Is that you?"

I snarled, lips peeling from my canines.

"W-wait, I can explain!"

I drew back his rifle and smashed the stock end into his forehead.

By the time I returned to Nadie, she was cold, her lips blue. She was coming in and out of our connection like a thinning flame. I jammed the M4 into the duffel bag, slung it over my back, and lifted her into my arms. I took off running, Nadie snug against my warm body.

One effect of our connection was that I had access to her history. As I ran, pieces came in flashes. Growing up in a pack, hunting, but taking only what they needed, hiding from humans—that had come to mean the Cree too, the tribe who had once worshipped the Masked Wolf People. For survival, Aranck had grown more despotic, restricting the pack's movement and eventually every aspect of their day-to-day lives. He met insubordination with violence. To Nadie—fiercely independent Nadie—it became unbearable.

The she-wolf had sensed my arrival to Old Harbor somehow, then tracked my scent to Berglund's cabin. In me, she saw a mate she could splinter away with and start her own pack.

Our next two meetings had been fast courtships, culminating in the moose hunt. The same damned hunt from my dreams of the past couple weeks. Only instead of offering the heart to Daniela—who had looked back at me with horror in the dream—I had offered the vital organ to Nadie. I remembered how our lips had touched when she'd accepted her half and swore at myself.

I crested the ridge where I'd met the she-wolf earlier, then raced down the far side toward the meeting point with Sarah and Yoofi. Rusty, who had a drone overhead, must have alerted them I was coming because they both got out.

"What happened?" Sarah called when she saw that I was carrying Nadie.

"She's been shot!" I shouted back through the snow. "We need to get her in the van!"

She nodded quickly and opened the side door. By the time I arrived, she had flattened the middle seat into a makeshift bed and covered it with a clean sheet. I lay Nadie down, checking where the bullet had gone in and grimacing at the ragged hole below her ribs where it had exited.

Yoofi, peering in from outside, made an ominous noise and turned his head away.

"Silver," I said to Sarah. "And there are still fragments in there. Did you bring more solution?"

"Yes, but give me some room." Steady as ever, Sarah opened a side panel onto a stash of medical supplies, transforming the van into a mobile treatment unit. "I'll start working on her."

I backed out and closed the door to keep the inside of the van warm. Yoofi came up beside me.

"Someone shot her, you said?"

"Yeah, Berglund contracted a group of hunters. They were armed for werewolves."

Yoofi looked off in the direction I'd come from. "Where are they now?"

"No longer with us."

His eyes went wide when they returned to mine, reminding

me how he'd reacted to the sight of me tearing out the throats of the death dog. "And Mr. Berglund?" he whispered.

I released a harsh breath, sending up a plume of vapor. After landing the blow to his head, I'd watched him collapse in a heap. Knowing he was ultimately responsible for Nadie being wounded, maybe mortally, the wolf in me had wanted to finish him. But he had acted out of the desperation to recover his girlfriend. He hadn't known it would be *me* the hunters would attack.

Plus, he was still our damned client.

Inside one of the trucks, I had found blankets and a towing chain. I wrapped Berglund in the blankets, secured him with the chain, and threw him into the backseat of his SUV. We'd pick him up later and hold him until the mission was over—for his own safety as much as ours.

"Sleeping," I answered.

When I heard Nadie moan, I turned back toward the van.

Sarah is a doctor, I said softly into the connection. *Let her help you.*

I thought I felt a nod of understanding. The moan subsided. If Sarah could get enough of the silver out, Nadie's own regenerative abilities would kick in. Closing my eyes, I said a prayer.

Then I walked around to the back of the van and opened the cargo hold. There, I swapped the M4 for my MP88 and loaded it. Nadie had never told me the meaning of the Prod 1's name, but that wasn't foremost in my mind right now. I was more concerned about her pack. If she *had* splintered from them would Aranck try to get her back? And how would he regard me, the one she'd splintered off with? I remembered his parting warning...

Do not become tempted by her, Wolfe. For I will know.

"Seems like we're fighting every damned thing except what we came here to fight," I muttered.

"Mr. Wolfe!" Yoofi shouted. He ran around to join me. "Rusty is calling for you!"

I'd almost forgotten about losing my earpiece, as well as the fact I wasn't wearing the suit I'd left up on the ridge. I nodded quickly, pulled a spare headset from the cargo hold, and turned it on.

"Go ahead," I said, fitting it over my ears.

"The surveillance grid just picked up something really frigging big!"

My heart sped up. "Can you see what?"

"It's pitch black and moving fast. I'm having trouble getting a clear visual on the feed, but it's heading straight for a cabin."

"And it's not a bear?"

"Way too big, boss."

"Get me there," I said, grabbing several spare mags. "Send Takara over too."

"Yes, sir."

"Are we moving out?" Sarah asked.

"I am. I want you to finish treating Nadie. Yoofi, stay on outside security. Join us when you can."

Part of wanting Nadie taken care of came from the pack bond we now shared—that was clear. But there was also a good chance she was the only one who would clue us into the creature's identity. And knowing what in the hell we were facing was the first step in stopping it.

"Rusty?" I said.

"You're two miles out. Take the road north."

With the duffel bag and MP88 secured to my body, I fell to all fours and launched away. As the wind screamed past my face, I could taste a hunger in the air that wasn't my own.

This was the thing we'd come to hunt.

17

With the energy from the moose still pulsing inside me, my wolfman form felt like it was hitting on all cylinders. Beneath my dense coat, muscles pumped and blood surged, propelling me at speeds I hadn't achieved before. The forest vibrated in my vision. I was aware of every creature hiding in trees and dens as I tore past them. Both Aranck and Nadie had said this thing couldn't be killed, but I was ready to test that theory.

"Hold that course," Rusty said. *"You'll get to the cabin about the same time as the Prod."*

"ETA?" I panted.

"A couple minutes."

I didn't want to reach the cabin at the same time as the Prod.

I wanted to head it off, then open up on it with everything I had without care or concern for human casualties. I was in no place to exercise restraint. Meaning if I couldn't find another speed, we needed to slow this joker down.

"If you get a clear shot," I said, "take it."

"*Should have one in a few secs. Still can't get a good look at him, though.*"

I remembered what Nadie had said about the creature's greed creating distortions around it. Maybe that's what Rusty was seeing.

"*She's away,*" he called.

The missile's impact rumbled through the ground.

"*Damn,*" Rusty said, "*he took the brunt of that, but he's still going full tilt boogie. Do you want me to hit him again?*"

"I'm almost there," I said, smelling wood smoke and the first traces of the person inside the cabin—the creature's target.

I lowered my head and charged on until I was breaking onto a road covered in a half foot of snow. Powder flew as I veered toward a pair of windows glowing warmly through the snowfall and trees. I could feel the creature I was on a collision course with—its strength, its size, its insatiable hunger. It seemed to resonate with a part of my own makeup, but in a much darker way.

Still, I wasn't ready for what I saw.

With the cabin fast approaching, the Prod burst from the trees. It was as tall as the meat cache that stood over our lodge, putting it at almost twenty feet. Its body was pitch black, its arms and legs lean bundles of tendon that met at an emaciated torso—stomach sunken, chest muscles drawn drum-tight above twin racks of flaring ribs. When it stopped and swung toward me, I found myself staring at a gaping mouth of razor-sharp teeth. Its head was a massive bull-like skull with segmented horns and skin stretched into every pit and hollow.

Thing's a demon, I thought. *Has to be.*

It regarded me from two swirling pits for eyes—starving, soulless eyes—while the surrounding air shimmered like heat from a blacktop in mid July. Only instead of radiating from the creature, the distorted air seemed to draw toward it. The demon reared back its head and released a piercing roar that felt like every nerve ending in my body being sand-papered at the same time.

I responded with a burst of automatic fire. The demon staggered back as silver-laced incendiary rounds detonated against its torso. But the holes being blown into its taut skin sealed instantly, as if by magic.

It roared again.

Demon or not, the being was made to consume—fangs for rending flesh, brick-sized molars for crushing bone. I had no doubt it was our Prod 1. Switching triggers, I sent a volley of grenade rounds at its mouth. The demonic thing flailed as the rounds exploded. Fragments of flesh and bone flew from its head before twisting into wisps of black smoke and dissipating. When the creature straightened after the final flash and thud, its head was fully intact.

Let's see how you like salt, I thought, switching mags on the rifle.

But the salt rounds that blasted into the demon's starved body seemed to do even less damage than the silver. With another roar, the creature lowered its head and charged toward me.

The door to the cabin opened. "The hell is going on out here?" a man shouted.

He couldn't have seen deep into the driving snow, but there was no way he could miss a twenty-foot-tall monstrosity bearing down on an armed figure with a wolf's head. I didn't need to tell him to go back inside. He did that on his own, uttering a string of profanities before slamming and bolting the door.

The motion, and probably the fresh scent of human flesh, caught the demon's attention. It veered from me and arrived at the cabin steps in two bounds. It shot an arm forward and, with jagged talons, clawed around the door frame. There was an imprecision to it that told me the creature relied more on smell, or some other sense, than its sight.

Unwilling to risk a shot from where I was standing, I switched to the flamethrower and unleashed a whooshing jet of napalm. The demon's prior roars had sounded like anger or frustration. This one was pain. The sound drove into my ears like steel picks, my eyes watering from the intensity. I clenched my jaw and sustained the assault, advancing toward the cabin.

So you can be hurt, you son of a bitch.

The demon retreated from the door, its body a suit of fire. It rounded toward me, flames crackling in the pits of its eyes and mouth. Raising an arm to shield itself from the blazing stream, it staggered toward the driveway, where a Land Rover was parked.

It can't sense me inside the flames, I realized. *Can't sense anything.*

The Land Rover rocked sideways as the creature's knee slammed into its side. Stooping over, the demon felt around the vehicle and then lifted it as if it were a battery-operated model for a kid. I swept the bottom of the Land Rover, hoping to catch the fuel line. Fire broke across the undercarriage. With another roar, the creature heaved it toward me. I leapt to one side. The vehicle crashed off to my right, and *that's* when the fuel line caught.

I spun from the explosion and landed hard, ears ringing. My right side was smoking and singed. When I tried to orient myself, everything wavered. The Land Rover was upended and spewing flames. Fire wrapped the front porch from my earlier assault, its tendrils starting to climb the walls.

Off to my left, I caught another flash of flames—the demon fleeing back into the forest.

I pushed myself to my feet. My MP88 was still slung around my body, but the duffel bag had come off in a trail of spilled mags. I grabbed the bag. Though I'd lost a lot of the ammo, there was no time to backtrack and scoop it up.

With my wounds healing in a prickling wave, I took off after the creature. Each stride felt surer, and by the time I hit the trees, I was nearing full strength again. The demon had a good lead. I could just see it through the trees, the flames over its body guttering out as if suffocated by the ravenous energy that surrounded it. And it was pulling away. By the time the flames extinguished entirely, I couldn't see the demon at all.

"Do you have eyes on the Prod?" I asked Rusty, before realizing I'd lost my headset in the explosion.

My nostrils flared. For the last half mile, I'd been trailing the harsh scent of burning napalm—and something else. Less a smell than a primal feeling. The hunger Yoofi had described. But with the fire out, I wasn't picking up anything.

I looked at the snow-covered ground. Where there should have been prints was pristine snow. Only by peering into the distant gloom could I see a line of tracks. Besides pulling away, they were closing in on themselves, like the wounds over the demon's body.

I'd never, in all of our training, heard of anything doing that.

I peered around. My pursuit of the demon was taking me in the direction I'd come from—toward the van, where I had left Sarah, Yoofi, and Nadie. A charge of urgency went off in my chest. I had denied the creature one victim, and now it was after another. And I had no way to warn them.

I picked up the sound of the drone high overhead. Unless Rusty was playing online poker, he would see where the creature was going. He would alert the others that it was bearing down on them. Just had to hope Sarah could get the van up to speed in time to outmaneuver it.

But in the next moment, the drone's engine rose in pitch. It zipped back and forth in an erratic pattern and plummeted. Within moments it was whacking through branches off to my left. It landed hard enough to detonate its remaining payload, which flashed through the trees.

The hell's going on?

Ears flattened, eyes squinted to the inrushing snow, I pounded on. If I couldn't close the distance, I needed to keep the demon from pulling too far ahead. Though I hadn't checked, I could smell the spare canister of fuel for the flamethrower in the duffel bag. The creature was heavy duty, but I had discovered a weakness: distaste for fire.

I was just hitting the road we'd arrived by earlier that evening when I heard automatic gunfire and the distinct sound of a bolt shooting from Yoofi's staff. The demon had gotten too far ahead of me, dammit.

"Fire!" I roared. "Use fire!"

But my call was buried beneath more gunfire and then the jagged peeling of metal. Another blast from Yoofi's staff sounded, followed by Sarah's shout.

By the time the van came into view, there was only one figure. It belonged to Yoofi, and he was pushing himself up from the ground. He didn't hear me coming. Instead, he stared into the whiteout ahead of the van.

"Where are they?" I asked.

I could see the chaos of tracks in the snow where Yoofi and Sarah had engaged the demon. The demon's own footsteps were already gone, but what remained of the van testified to the thing's violent presence. Amid a fury of gashes, the entire passenger door had been torn back so that it stood at a ninety-degree angle to the body.

I thrust my head inside. Where Sarah and Nadie had been was empty space. Medical bandages and bottles littered the floor.

I turned back to Yoofi. His helmet had come off, and he was bleeding between two lines of cornrows. He looked at me with dazed eyes.

"Did it take them?" I demanded.

Yoofi nodded.

I clenched my jaw. "Which way?"

He pointed in the direction he'd been staring when I arrived. "I'm sorry, Mr. Wolfe. I tried to stop it."

"Is Rusty on your feed?"

"We lost the feed a few minutes ago. Static and then nothing."

About the time the drone crashed, I thought. "Stay here," I ordered. "Keep trying Rusty. If you get him, send him my way."

I set off in the direction the demon had taken Sarah and Nadie. I could have used backup, but Yoofi wouldn't have had a chance in hell of keeping up with me. And I was having a hard enough time keeping up with the creature solo.

Maybe the extra weight will slow it down.

I hadn't gone far when I noticed a fog gusting in on my right. A muscular appendage wrapped my waist and slammed me high against a tree. I tumbled to the ground. An elephant reared above me, front legs pedaling air. It trumpeted as its massive feet fell toward my head.

Not these fuckers again.

Fortunately, my rifle was still loaded with a salt mag. I kicked backwards and unleashed a burst of automatic fire into its belly. As the elephant's legs crashed down, the entire animal burst apart in smoke. But like last time, more animals were arriving. And I could hear that damned drum.

The god, Muluku, was making another go for Yoofi's staff—and at the worst possible moment.

As I gained my feet, two large crocodiles appeared. I blasted one into smoke and jumped as the other one lunged. I landed with a foot on its neck, pressed the barrel to its craggy head, and fired twice more. I didn't have enough salt rounds to keep this up, but the god was in my way now.

I plunged into the fog, toward the drumbeats. Whiteness and a sensation of displacement closed around me. I was between worlds, but I could give two craps. My only thought was recovering Sarah and Nadie and blowing apart anything that came between us.

Animals raced past me going the other direction, presumably

for Yoofi's staff. Gorillas, lions, elephants, crocs. Those that so much as looked at me got a salt round to the face. They were Forms, as I understood them. Ideas. They could be dispersed but not destroyed, so I felt no guilt about blowing them apart.

Slowly, the god Muluku took shape through the mist.

I aimed at his drum. A giant gorilla landed in front of me, forcing me to use up scarce rounds to blow it out of my way. When a second gorilla appeared, I dropped it with my final two rounds.

Dammit.

I dug a hand into my duffel bag, but I was out of salt mags. I slotted home a mag of conventional ammo and took aim at the god again. But when I squeezed off a burst, the rounds passed through him and his drum.

Grunting in frustration, I dropped the MP88 onto its sling and charged Muluku.

The god was bigger than he'd appeared from a distance, and the drum Takara had shot to shreds earlier was back underneath his arm. He raised his club and brought it down in a methodical beat. I needed to take care of it, somehow. Without the incessant sound, the animals would return to their realm. Then it would be Yoofi's job to make sure they stayed there.

When I was within range, I leapt for the drum, talons slashing toward its taut skin. I met empty air, god and drum no longer there. I turned to where the drum continued to sound its ominous beat. Muluku had reappeared a short distance away. Judging by his hooded eyelids, he wasn't concerned by my presence. He stared past me, as if seeing something distant.

The corners of his lips turned up. He brought the club down in a faster beat, eyes sparkling until they looked almost maniacal. The animals that had been emerging started to return, disappearing into the mist at his back.

I crouched, ready for a fight, but the animals never gave me a second glance. I didn't like what that suggested. Amid a riot of hooting, a gang of bloated chimpanzees jumped into view. The lead one pumped Yoofi's staff overhead like a prize, while the others hopped around, clamoring to hold it. I was prepared to let them keep it—maybe that would put an end to these damned gods interfering—until I picked up Yoofi's voice.

"Mr. Wolfe!" he cried. "Mr. Wolfe, the staff! We will need it against what we're facing!"

How would he know that?

"Mr. Wolfe!" Yoofi cried again.

For the love of God. "On it!" I roared back.

I sprang toward the chimpanzee pack, my talons slashing. "Sorry to break up your party, guys," I said as I caught the chimp hoisting the prize. He screamed as smoke gusted from the wound across his chest. I grabbed for the staff, but he had already tossed it to another chimp. That chimp backed away and jutted his bristly lips at me.

I snarled and leapt toward him, but he tossed the staff to a third chimp. They were surrounding me now, hooting and jumping up and down. I faked toward the chimp with the staff and then lunged in the direction I'd thought he was going to throw it. But he anticipated the move and held on. As I stumbled off balance, the other chimps screamed with laughter.

A hard double drumbeat sounded, and the chimps turned toward Muluku. He was telling them to stop screwing around and bring him the staff.

I was preparing to head them off when something crushed my ankle and twisted me to the ground. Pain speared through my leg. My foot was clamped in the mouth of one of the crocs. I kicked its rock-hard head with my other leg as the chimps scampered off. When the croc didn't relent, I took its snout and chin in my hands and, snarling, pried its jaws open. I withdrew my mangled ankle and swung the flailing croc off into the mist.

I pulled my weapon back around, swapped mags, and sighted on the lead chimp. A burst of conventional rounds dropped him, but another one grabbed the staff. I took aim, but now I was being butted and pummeled as other large animals came between me and my target. I hopped to one side and the other on my healing ankle, looking for a clear shot.

Too much interference.

Dropping my weapon back on its sling, I made a dash for the chimps. I slipped between two gorillas and leapt over a lion that managed to rake its claws down my side. Even with the suit's protection, I staggered. That gave a group of elephants time to lumber between me and the chimps. When I tried to skid underneath one, the elephant pinned me with a foot.

My ribs crackled as its weight bore down on my chest. I grunted, struggling to twist its leg off me. A distant jack-hammering sounded. The elephant staggered and came apart in an explosion of smoke. I drew a painful breath. The other elephants rounded toward the sound before being chopped into oblivion.

Salt ammo, I thought.

The chimps paused to look back. Amid the sound of automatic fire came the revving of an engine. And now I could make out our cargo van, headlights cutting through the mist. Takara was driving.

Gunfire burst from the roof-mounted machine gun. Through the window, I recognized the thick figure manning the weapon.

"Olaf!" I shouted. "The chimps!"

He redirected his fire. One by one the screaming chimps went up in bursts of smoke. Finally, the salt rounds lit into the chimp holding Yoofi's staff. He grasped for it even as his hands were coming apart.

I was already in motion, ears pinned back, determined to catch the staff before it hit the ground. Olaf continued to fire, now aiming at the god who had been striding forward to meet the returning chimps. Rounds flashed off the rim of his drum before punching through the stretched leather. Absent the beat, our space underwent a sudden change in pressure.

I caught the end of the staff at the same time Muluku grabbed the hilt beneath the blade. Snarling, I glared into his hooded eyes as we struggled for control. I brought my other hand beside my first and he did the same. We were at a stalemate, but it didn't last. As the mist world collapsed around us, it felt as if Muluku had an anchor in our tug-of-war for the staff.

I roared as the staff began to slip from my grip.

With a final wrench, Muluku disappeared into the swirling fog, and I found myself prone in the snow, hands empty. Headlights grew over me as the van roared up and came to a stop. I got to my feet at the same time Yoofi ran up in his heavy, clinking coat. He peered all around, eyes large and desperate.

"My staff, Mr. Wolfe?"

I shook my head. "Muluku got it."

Yoofi searched the ground as if he might spot it sticking out of the snow. A part of me wanted to grab him by the coat and give him a hard shake. Twice on this mission he'd sworn Dabu wouldn't be a problem, and twice now we'd had to deal with his shit show. But Yoofi already looked devastated enough.

While Olaf kept his position at the gun's controls, Takara stepped out of the van. "Where's Sarah?" she asked.

"The Prod took her and one of the wolf shifters that way."

"How long ago?"

"A few minutes." I burned to take off after them, but the creature had too far a head start, and I'd just be chasing blindly. I needed eyes in the sky. "Yoofi, were you able to bring Rusty up?"

"No, Mr. Wolfe."

"The whole commo system went down on my way here," Takara said.

"The *whole* system?" I asked.

When Takara nodded, I swore. Had Berglund gotten out of his confinement somehow and called Beam to cancel the contract? There was no way. Not in that amount of time. Whatever the issue, I'd no doubt Rusty was already working on a solution to get everything back up.

I turned to Yoofi. "You said we'd need the staff against this thing. What did you mean?"

"Yes, Ms. McKinnon was talking to the she-wolf. I could not hear what they were saying, but very soon she comes out of the van and asks whether I can cast a reveal spell. When I asked why, she said we would need it to see where the Prod had put Ms. Welch. And then the creature appeared. Ooh, I never see anything that big and scary. I hit it with the bolts, but they did nothing."

Nadie must have recovered enough to tell Sarah the meaning of the creature's name, a meaning Sarah had interpreted.

"Did Sarah tell you the name of the Prod?"

"No, Mr. Wolfe."

I waved Olaf over and screwed a fresh fuel canister into the port of my MP88. "We're going to start a search for our teammate," I announced. "The Prod doesn't like fire. There are flamethrowers in the other van."

Using my sat phone, I called the quick reaction force and ordered them to perform flyovers of the area. Visibility was shit, but it was what it was. The rest of us set out on foot in pairs, me and Yoofi and Takara and Olaf. I felt responsible for Sarah as a teammate, but with Nadie, I felt a strange loss. It was our lupine connection, I told myself. There one moment—a growing, organic presence that embraced the being I'd become—and snatched away the next.

After an hour of finding nothing, and conditions worsening, I called a halt to the search. We were going about it the wrong way. As I squinted into the vast expanse of a wilderness cut through with wind and driving snow, my captain's mind was telling me we needed to regroup, to form a coherent plan. I judged our distance to the cave where Aranck was waiting. Could he and his pack help, or would they attack us for failing to return Nadie?

I'd consult Prof Croft, I decided. He'd know what we were up against. Plus, Sarah's exchange with Yoofi suggested that magic would be essential to mission success.

"Back to home base!" I called over the storm.

18

"I am so sorry, Mr. Wolfe," Yoofi said through chattering teeth. I looked over at him. Even though I'd bent the passenger door back into place and turned up the heat, snow blew in through the seams. A powdery frost gripped Yoofi's braided hair. I'd wanted him to ride in the cargo van with Takara and Olaf, but he insisted on coming so he could explain himself. I turned my face back to the onrushing road.

"We're not going to dwell on it," I said. "It's done."

"I thought Dabu would protect me," he pressed. "That was what he was telling me, but now he is telling me he has set a trap for Muluku. He *wanted* Muluku to get the staff. He put bad magic into it—that was why it was acting funny at the cabin. He kept it a secret to trick Muluku."

"Is he going to give you a replacement?"

"No, but he is promising that when he has defeated Muluku and sent him away, he will return the staff."

"Does he have an estimate on when that will be?"

Yoofi giggled.

I glared at him. "Something funny?"

"Sorry. Dabu just tell good joke."

"Well, I'm glad someone's in a happy mood," I growled.

"He does not know when, Mr. Wolfe."

I grunted. I was annoyed, of course, but Yoofi wasn't entirely to blame. He was a pawn in a squabble between gods. Caught up in their own shit, they couldn't care less about our mission. It was the price of Yoofi being able to channel Dabu's powers in the first place.

We all had our tradeoffs. Olaf's body could heal from almost anything, but someone who preferred death could well be trapped inside that body. Takara wielded awesome powers, but they came with disfigurement and excruciating pain. I thought of my change into a wolf—one with mind-boggling abilities, but there was my isolation from Daniela, not to mention my recent reckless behavior. I could still feel a desperation to recover Nadie and restore our connection. It clawed at the back of my mind like an unfulfilled need. Or was it desire?

"Then we'll hope for the best and work with alternative resources," I said. "Just stop beating yourself up."

"I will try, Mr. Wolfe."

We arrived at the lodge a few minutes later and piled out of the vans. Even before I opened the front door, I could hear Rusty swearing inside. I directed the others to the kitchen when we entered. "Hydrate and calorie up. We'll meet at the planning table in five."

Still full from the moose, I followed the trail of choice words to Rusty's command-and-control center.

"What's going on?" I asked.

"We're offline is what's going on, boss," he said, attacking a keyboard with his fingers.

Anger gripped my neck. "Did Beam take us down?"

"Not exactly..."

I had already picked up my private sat phone to call Beam. I paused.

"What do you mean 'not exactly'?"

"I was playing with the workaround. I had a model for testing and a block of code on standby. I was running a test on the model—I thought. Turned out it was the real McCoy. Which would have been fine if Centurion's system hadn't detected it. Locked us out of the subnet. We lost the commo system, access to the databases, and the linkup to the drones. I was able to land Drone 1, but I lost contact with 2. Probably crashed somewhere."

"Yeah, near me."

"I'm trying to get us back up, but the system thinks I'm a hacker now."

"Stop," I said, not wanting him to make a bad situation worse. "I'll call Beam and have them restore it on their end."

"Yeah, but then they'll know what I did."

"What I *ordered* you to do," I reminded him. "This is on me."

I stepped from the room and dialed Beam.

"Yes?" he answered.

"It's Captain Wolfe."

There was a pause as my voice went through a recognition protocol. A click followed. "Security pin?"

I recited it to him.

"Are you calling to explain why I don't have any new updates?"

"No, I'm calling because our system is down. We need it back up."

"The system's down?"

I took a deep breath. "I ordered my team to create a workaround in the event of a shutdown."

There was a pause on his end. "Oh, you mean in the event *I* shut you down."

"I wasn't going to have my team made vulnerable mid mission."

"And now look what's happened."

"The workaround triggered some sort of kill switch," I continued, trying to ignore his condescension. "We need it reset ASAP."

"I'm sure you do, but here's the thing, Captain. There's a built-in protocol on that system. When it senses it's been compromised, not only does it shut down the subnet, it goes into lock down. You can't just turn a key to restore it. It's one of the most secure systems in the world. The process takes time."

"How long?"

"Probably a question you should have asked before ordering your team to illegally hack the system. Not only did you violate my trust, Captain. You violated your contract. And so did anyone who followed your order."

"Leave them out of this," I growled.

"I wish I could, but they're bound by the same terms as—"

"Sarah's been taken, goddammit."

"Taken?"

"The Prod we're hunting has her."

"How did that happen?" he demanded.

"How do you think? During a confrontation with the Prod 1." When he tried to cut in, I said, "You wanted the latest SITREP. Shut up and let me give it to you. Our communication is down, and with the storm, we're facing near white-out conditions. I need your engineers to restore the system. I have a sat phone and can requisition other modes of commo in the meantime."

"Secure modes?"

"Not a priority. We need to ID the Prod 1."

"They're werewolves," he said, as if Centurion's early assessment was infallible.

"Not werewolves," I snarled. "Pretty fucking far from it, in fact. Which brings us to the next item. Sarah seemed to have an idea what we were facing, but with her not here, I need two things: a contact number for someone who can access the Prod 1 database, and permission to use an outside expert."

"I'll get you the first," he said begrudgingly. "Who's the second?"

"Everson Croft, a magic-user based in New York City. He gave us crucial intel during the El Rosario mission. Sarah submitted a clearance request following, but at last check it was still working its way through your pencil pushers. I need him cleared in the next ten minutes."

"How critical is Croft to *this* mission?"

"If we want to recover Sarah and Ms. Welch, very."

"Yoofi's a magic-user," he pointed out.

"With limited knowledge, and he's currently without his staff."

"What happened to it?"

"It doesn't matter. Do I have permission to contact Croft or not?"

He sighed in a way that said he knew I'd call him anyway. "I'll give a tentative okay, but I'm not happy, Captain. I'm not happy about any of this. I don't imagine Berglund is either. Is he still safe, at least?"

"I had to detain him."

"Detain? What the hell are you talking about?"

"He contracted a second team of hunters that attacked while I was meeting with an asset. They critically wounded her. I had no choice but to neutralize them. Berglund's lucky to be alive."

I could hear Beam's breathing pick up as he realized his payment was in jeopardy. "Listen to me, Captain. You need to release him this instant."

"He's a liability. We already have five dead mercs that we're going to have to explain." Now that I was back in control, my conscience was prickling me about the hunters—former military, like me. Not that they would have fared much better against Aranck's pack. "I've made mistakes, but I'm not the only one. Telling Berglund that werewolves had taken Ms. Welch and then letting him write himself into the mission are on Centurion."

"Captain—"

"I want him out of here," I said over Beam. "I'm going to give you his location. Have the backup force retrieve him. He has a head wound so they can hold him under the pretext of treatment."

"Where is he?" Beam demanded.

"First I want your assurance that there'll be no repercussions for the system going down. Not for my teammates. Not for anyone." But for Daniela, I wouldn't have cared what they did to me.

"We'll discuss it after the mission."

"It was just an unfortunate misunderstanding," I added.

"You violated the terms of the contract, Wolfe."

"Then what do I have to lose?"

"A lot," he said in a lowered voice. "Believe me."

"Did I mention Berglund was chained up in the back of his vehicle?"

"Goddammit," Beam barked. "All right, I'll give you your damn pass, but on the condition you complete the mission *and* Berglund comes through with the rest of the payment."

"Smart move," I said, and gave him the coordinates of Berglund's Suburban.

I could hear him tapping them into a device. "I already have a team working to restore the system," he said in the distracted voice of someone texting. "It's going to be an hour or two. Until then, I'll have someone contact you so you can query the database."

"Glad we're on the same page again."

"This isn't over," he promised.

I ended the call and stepped back into the computer room, where Rusty was staring at the main monitor with a hangdog expression. "It's going to take time, but they're working on getting everything back up," I told him.

"I fucked up again, boss."

"No more than I did. There's nothing any of us can do in here till the system's restored. C'mon."

I led the way to the planning table, where the others were waiting. Olaf and Takara were eating from pouches of MREs, while Yoofi clasped a steaming mug of tea in both hands.

"Here's the situation," I said, leaning my fists against the spread-out map and looking around at my teammates. "Sarah is missing, our system is down, and we need three crucial pieces of info. One, what the Prod 1 is. Two, how to find where it's keeping its prey. And three, how to kill it. The creature's pattern suggests we have a window to reach Sarah, but not much of one. Rusty, before the system went down, did you overhear anything coming through Sarah's feed? The she-wolf might have told her what this thing's name means."

Rusty perked up so suddenly that under different circumstances I might have cracked a smile. "I had an eye on the drone monitors, so I was only half listening, but yeah, yeah, the she-wolf said a word and Sarah repeated it. 'Cannibal.' Then the system went down, and I forgot all about it."

"I think Sarah knew what that meant," I said. "She stepped out to ask Yoofi about one of his magical capabilities."

"Yes, when I still had my staff." Yoofi took a sullen sip of tea.

"We'll work with what we have," I reminded him. "I'm going to start by calling Croft, the wizard who helped us with the El Rosario case. Keep eating and getting fluids down."

I dialed Croft's number from memory and waited, but not even his cat picked up this time. The call went to his voicemail. *Dammit.* I knew he was busier than ever these days, but I'd been hoping to catch him in. I left a message explaining our situation and ended by giving him my number.

Moments later, my phone rang. "Captain Wolfe," I answered hopefully. But I recognized the pause and subsequent click of Centurion's voice recognition protocol.

"This is Megha Shah," a woman's voice said in a British accent.

"I'll be assisting you with your queries."

"Pin?" I asked mechanically.

The electronic distortions that squiggled around her alphanumeric response were another layer of security from her end to ensure no one could eavesdrop on our conversation.

When she finished, I said, "Thanks for helping out. Do you have the case information?"

"Yes, it's already entered."

"Then let me give you a description of what I saw." I went on to tell her everything I remembered from our encounter—the Prod 1's appearance, abilities, fear of fire. I made sure my teammates could hear me as well. I'd only had time to give them basic info prior to our search. As I spoke, I could hear Megha tapping through the connection. "A local asset told us its name means *cannibal*," I added. "Query as many iterations of that info as you can and get back to me."

"Our software does that automatically," she said before I could disconnect. "Nothing's returning from the main databases, but hold on." Her young voice carried a note of interest I was unaccustomed to hearing among Centurion's rank and file. "We have another database that contains Prod 1s whose existences have yet to be verified," she explained. "A skunk database."

"I'm going to put you on speaker so the rest of my team can hear."

"Go ahead ... There!" she exclaimed. "Your Prod 1 is returning 94.9 percent for Wendigo."

"Wendigo?" I couldn't remember Sarah ever talking about a creature by that name. "What can you tell us about it?"

"According to the data, it comes from the myths of the

Algonquin-speaking people." *Which would include Cree,* I thought as I pictured Megha reading from a monitor on her end. "A person becomes a Wendigo in a ceremony that involves eating human flesh. And the description here lines up with what you told me. Large and gaunt, head with horns, empty black eyes, cannibalistic ... Now this is interesting."

"What's that?"

"Per the myths, it grows in proportion to what it eats, which keeps it from ever being sated. In fact, eating only makes it hungrier. Knowing this, it stores its victims to stretch out the time between meals."

That jibed with Nadie's intel. It also explained why the sizes of the claw-marks were different between the abduction scenes.

"The Algonquin-speaking people don't like to say its true name," Megha continued, "so they call it 'the Evil Spirit that Devours Mankind' or simply 'the Cannibal.'" The more she talked, the more animated her voice became. If most of her work involved data entry, getting to contribute to an actual case was probably a thrill for her.

"Where does a Wendigo keep its victims?" I asked.

She fell back into her data-skimming voice. "Wendigo is a spirit ... Someone has to call it into them for it to take form ... ceremony with human flesh ... The Wendigo enters and leaves its host as its hunger dictates..."

"Why would anyone invite a Wendigo into them?" Yoofi interrupted.

"Its exclusion from the main database suggests it's not common," I replied. At the same time I remembered Aranck's remarks about stupid men from across the water, suggesting there had been an episode in the past. Knowing how that episode had ended could be a big help.

"Let's see ... victims ... victims ..." Megha was saying. "Ah! It says here that a Wendigo makes its lair in a cave between the material and ethereal planes where it, and its victims, are hidden from both. Exposing a Wendigo's lair requires special magic."

"Explains why no one's located the vics," Takara said.

Must also have been why Sarah was asking Yoofi whether he could cast a reveal spell, I thought. But how had she known about the Wendigo if it wasn't on the main database? Had she known about the skunk database, and if so, why had she never mentioned it? If it hadn't been for this call, I wouldn't have known the database even existed. But this wasn't the time to dwell on it.

"Are there places that lend themselves to that kind of transparency between planes?" I asked.

"I'm not seeing anything in the database," Megha replied.

"Yes, there are, Mr. Wolfe," Yoofi said. "Back home, the priests do their best magic in the sacred places. These are where rituals have been performed for many, many generations. The magic passes back and forth much easier."

I nodded. We'd seen something similar in El Rosario, where the shaman had gone to a special mountain to invoke a local god, but unwittingly called forth an ancient creature that had infiltrated the god's space. It made sense that the Cree's sacred places would offer a similar thinning of the layer between worlds—and the most opportune spaces for something like a Wendigo to lair.

"But the person would have to have Cree blood," Yoofi added. "And be a strong believer."

"We'll need to ID the Cree's sacred sites in the area," I said.

"I can do a records search when we finish here," Megha offered.

"That would be great. What does the database say about killing a Wendigo?"

"According to the legends, they can't be killed," she replied. "At least not while they're in possession of their hosts. You mentioned an aversion to fire, which makes sense. In addition to famine and starvation, a Wendigo embodies winter and coldness. But fire won't destroy it. The only way to stop a Wendigo is to wait for it to leave the host and then destroy the host."

"Make it so the Wendigo can't return to that particular body," I said.

"That's my read. It remains in the spirit world until someone else calls it."

"Is there anything about *driving* a Wendigo from the host?" I asked.

"Ooh, if I only had my staff," Yoofi lamented.

"Not according to the data," Megha replied.

"All right," I said, "see what you can learn about the sacred sites in the region."

"I will."

"Not bad, boss," Rusty said as I ended the call. "Five minutes after laying out the situation, and we know what the thing is, an idea of where to find its lair, and how to kick its head in."

"Wendigo," Yoofi repeated in a mixture of wonder and dread.

"Recalling that exchange between Sarah and Nadie helped set off the avalanche of info," I said to Rusty. "And Yoofi had the insight on the sacred spaces. Good job, guys." For the first time since the Wendigo had taken Sarah and Nadie, I felt like we had at least a few finger holds on the situation. "I'm going to try Croft again. See if he can help us cut down the search time."

But before I could dial him, Takara stepped forward.

"Don't you want to hear what I found?"

19

I hadn't forgotten that I had sent Takara to see what she could learn about the mayor. But when she hadn't volunteered anything, I'd assumed the assignment had been a bust.

"Go ahead," I said.

"The mayor and warden are involved in drug-trafficking—heroin, some meth. Grimes is the purchaser. Wabberson distributes the drugs in his bush chopper. It's nothing huge, but it would explain why they didn't want the Mounties up here."

"How did you learn that?" I asked.

"I took up a position outside Grimes's office and paired to their phones," Takara replied. If she was still upset about how our earlier conversation had ended, she didn't show it. "You were right.

Your visit shook them up. They were speculating on the strength of our ties to the Canadian government. With the storm, they had to rearrange some logistics relating to pickups and deliveries. They might as well have mapped out their entire operation."

"So they played down the attacks for personal reasons," I said. "What about the mayor's wife?"

"With Grimes at the office, I found her alone at their house. No security except for a kennel of hunting dogs. I put them to sleep and entered through the back door. Mrs. Grimes was sitting by a wood stove, listening to the radio. She had a revolver holstered at her waist."

"Ooh, did she see you?" Yoofi asked.

"'Course not," Rusty said. "T-cakes is a flipping ninja."

Takara gave Rusty a withering look. "And Mrs. Grimes is legally blind."

I grunted in surprise. The blindness had to be recent if she had been researching the area's history.

"She was wearing tinted medical glasses," Takara continued.

"Might explain her husband's protectiveness," I said.

"Her library was off the living room. Shelves of books, notebooks, journals. I had two choices: search through the library for something relevant to our mission or talk to Mrs. Grimes herself."

"You didn't," Rusty said.

"I left the house and knocked on the door. When she answered, I told her I was researching the settlement's history and that her husband had sent me to interview her. Mrs. Grimes tried to call him, but I had already scrambled her phone. She then said she wanted to wait for him. I told her that with the weather, I only had a narrow window."

"Very tricky," Yoofi said approvingly.

"She asked several times to make sure her husband had sent me before inviting me inside. Once we began talking, she relaxed. She even lit a joint. The history of the region had been her life before she'd lost her eyesight to glaucoma. After a couple of general questions, I told her I had heard a rumor of killings in the early days of the settlement. She asked again whether her husband had given me permission to talk to her. I assured her he had, that I wouldn't have known who she was or how to find her otherwise. That convinced her."

"Let's hear the relevant info," I said to speed her along. Sarah was still missing, along with Nadie and Ms. Welch, and the Wendigo's appetite was only going to grow.

Takara narrowed her eyes at me. "It's *all* relevant. In the settlement's beginnings, fur traders did business with the Cree. There was a dispute, though, and the settlement captured a Cree chief and held him hostage. Some wanted to execute him to make their point. But the chief escaped under mysterious circumstances. His guards were found dead, savaged by a mysterious animal. Shortly after, settlers began to disappear. They blamed the Cree and war broke out. By the time the conflict ended, more than twenty settlers had gone missing."

"Did she say what had taken them?" I asked.

"We didn't get that far before I was called to the Wendigo attack. But she said that the Cree chief who escaped was later sacrificed by his tribe for unknown reasons. A new chief was appointed. I didn't make the connection between that and what we were hunting until hearing what Megha told us."

"The Cree chief could have escaped by calling the spirit of

the Wendigo into him," I said in understanding. "Then the chief confessed to what he'd done or the tribe found out. Either way, they sacrificed him to be rid of the creature."

Takara nodded. "The difference between then and now is that the Cree *knew* who the host was."

"But we have a lead," I said.

Rusty's head had been turning between me and Takara during the exchange as if he was watching a tennis match. Now he stopped so suddenly that his eyes jittered for a moment.

"We do?" he asked.

"Megha said the Wendigo ceremony requires the host to eat human flesh. In Takara's account, the guards looked like they'd been savaged by an animal. But I bet if someone had taken a close look at the first guard, they would have found a human bite mark. That was the chief."

"But how is that a lead in *this* case?" Yoofi asked.

On the map, I pointed to the photo of the young man with the military cut, Connor Tench. "We know who the first victim was."

"So you think someone, what, snatched this guy and used him in a Wendigo ceremony?" Rusty asked.

"More likely the perp knew him," I replied.

"Then we're looking for someone with Cree blood, yes?" Yoofi asked.

"If that's who you say is most likely to perform this kind of ceremony," I replied. Yoofi nodded vigorously. "The mayor mentioned earlier that his older son was best friends with the vic. If Connor was close to any Cree, Austin would know. We need to talk to him."

"I learned something else during my visit," Takara said. We

stopped and turned toward her. "Mrs. Grimes has First Nation features. When I asked, she told me she was half Cree."

That meant Austin had Cree blood too. I thought about the books and notes in Mrs. Grimes's library, some of them undoubtedly on Cree beliefs and ceremonies. Austin would have had access to them. I also remembered his hostility toward me and Sarah when we'd visited the office earlier. There was a good chance the perp had been standing right in front of us.

"Let's go," I growled.

The mayor's and warden's trucks were still parked in front of the office when we pulled up. I had tried Prof Croft again en route. This was the second mission where I was having to lean on him—third if I counted the White Dragon—and a part of me didn't like it, but we were dealing with another being beyond Centurion's understanding. I reached his voicemail again.

"Are you sure Austin wasn't here earlier?" I asked Takara.

"No," she replied impatiently—I'd asked her already, but I wanted to make certain. Just because I couldn't smell him didn't mean anything. The whipping wind and driving snow were playing havoc with my senses. There was also my broken connection with Nadie to distract me.

I turned to the back of the van, where the rest of the team sat. "At least two men are inside. Both armed and edgy."

"Stack and enter?" Rusty asked eagerly. With the system still down, I'd decided to bring him along. He was sufficiently trained in tactics, and I needed boots on the ground.

"I'll breach," I said. "Olaf and Rusty cover the room in sectors, left to right. I'll come in behind. Takara will make sure no one escapes out back. And Yoofi..." I still didn't like the idea of him using a gun instead of his staff. "Just hang back. You'll be on rear watch."

"Yes, Mr. Wolfe."

We stepped out into the storm. While Takara went around to the rear of the building, the rest of us approached the front door in a column. When we were in position, I kicked the door open.

There was a mad shuffle inside, but Olaf and Rusty were already entering, covering Mayor Grimes and Wabberson. They had been sitting on opposite sides of a table, consulting a spreadsheet. Wabberson threw his arms up when he understood what was happening, but the mayor fumbled for his holstered sidearm.

"Show your hands!" I roared.

When the mayor didn't comply, Olaf drove the stock end of his MP88 against his temple. The blow was just hard enough to daze him. Olaf then disarmed the mayor and secured his wrists with plastic cuffs. I moved past them to a back corridor. The two rooms and bathroom off it were empty, confirming what my nose had already told me.

"We're clear," I called.

I returned, ensured the two men were fully disarmed, and secured Wabberson's wrists.

"You're done here," Grimes seethed at me from across the table. "You know that don't you?"

"Where's Austin?" I asked.

"None of your fucking business."

"I'm going to ask you again, where is he?"

"You don't have any authority here, and I'm ordering you out."

I walked around, palmed his head, and brought it against the table. "We know about your operation, pal. You were wondering about our connection to the Canadian government?" I paused long enough for him to understand we'd been listening. "If you want to stay in business, you're going to start answering questions. If not, we'll clean you out and turn you over to the Mounties. We're under no obligation to them, but we'll do it for shits and grins."

"Why do you want to know where Austin is?"

"He was friends with the first vic, and I have some questions."

"He's got nothing to do with the killings."

I pressed down on his head. "Where is he?"

"The house, probably," the mayor grunted. "Left here a few hours ago."

But there had been no one else at the house when Takara had talked with Mrs. Grimes.

"He wasn't there an hour ago," I said.

The mayor struggled against his confinement. "You went to my house? You went to my house when I told you not to?" He thrashed some more, but I held him easily.

"Where else could he be?"

"Hell if I know. Kid does what he wants."

Yeah, I bet, I thought. *Especially lately.*

"Mr. Wolfe!" Yoofi called from outside.

I left Grimes under Olaf's watch and stepped out into the driving snow. A pickup had slowed like it was going to stop in front of the mayor's office, but now it was trying to gun off again. I sprinted past Yoofi, who was shouting at the driver and aiming his Beretta with both hands.

"Hold fire," I told him.

I caught up to the vehicle and threw a shoulder into its right flank, above the taillight. The tires skidded over the snow. Before the driver could correct, the truck went into a full spin. It jounced off the road and came to a rest at an angle, its headlights facing me. I raised my MP88 to the silhouette beyond the glass.

"Exit with your hands in view!" I shouted.

The door opened, and a tall, lanky figure stepped out showing his gloved hands. For a moment I didn't recognize the man in the hunting cap. When I caught his scent, I realized it was the mayor's younger son, Sean.

"Where's your brother?" I asked him.

"I-I don't know. He left the office earlier, and I ain't seen him since."

"Where are you coming from?"

"Fort Smith. My dad wanted me to get some more fuel before we were socked in."

Sean had Cree blood too—and the same access to his mother's research as his brother. But my nose was picking up the scent of propane from the covered truck bed. "Why did you try to drive off just now?"

"I saw that guy standing out front with a gun." He nodded past me. "Sort of freaked me out."

I looked over at Yoofi. Kid had a point.

"Do you know where Austin went?"

"I never know where he is half the time."

"How's he been lately? Acting any differently?"

"Differently? No, sir. Not that I'm aware of." His eyes cut down and to the right—usually a sign someone was lying. Plus the scent coming off him had changed, grown sharper.

"I heard him hit you earlier. Is that normal?"

"He's been acting more irritated, I guess. Keeps telling me not to go out into the woods by myself. Then he takes off on these hunting trips on his own, and without telling anyone where he's going."

"I understand he was friends with Connor Tench."

"Yes, sir."

"Were they together around the time of his disappearance?"

"Austin took him hunting sometimes. I don't know about that night."

There was no info in the file about what Connor had been doing on the night he'd disappeared. Home had been his father's house. Drunk most of the time, his father had been no help in Centurion's preliminary investigation. But a hunting outing would have been a good excuse for Austin to get Connor alone.

"I'm going to ask a question and I want an honest answer." I stepped closer so I could smell him better. "Do you think your brother is involved in the recent disappearances?"

Sean's eyes widened in alarm. "You think Austin's got something to do with them?"

"I'm just asking."

"I mean, I've never even thought about it. He'd have no reason to hurt Connor. They were best friends. He was all the time helping Connor after he came back from the war. He was in bad shape." Sean's scent remained sharp but that might have had more to do with the fact that someone seven feet tall and armed was interrogating him about his brother.

"Has he shown any interest in Cree beliefs?"

"He's always thought that stuff was cool, yeah." He stopped. "A couple weeks ago, I heard him and my mom arguing about a book. One was missing from her collection. My mom said something about hundreds of hours of interviews, so I knew it was the one about the Cree. That book was her life's work before her eyes went bad. Is that important?"

The info was adding up, but I wanted to be as close to a hundred percent as possible before taking Austin out.

Right now we needed to talk to Mrs. Grimes. I still hadn't heard back from Megha, and with Nadie captured, we had lost the Masked Wolf People as a source of intel on the Cree. With Mrs. Grimes, we might not only be able to learn the location of sacred Cree sites in the area, but which one her son would use as a lair, assuming he *was* the Wendigo.

"Could be," I replied.

20

I brought Sean to the mayor's office. I zip-tied his wrists, though I hated doing it, and walked him to the table to join his father and the warden. With so much at stake, I couldn't risk them interfering—especially with the trail to the Wendigo now leading through the mayor's family.

"Did you send Sean out for something?" I asked the mayor.

"Yeah, propane. What's he got to do with any of this?" he demanded.

I gave Sean's shoulder a reassuring squeeze as I sat him down. He glanced nervously at his father, whose own eyes remained fixed on my visor. For his part, the warden looked down glumly, seeing the situation for what it was. Not much you could do against three heavily armed men.

"I asked you a question, *Captain*," Grimes pressed.

"This is for everyone's safety," I replied. "We're going over to interview Mrs. Grimes."

"No you're not!" he roared. He tried to thrust himself to his feet, but Olaf clamped a meaty hand on the back of his neck and pushed him back down. "Let go of me, you ugly sonofabitch. No one talks to her! Do you hear me?"

"It's just an interview," I said.

"She's not well, goddammit!"

"She has information that could help us stop the killings. Isn't that what you want? For everything to go back to normal around here?"

The mayor struggled until his face was beet red. Finally, he banged his forehead against the table three times and left it there. When his body began to hitch, I realized he was sobbing. The warden cocked an eyebrow, while Sean, who had probably never seen his father made powerless like this, didn't seem to know where to look. I felt sorry for the young man.

I waved Olaf over to a corner out of their hearing. "I want you and Yoofi to watch over them. The son and warden shouldn't be a problem, but keep a close eye on Grimes." Olaf's dull gaze shifted past me to where the mayor continued to sob. "Restrain him if you have to, but no excessive force."

Olaf gave a nod and returned to his position behind Grimes.

I called Yoofi inside and gave him the same instructions. I picked up the mayor's sat phone from the table and programmed the number into my phone. Then I called it so his phone would grab my number.

"This is our communication system until ours is back up," I said, handing Yoofi the mayor's phone.

I expected Grimes to react, but he remained with his head on the table, defeated.

I jerked my head for Rusty to follow me from the office. Outside, I called Takara from the back, and the three of us boarded the van. Rusty took the wheel. As the engine started, the wipers beat to life, shoving away the snow that had accumulated on the windshield. More snow sliced past the van's head beams. I decided to keep the machine gun in the cargo hold for the short ride and took a position beside the window with my MP88.

The mayor's house was only a mile from the downtown. It was a cabin, like most of the housing around Old Harbor, the rooftop piled with snow. A window in the front room glowed with warm light. As we pulled up, I listened for the kenneled dogs Takara had mentioned, but they were quiet.

"Takara and I are going in," I said. "Rusty, you'll be on outside security."

"Sure thing, boss, but how am I supposed to alert you?"

"Shout," Takara said.

"Yeah, shout," I agreed.

We stepped out of the van. "Knock on the front door like you did last time," I whispered to Takara. "I'll enter through the back in case Austin's returned." She nodded and we split.

I chose the lee side of the house, where there wasn't as much snow. Ducking beneath the windows, I made my way toward the back. The fenced-in area with the kennels was just coming into view when I heard Takara knock. I took a position beside the back door, ready to pounce if Austin tried to slip out. But no one had emerged by the time the front door opened, Takara and Mrs. Grimes exchanged greetings, and the door closed again.

I wasn't picking up a fresh scent on Austin either.

I cocked an ear toward the kennels. Still quiet. I hesitated when I realized it was too quiet. I couldn't even hear breathing. I stepped toward the fencing until I could make out several of the dogs inside their shelters. They were lying on their sides as if sleeping, but I could see their mangled necks. Hackles stiffening, I raised my muzzle but I was upwind from them.

"Wolfe," a familiar voice called.

Dammit. My rifle was loaded with conventional ammo. I began swapping it for a silver mag when the enormous figure of Aranck rounded the fencing. He strode toward me on all fours, unafraid.

"What have you done with my daughter?" he demanded.

In the trees beyond the kennel, the gold eyes of the pack glowed in and out of view. I could barely make out the wolves' bodies in the driving snow. I was wondering how they'd found me when I remembered the binding power of our agreement. Aranck had a lock on me. But he was risking a lot bringing his pack to Old Harbor—a risk he'd tried to mitigate by killing the sleeping dogs. Still, the pack's presence in town told me how badly they wanted Nadie back.

"I haven't done anything with her," I said. "She—"

"Liar," Aranck growled. "She broke her connection to us, which could only have happened if she'd found a mate—and the mate *accepted* her." Though the barrels of my weapon were pointed at him, he rose onto his hind legs as he arrived in front of me, exposing his muscled belly.

"I hunted with her," I snarled, removing my helmet. "I offered her the heart as a courtesy. I didn't know what it meant."

"How dare you, *whelp!*"

Before I could react, rock-hard knuckles cracked across my jaw and knocked me into a backward stumble. My healing quickly absorbed the pain that flared through my mouth.

In its place grew a lupine rage.

With a savage roar, I threw my weapon aside and launched myself at Aranck. I ducked beneath his next blow and plowed into his chest. The force sent him back with a grunt. Locking my hands behind his thick waist, I continued to drive with my legs. With a jump and hard thrust, I pile-drove him against the ground, head first. The other wolves barked excitedly.

The snow that flew around us turned red as we rolled back and forth trading blows and slashes. I was in full wolf mode, reacting to his attack, but I felt the lupine in me fighting for something else—proof I was worthy of his daughter.

That extra motivation put us at a dead heat.

What the hell are you doing? I demanded of myself, even as I tore at Aranck's shoulder with my teeth. *This has nothing to do with the mission.* But it was like telling a missile in flight to back off. I was going too fast, too hard. As much as I tried, I couldn't regain control.

I fended off Aranck's lunge at my throat and hammered him beneath the ear. With an angry roar, he flipped me. We launched into another series of rolls, blood trailing from our closing wounds.

A shot cracked, searing the air with the bite of silver.

Aranck and I stopped mid-roll and looked over. Expecting to find Takara, I was surprised to see Rusty standing at the corner of the house, M4 at his shoulder. He'd fired a warning shot, but now he leveled the barrel at Aranck. He looked from the Alpha to the ring of wolves and back.

"Should I plug him, boss?" he asked in a trembling voice.

Aranck growled and tried to lunge toward Rusty, but I grabbed the wolf's legs and pinned him. We had both moved at preternatural speeds, making Rusty's reaction—shuffling backwards—appear delayed. The sudden end to the fighting coupled with the threat to my teammate restored me. I panted as I continued to hold Aranck, who had exhausted himself as well.

"Keep your aim on him but hold fire unless he attacks," I told Rusty.

"You're too merciful," Aranck snarled. "Nadie and her offspring would never survive with you leading them."

Defiance surged fresh inside me, but I forced it back down. "I've made no commitment to your daughter, but that's the least of our problems right now. She's been taken."

Aranck twisted so he was facing me. "Taken?"

"By the thing we're hunting. The Wendigo."

He stiffened at mention of the name. "How did this happen, Wolfe?"

"A group of hunters wounded Nadie. I carried her to a teammate to be treated. The Wendigo attacked them. It took Nadie and a teammate named Sarah." I opened my mind to the collective so Aranck and the others could see the truth of what I was saying. Mournful howls rose from the pack.

Aranck bared his bloody teeth. "Then she is gone."

"No, she's in the Wendigo's lair, with Sarah. We're trying to learn its location. We think it's at one of the sacred Cree sites in the region. Are there any nearby you know about?"

But Aranck was shaking his head, the fight from earlier seeming to have drained from his heaving muscles. "No, Wolfe. You are not understanding. When a shifter crosses the plane from this world, that shifter can never come back. Nadie has returned to the One Who Sits Above. She is gone."

A desperate anger burned in my chest. "How do you know?"

"Because it is the way of the world." Aranck stood and shook the snow from his body. His fur was bloodied, but his wounds had healed. Head hung, he plodded from me toward his pack.

His posture resonated with the widening hole in me where the connection with Nadie had once lived. But while the wolf in me grieved, I was struck by the sudden fear that Sarah might not be able to return either.

"What about my teammate?" I called after him.

"I care not for humans," he rumbled. "They're the reason the Cannibal is here."

I watched his massive silhouette merge into the others. The pack disappeared into the snow and trees.

"You all right, boss?" Rusty asked, snow crunching under his boots as he hurried toward me.

I straightened and turned toward him. "Already healed." Before I could thank him, my sat phone rang. It was the database tech from Centurion.

"Megha," I said. "What'd you find?"

"A lot of mentions of sacred Cree sites in the region, but no locations. And I'm afraid I've exhausted all of my resources. Most of that information is oral. You'll need to consult a Cree."

"We might have the next best thing," I said, glancing toward the house. "Thanks for all of your help."

"Anytime. It's been an honor."

As we disconnected, I locked her number away in my mind. Having a resource on the inside could come in handy down the line. I didn't trust Centurion to always come through for us, and it still bothered me that Sarah had kept me in the dark about the skunk database.

The backdoor opened and Takara appeared. I'd glimpsed her in an upstairs window right after Rusty had fired his shot. She had taken an overwatch position, her barrel trained on Aranck's head. The Alpha was lucky to be alive.

"Everything all right?" she asked.

"Yeah, just a visit from Aranck and his pack. They were looking for Nadie. When I told him about the Wendigo, Aranck said she was gone for good—something about shifters leaving our plane."

"And Sarah?"

"I doubt the same rules apply to humans, given that the remains of the Wendigo's other victims turned up. We still have a good shot of recovering her."

"Mrs. Grimes is waiting. I told her my assistant would be joining me."

I cocked an eyebrow. "Your assistant?"

Takara turned to Rusty. "Remain on outside watch."

"Yes, Mein Fuhrer," he muttered.

"Thanks, Rusty," I said as he trudged off.

I used a handful of snow to scrub the blood off my face before securing the helmet back over my head. Retrieving my MP88, I followed Takara inside. The warm cabin held the homey scent of smoke baked into wood. Takara led me to the living room, where I got my first view of Mrs. Grimes. The middle-aged woman was sitting in a recliner in layers of robes and thick socks. Medical glasses hid her eyes while an oxygen line ran from a cannula in her nostrils to a small tank she wore over a shoulder. I saw what Takara meant about her Cree features. Her skin was the color of leather, her jaw strong and square.

"Mrs. Grimes," Takara said. "This is Jason."

"Was that you shooting out back?" she asked.

I shook her outstretched hand with a thumb and two fingers. "Yeah, thought I heard a wolf prowling."

"Surprised the dogs aren't going crazy." She cocked her head as if listening for them.

"As I was saying, Mrs. Grimes," Takara spoke up, "I just had a few follow-up questions." She had altered her voice to sound like a young academic, and it was entirely convincing.

"I can't believe you're still out here in this weather." Mrs. Grimes oriented herself to Takara. "Forecast says it's going to drop another foot."

"What do you know about the Cree's sacred sites?"

"Which ones?" Mrs. Grimes asked. "There are dozens around Old Harbor alone."

Dozens? There wasn't time to search that many. I thought about the direction the Wendigo had fled after taking off with Ms. Welch as well as with Sarah and Nadie.

"How about north of the Platt River?" I asked.

"That's where most of them are," Mrs. Grimes said. "The mountains and caves made good sites for ceremonies and vision quests. Many of them are still marked with old cairns and petroglyphs."

"Do you have a map of their locations?" Takara asked.

"I did." Mrs. Grimes's face seemed to darken. "It was in a notebook I'd spent years putting together."

"What happened to it?" I asked.

"Went missing."

I remembered what Sean had said about an argument between his mother and older brother regarding the whereabouts of the book. I wanted to probe further, but I could feel her shutting down. And she was our last source of reliable info. "During your research, did you come across a being called a Wendigo?" I asked.

That seemed to bring her back. "I'd heard about the legend, but none of the Cree would talk about it. It wasn't until I visited a reservation near Ennadai—that's way out on the edge of the province—that I met an old man who wouldn't *stop* talking about it. He lived in a beat-up Airstream at the end of a dirt road. The locals considered him a kook, but he was also rumored to be the oldest living Cree. So old that no one else on the reservation really knew him—he'd outlived everyone. He told me he practiced religious medicine at one time but was infected by White Man's poison until he couldn't practice anymore."

"White Man's poison?" I asked.

"Alcohol. Claimed it killed his connection to the spirit realm and made his hands shake. By the time I visited, his whole body was shaking. After answering some questions about the healing ceremonies he used to perform, he started talking about the Wendigo. Asked if I wanted to learn the ceremony to call it up. He had such a crazy look in his eyes, I almost told him no, but I was curious."

She paused to cough into a handkerchief and fix her nasal cannula.

"He claimed the Wendigo was misunderstood," she continued, "that it was nothing to fear. To call one involved eating human flesh, sure, but only because humans were the highest form of life. It was the ultimate offering. As such, it would bring god-like powers to anyone ready to 'ascend,' as he put it. That's not what the legends say, though," Mrs. Grimes said in a lowered voice. "The legends say the Wendigo will turn the person into a raving cannibal. I didn't challenge him," she continued. "Just wrote down the steps as the old man described them. It was all myth anyway. When he finished, he laughed and told me to share it widely. By then I was convinced he *was* a kook, but I kept the info anyway."

"Did he say how to stop a Wendigo?" Takara asked.

"Not that I can remember," Mrs. Grimes answered. "Just how to call it up."

I thought about that. Had the Shaking Man wanted to inflict the curse of the Wendigo on the people he blamed for making him sick? To have Mrs. Grimes be the carrier? "Is there a way to reach this guy?" I asked.

"He didn't have a phone or anything back then. And given it was twenty years ago, I doubt he's even alive."

I nodded to myself. "Do you still have the info you took down?"

"It was in the same notebook as the maps."

"Did the book have a name?" I asked.

"I labeled it 'Cree Beliefs.'"

I stood. "Is there a restroom I can use?"

"Go to the kitchen and take a left. First door on the right."

I signaled for Takara to keep her talking as I made my way toward the back of the house. But instead of going to the bathroom, I continued down the hallway. I had picked up Austin's stale scent upon entering the house, and it wasn't hard to find his bedroom. It held a bed with a pine-wood frame, a dresser, and a scattering of clothes. I removed my helmet and sniffed. Amid the tapestry of smells, I honed in on a particular scent—a combination of paper and pen ink—and followed it to his closet.

In the wall above some shelving was a vent with a protruding corner. I worked my talons around the seam and pulled. The vent removed easily. I reached into the large duct and pulled out a pile of girlie magazines. Underneath them was a thick notebook. I turned it right side up and read the title.

Cree Beliefs.

I flipped through the pages of handwritten notes and pictures, but this wasn't the place to go through it. Stashing the notebook in my pack, I stopped off at the bathroom to flush the toilet before returning to the living room. Mrs. Grimes turned her head toward my heavy footfalls.

"When did your book go missing?" I asked.

"About six months back. I wanted to show it to someone, but it was gone."

Enough time for Austin to learn the ceremony, I thought.

"It could be really helpful for my research," Takara said. "Any idea who might have taken it?"

"Austin used to show it to his friends. He was proud of being part Cree. Believed all the myths, even though I told him they were stories and superstitions. He probably lost it somewhere."

"When was Austin last here?" I asked.

"This afternoon. He cleaned out half the fridge, then said he had to go somewhere. I tried to tell him about the storm, but he wouldn't listen." She gave a resigned sigh. "'Course he doesn't listen about the bear either. Claims that's not what's killing people."

Takara and I exchanged a glance.

"Did he say what *was* killing people?" I asked.

She shook her head. "He doesn't say much these days."

"Did he at least mention where he was going?" I pressed.

Mrs. Grimes started to shake her head again, then stopped. "You're not researchers, are you?" The muscles around her square jaw stiffened. "You're those investigators my husband told me not to talk to."

Before Takara could answer, I said, "Yes, we are."

I expected her to scream at us to leave, but she laced her fingers across her small paunch and said, "Fine. What do you really want to know?"

"We agree with your son that something other than a bear is killing people," I said. "He might be in danger. We need to find him. Did he ever visit any of the sacred sites north of the Platt River?"

"There was one place he liked to go. Locals call it Cavern Lake. You'll find it on a survey map. The Cree used it for warrior ceremonies, something that fascinated Austin. He'll often camp there when he goes on his overnight hunts."

I nodded at Takara. That was it.

"Now please get out," Mrs. Grimes said.

21

"Dammit," I growled.

"What?" Takara asked from the passenger seat.

I had been flipping through Mrs. Grimes's thick notebook as Rusty grunted and plowed our van over the snow-covered road. A section of the notebook had been removed. When I referred to the table of contents, I saw which one.

"The notes on the Wendigo are gone."

"Mrs. Grimes said there was no info on how to destroy it," Takara said.

"I wanted Yoofi to look over the summoning ceremony anyway. Could have been similar to something he was familiar with, given him some ideas on how to put it back down."

"Killing the host will do the job," she said.

"And if the host is Austin Grimes?"

"Is there any doubt at this point?"

I thought about the evidence: his unexplained absences, his change in behavior, the hidden notebook with the pages on the Wendigo ceremony removed. "Maybe not, but you heard his mother's story. The Shaking Man deliberately told her how to summon the creature. He wanted her to spread the info like a virus. And he lied, claiming the ceremony would bring the summoner power."

"Austin murdered his friend for that power," Takara pointed out. "He's not innocent."

She was right, of course. I was thinking of him as a fellow man-turned-beast. But where I had been chosen—and Takara cursed—Austin had brought on his transformation through an unspeakable act, and with full awareness of what he was doing. I thought of Connor's picture. A soldier.

"No, he's not," I agreed.

When we got to the mayor's office, I found the scene much as we'd left it. The mayor was sitting up again, but his eyes remained bloodshot and puffy. He turned his head at my entrance.

"Get what you wanted?" he asked quietly.

He showed all the signs of submission, but I knew it would be dangerous to assume he'd stay that way.

"Here's what's going to happen," I said, looking from him to the warden and Sean. "Mayor Grimes and Wabberson will take one vehicle back to the house, where you'll stay put. Olaf will follow with Sean in Sean's truck. He'll remain with you for your safety." I wanted to avoid a repeat of the El Rosario mission where the preacher had tailed us to the cave and mortally wounded the shaman. I was putting the family and Wabberson on the equivalent of house arrest with Olaf standing guard. I hated not having Olaf along for the final push, but I needed the others for their specific skill sets. And I wanted Olaf at the house in case Austin returned.

Grimes blinked slowly. "What are you going to be doing?"

"Recovering two missing persons." There was still a hole in my wolf being where Nadie had been, but at least she had returned to her realm. Sarah and Ms. Welch were God knew where.

"You think Austin's wrapped up in this, don't you?"

"We're going to try to find him," I said, which wasn't a lie.

But Grimes read between the lines. When he spoke, it was with eerie calmness. "You harm one hair on his body, and I'll kill you."

"Olaf," I said, jerking my head. He plodded after me to the far corner of the room. "Did you catch what I said?"

"I follow them to house and stand guard."

"That's right. I rounded up the weapons before we left and hid them out back. Mrs. Grimes is still armed. Revolver, holstered on her left hip. You'll disarm her without force and requisition her phone—it's the only working one in the house. We'll stay in contact that way. When everyone's inside, disable the vehicles." If Grimes or the other two slipped out, I didn't want them to have transportation. "Do you follow?"

Olaf's dull eyes remained fixed on my visor. "Yes. Anything else?"

"One more thing." I pulled out my tablet. Though the system was still down, I had the info from the mission file uploaded to the device. I opened a folder and scrolled through the images. In my peripheral vision, I could see Mayor Grimes watching us. When I arrived at Austin's picture, I angled the screen toward Olaf.

"If he shows up," I whispered, "put him down."

Except for Takara, Olaf was the only one I trusted to take a lethal shot without flinching.

"Yes," he said.

After searching the mayor's vehicle to ensure it was clear of weapons, I signaled for Grimes and Wabberson to climb in. They did so wordlessly while Sean and Olaf got into the young man's truck. The vehicles ground off slowly through the snow. The rest of us climbed into the van and headed back toward the lodge.

We had a location—Cavern Lake—but without Yoofi's magic we wouldn't be able to penetrate the veil where the Wendigo had stashed Sarah and Ms. Welch. And I still hadn't been able to get ahold of Croft.

"Where are we with Dabu?" I asked Yoofi.

He shook his head. "Dabu's trick did not work. Muluku neutralized the bad magic, and now he is using the staff to keep the death dogs back. Dabu is trapped in the bottom of the underworld."

"Is there anything else you can use to channel his power?"

"Yes, but Dabu says he can spare no magic. He must use it to keep Muluku back." Yoofi shook his head some more. "It does not look good, Mr. Wolfe."

"You mentioned taking trips to the underworld," I said.

"Oh, yes, but I never like to go. I get very nervous down there."

I thought of our armory back at the lodge. We still had plenty of salt rounds.

"I want to make a deal."

"A deal?"

"Tell Dabu I'll help fight Muluku off and recover your staff, but then he has to help us with the Wendigo."

Yoofi closed his eyes and took several puffs from a cigar. A moment later, he giggled through the smoke. "Dabu is saying he wonders why he never thought of that."

Probably because he's a self-absorbed dick, I thought.

"Yes," Yoofi said decisively. "Dabu agrees."

"Good. What will it take to get us there?"

Rusty looked back nervously. "The underworld?"

"You won't be going. It'll just be me and Yoofi."

Eyes still closed, Yoofi began to speak in rapid Congolese. Soon his face creased and he raised his voice in anger. He shook his head and opened his eyes again. "Dabu says we need to go to a place that honors him, even though I tell him that there are none here. He only knows my country. He does not understand that there is a whole ocean between Canada and the Congo."

"Well, what happened during the exercise last night?" I asked. "There were no places like that at the compound for the dogs to come and go."

"Yes, because the power of the staff created the portal. It pulled from this side and Dabu pushed from that side. To get there, we must do the opposite. But without the staff, there is only Dabu to pull and nothing to push. It is not enough. The *kuna* between our worlds is too thick."

"*Kuna?*"

"Yes, it is like a rind of energy."

"Well, if the issue is Dabu needing us at a spot where the rind is thinner, would a Cree site work?" When Yoofi gave me a skeptical smile, I said, "We have to get that staff somehow."

"We can try, Mr. Wolfe. But do we know where any of these sites are?"

I held up Mrs. Grimes's notebook. "We do now."

An hour later the four of us were on foot, descending into a bowl-shaped depression north of our base. When we arrived at the bottom, I peered around through the storm. At the cardinal directions, snow-covered humps showed where large stone cairns had once stood. I referred back to the notebook.

"This is the place," I said.

"Yes," Yoofi said, his coat billowing around his suited body. "I can feel the power here." He spread out several woven blankets that he had insisted we would need for the ceremony, then began pinning their corners with rocks. Rusty and I helped.

En route, we had stopped at the lodge to arm up. We would proceed to Cavern Lake once we recovered Yoofi's staff. Two hours had already elapsed since the Wendigo had grabbed Sarah, and there was no telling how long our round trip to the underworld would take—assuming we could even get there.

Rusty adjusted his grip on his weapon so he could bury his other hand into his coat pocket. "Just the two of you are going, right?" he asked through chattering teeth and for the third time.

"You and Takara are staying up here for security."

Yoofi nodded. "Yes, very important, in case anything tries to come out." Yoofi knelt and planted the wooden idol of Dabu in the snow at one end of the blankets. "Mr. Wolfe, I am ready for you to lie down."

I had removed my helmet—I didn't want anything obstructing my senses—and set it to one side. I then did as Yoofi said, lowering myself onto my back. When I braced my MP88 across my chest, I felt like I was posing for my own funeral. I hoped Yoofi knew what he was doing.

He chanted over the idol for several seconds, then lit a thick cigar and held it toward my muzzle. My nostrils wrinkled from the pungent smoke. "Is that really necessary?" I asked.

"Yes, it will help Dabu to find us," he said.

I took the cigar between my lips and puffed shallowly. Yoofi lit a cigar for himself and walked in a circle around the blankets. When something splashed across my face, I realized he had opened a flask and was tossing brandy on me. It was much stronger than the brandy he normally drank.

"How long does this ceremony go on?" I asked in annoyance.

"Okay," Yoofi blurted. He joined me on the blankets as if he had just set up a countdown on a camera and was rushing to beat the timer. He lay beside me with his head at my feet and clasped my hand. "Close your eyes, and do not let go of me, whatever you do. Otherwise, you will get lost in the *kuna*."

He picked up the chanting again, this time in a voice that rose and fell like a drumbeat. I caught a trembling snort from Rusty— I'm sure we looked ridiculous. I was doubting this would even work. Then we began to spin.

I squinted my right eye open, expecting to see the sides of the basin rotating, but everything was still. Yoofi squeezed my hand in warning, and I closed my eye again. The spinning resumed, picking up speed. I didn't like the sensation. I clutched my MP88 hard. In the next moment a lightness came over me and we were lifting off the blankets. I fought the urge to peek again.

When we landed with a jolt, I realized Yoofi had broken off the chant.

"Okay, Mr. Wolfe," he said in a whisper. "You can open your eyes."

"Are we there?" I asked. But when I looked around, we were still in the snowy basin. I released Yoofi's hand and pushed myself up. My hackles rose suddenly when I realized Takara and Rusty were gone. I heaved my MP88 into position and scanned the basin rim.

"We are through the *kuna*," Yoofi said.

My nostrils flared as I stalked from the blankets. Beyond the stink of the cigar that still smoked from my lips, the smells here were more intense, more alive. The landscape seemed to shimmer.

"We're not in Canada anymore," I said in understanding.

"We are in the Cree realm. Now we must wait to see if Dabu can find us."

"And if he can't?" I asked around the stogie.

"Then we go back. His idol will guide us."

Yoofi's eyes clamped closed.

"What is it?" I asked.

But instead of answering me, Yoofi spoke Congolese. Apparently, he was in another argument with Dabu. I picked up movement in my peripheral vision and spun toward it. A young man's painted face was peering over the rim. His eyes flashed with white light as he ducked out of sight. I didn't know much about the Cree, but something about his face paint suggested warrior.

"Ugh," Yoofi complained. "Dabu is being difficult."

"In what way?" I asked, scanning the rim of the basin for others.

"He is worried now that it will take too much of his energy to bring us to the underworld. And if we are unable to defeat Muluku, then he will not have enough power to fend him off."

"We had a deal," I growled.

As Yoofi resumed his argument with Dabu, another warrior's face rose into view. I could smell them now. There were at least a dozen, and they had pegged us as intruders. Their earthen scents hummed with a power not of our world. I kept my finger on the trigger guard.

"Tell him to get us down there," I said. "Now."

The warriors crested the rim, bows in their grips. The dozen-odd men were idealized forms. The handsome animal skins they wore complemented their bronzed, muscled bodies. White starlight gleamed from their eyes. They came down the sides of the basin smoothly, swiftly. I switched my aim from one to the other, but I couldn't bring myself to squeeze off a shot.

"Yoofi?" I shouted, losing my cigar.

He remained pitched in debate with Dabu. And with his eyes closed, he was oblivious to the danger closing in. With a final cry, he spiked his own cigar against the ground. Fire plumed up where it hit, sending smoke and sparks into the night sky. The warriors paused in their advance.

"This way, Mr. Wolfe," Yoofi called.

There was a hole in the snow and earth where the cigar had struck, reminding me of the portal to the Chagrath's realm.

"Quickly! Dabu has agreed, but he will not keep the way open forever." Yoofi had been waving at me, but now he straightened and blinked around at the warriors. "Who are *they*?"

"Not happy we're here," I said, hustling toward him. "Do we just jump in?"

"Yes, yes!"

Without breaking stride, I seized him around the waist and stepped over the opening. We plummeted with a force greater than gravity. I felt my body stretching like taffy. Even my weapon seemed to be pulling apart. Above the rush, I could hear Yoofi screaming.

Like with the Chagrath's realm, we didn't land so much as materialize in another world. I checked to ensure I was intact before peering around. To all sides of us were animals—elephants, lions, chimpanzees—and they were clashing with hordes of two-headed dogs. A dark force I'd come to associate with Yoofi's staff warped the air like an approaching storm.

Dabu had pulled us right into the middle of his damned war.

22

Dabu's realm wasn't what I had expected. Instead of a system of caverns, we were in a broad valley beneath an orange sky, cliff walls rising to either side. My first impulse was to start shooting, but I had no sense of the battle. I needed to get to higher ground. Still carrying Yoofi, I sprinted for an opening.

I raced through the confusion until I was scaling the near wall, talons knifing into crevices. When I reached a shelf, I set Yoofi down and looked over the battle while he clung to the wall.

"This is Dea-Dep," Yoofi said. "And that is the Dombola River." He pointed quickly to a dark river that snaked through the barren valley. "It leads there." I followed its course to a massive stone complex that could have been a feature of the landscape. "That is where Dabu rules. All of the great ancestral families have houses inside. It is a beautiful place except for the death dogs."

I listened for a drumbeat. "Do you see Muluku?"

Yoofi squinted around. "There," he said, pointing him out.

Muluku was seated atop an elephant that lumbered in the middle of a large formation wedging its way through the death dogs. Instead of a drum, Muluku wielded Yoofi's staff. A globe of dark energy warped the air around the blade. Though some dogs were trying to clamber past the protective wedge to reach the staff, the majority were snarling and backing from its power.

"Dabu has moved all the death dogs out here to slow down Muluku," Yoofi said. "If he reaches the inside, there will only be his staff to protect him. He says we must recover my staff before that happens."

Which was what I was trying to figure out. Muluku was about two hundred meters away, within range of my weapon. But if I took him out from this distance, one of his chimps could just grab the staff like last time, and Muluku would call the whole zoo back to his neck of the god realm.

"We're going to create a diversion," I said.

I reached into my vest and started pulling out salt grenades and handing them to Yoofi.

He took them reluctantly and placed them in his pockets. "Oh, I don't know, Mr. Wolfe. You have seen me in training. My aim is not very good."

"It doesn't have to be. I'm going back down. When I reach that spot, I want you to arm the first grenade and throw it as far as you can, out ahead of Muluku. Count to ten and repeat. Keep going till you're out."

Yoofi nodded uncertainly.

Slinging my MP88 around to my back, I descended. When I reached the valley, I opened fire, blowing a lane through a knot of death dogs. I plunged into the smoke of their dispersing bodies, passing the spot I'd pointed out to Yoofi. Seconds later, the first grenade detonated more or less where I'd wanted it to. Creatures went up in explosions of smoke. Muluku's wedge stopped and wobbled.

I used the confusion to approach the god from behind. I dodged the animals I could and blew apart those I couldn't. When the second grenade detonated, animals began breaking from the wedge.

At the rear of the formation, I leapt onto one of the elephants that remained in place and jumped from one to the other toward Muluku. The god looked around until his hooded gaze fixed on Yoofi, who was waiting to arm another grenade. Before I could reach him, Muluku raised the staff and a black bolt spiraled from the blade. I heard Yoofi shout as the bolt disintegrated his ledge and swallowed him in thick smoke. Yoofi plummeted with the ensuing rock slide.

I winced but kept going. I'd have to check on my teammate later.

When I was one elephant away, Muluku sensed me. He turned, but I was already to him. I slammed an elbow into his neck and ripped the staff from his grip. Good thing I could get my hands on him down here, because I was pretty fucking fed up with this family feud.

The elephant trumpeted and reared up, but twice now I had clung to dragons mid flight. This was child's play. I dug my heels into the elephant's sides and pinned Muluku harder. He grunted beneath me.

"You attack my teammates again," I said into his ear, "and I'll jam this staff down your throat till it comes out the other end."

I brought my MP88 around, but with Muluku no longer powering the staff, the death dogs had rediscovered their ferocity. They slavered and climbed over one another to get at the invaders. I would need the ammo to get out of here. Giving Muluku's head a final shove, I jumped down and blew open an exit route. I broke through the smoke to escape what was turning into a massacre.

When I reached the valley wall, I found Yoofi pushing himself up from the rubble. I helped him to his feet.

"You all right?"

"Yes, Dabu softened the landing." He gazed up the cliff wall to where he'd been perched and shook his head. "This is why we do not like heights, Mr. Wolfe."

"Here," I said, handing him the staff.

He stared at it for a moment, then took it and stroked the dark length of wood. Back at the battle, the dogs had reached Muluku and were tearing him from his perch. The god looked over at me, his eyes wide in terror. A moment later, he and his animals disappeared in explosions of white smoke. The assault on Dea-Dep had ended, prompting Yoofi to giggle.

"Dabu must be happy," I said.

"Very happy. He would like us to feast with him now."

"There's no time. We have to get back."

Yoofi lowered his voice. "Ooh, very insulting to refuse a god's feast."

"Then tell him we'll take a rain check. He still needs to help us, and right now that means getting us back to the others."

Yoofi closed his eyes and communicated the message. I eyed the valley. With the intruders gone, the death dogs had begun to take an interest in us. Their twin faces shook with snarls as they stalked in our direction. I could see why Yoofi didn't enjoy coming here.

Without warning, Yoofi seized my hand and we were spinning again. This time we did land—hard. I opened my eyes to find us back in the basin. We had missed the blankets by several feet and were lying in snow. Thinking we were in the Cree realm, I brought my MP88 into position in case the warriors were still around, but a moment later I smelled Rusty and Takara.

Rusty hustled up from behind. "Did you get it, boss?"

Though Yoofi was covered in snow, he held up the staff triumphantly. Then he grimaced and rubbed his tailbone. "Dabu did not take the refusal to feast with him very well." He struggled to his feet and pulled the idol from the snow. He clucked at it before dropping it into a pocket.

"How long were we gone?" I asked.

"About an hour," Takara replied.

"You didn't miss much," Rusty said. "The system's still down."

"Any word from Olaf?"

Takara nodded. "He called to say they were at the mayor's house. No sign of Austin."

"Then it's time we got to Cavern Lake."

We were climbing from the basin when I heard something large crunching through the snow beyond the rim. I raised my nose, but the wind was gusting in from the other side. The footsteps sounded wolfish. Had Aranck returned?

Signaling for the rest of the team to remain behind me, I switched my salt mag for a silver one and advanced in a hunker. When I reached the rim of the basin, I peered into the trees.

Gold eyes peered back at me.

"What do you want?" I demanded, raising the MP88 into position.

Something flickered in my mind before filling with a familiar voice.

It's me, Wolfe.

I stopped, heart thudding. *Nadie?*

I stepped from the basin, and she trotted toward me. I could see her markings. It was her. When she reached me, I knelt and let her push her head against my face. She was solid, material. I brought an arm around her neck, the wolf in me overcome by her sudden return.

What happened? I asked. *Your father said you were gone, that you'd returned to your realm.*

It was close, she said. *The Cannibal almost destroyed me.*

I noticed that she still wouldn't call the Wendigo by its name.

As our connection continued to reform, I could feel her opening herself until I was experiencing what she had. Darkness. My body jostling in the grip of something hungry and powerful. Side burning where the silver bullet had torn through. Eyes opening to find myself in the foul arm of the Wendigo, Sarah in its other arm, head gashed where the being had struck her. The Wendigo was carrying us through the forest, the world beyond its aura seeming to bend and distort. When it sensed I was awake, it brought the pits of its eyes toward mine and stared. Their hunger stole my consciousness. Everything went dark again.

Movement startled me from the experience. I turned to find Takara peering from the basin, M4 in firing position. My head swam a little as I rose from Nadie.

"It's okay," I said to Takara. "She's an ally. Everyone can come up."

Takara strode toward us and gave me an inquisitive look. She had seen me holding the she-wolf. Moments later, Yoofi and Rusty came hustling over the rim of the basin.

"This is Nadie," I said. "She was captured along with Sarah, but she escaped."

"How?" Takara asked, her voice sharp with suspicion.

"She'll tell us on the way to the van," I said.

Nadie walked beside us as we made our way through the snow. The tracks we had created on our arrival were mostly filled in now.

"What happened after you lost consciousness again?" I asked.

"I slept and dreamt nightmare dreams," she said, loud enough for everyone to hear. "Dreams of being attacked, but not being able to fight back. The stare of the Cannibal stole my will, among other things." She was referring to our connection, which explained why Aranck and I hadn't been able to sense her. "When I felt my body turning to mist, I knew I was crossing over. That awakened something. It wasn't my time to leave. I fought with everything I had until I was back in the Cannibal's clutches. I found myself tearing into him, ripping out mouthfuls of his arm, his body. We were in a cave, near water."

"Cavern Lake?" I asked.

"I've heard it called that, yes," she said. "The creature had placed Sarah in the water and was about to do the same to me."

"The veil is over the lake?" Yoofi asked.

"Yes."

Yoofi's brow wrinkled as he appeared to ponder that.

"The Cannibal and I fought furiously," she continued, "but I couldn't hurt it. Seeing a narrow cave in the rocks, I sprinted to it, then shifted to my human form and wedged myself into the very back, where the Cannibal couldn't reach me. It tried for a long time, its talons coming within inches. Eventually, it returned to the water. When it passed through the veil, I made my escape." She looked us over before her eyes returned to mine. "What do you intend to do, Wolfe?"

"Yoofi's magic can pull back the veil. Then it's a matter of keeping the Wendigo at bay with fire until we recover Sarah and anyone else it's taken captive. Is there anything else we should know?"

"The being is more than just a Spirit That Devours Mankind," she said.

"What do you mean?"

"I felt its essence. The ceremony that brought it into being was not a traditional summoning ceremony. It is what's known as a celestial ceremony. Whoever performed it called down its primal form."

I remembered the beam of blue light the old man at the bar had described. That would have been about the time the Wendigo had come into being.

"What's the difference?" I asked.

"Its primal form is the most powerful expression of the Cannibal." Foreboding shook through our connection. "Even if you destroy the human host, the Cannibal will continue to hunt and kill."

23

"How was it stopped in the past?" I asked, refusing to believe that anything was indestructible.

"It's never manifested down here before," Nadie replied. "Not like that. Only the Cree masters knew the primal ceremony, and it was highly secret, requiring very powerful magic."

I thought about the Shaking Man, who had described the ceremony to Mrs. Grimes. *If there's a way to send it back, he would have known. We need to find the missing pages from Mrs. Grimes's notes. Could be something in there she didn't remember taking down.*

"But the person who summoned it is just a boy," Takara said.

"Things have changed," I pointed out. "A being tried to invade last summer. Chaos. Croft's magical order kept it from breaking through, but it created tears around our world. That's how the Chagrath was able to get through in El Rosario. Might also explain this version of the Wendigo."

"I've felt the changes," Nadie agreed as we arrived back at the van.

"It doesn't alter the basic plan, though." I said. "Expose the lair and recover the vics. Destroying the Wendigo is a secondary concern right now. We'll figure it out once Sarah and Ms. Welch are safe." I opened the cargo hold and handed flamethrowers to Rusty and Takara. Then I lifted out the medium machine gun and mounted it atop the van. I checked my sat phone, but Croft still hadn't called back.

As my teammates climbed into the van, Nadie arrived beside me. "I'm coming too."

"Go back to your father."

"I'm no longer his to command."

I felt the connection between us pulsing warmly, enticingly. But I stood my ground. "There's nothing more you can do. You said it yourself—the Wendigo is indestructible. You're lucky to be alive."

"A she-wolf hunts with her mate."

"I'm not your mate. Return to your pack."

It took all of my willpower to remain cold and formal. Turning from her, I climbed into the van and sat beside Yoofi.

"Let's go," I said.

Rusty eyed me in the rearview mirror to make sure we were leaving without Nadie. When I gave a single nod, the van ground into motion.

"Estimated time to arrival?" I asked.

Rusty consulted the top of the dashboard where he'd spread out a map. "Let's see ... eight miles by road and then a two mile walk, and in these conditions?" The headlights were barely penetrating the heavy snowfall. He scratched a cheek. "Forty, forty-five minutes?"

I swore under my breath. It felt like everything was going in slow motion—and with our systems down and against a foe that seemed to be growing more formidable by the minute. I was pulling out the sat phone to try Croft again when something struck the back of the van.

"What the...?" Rusty said, squinting toward the side mirror.

For a moment I thought it was Nadie, but then something else raked the van's side in a screech of stone on metal.

"What are you seeing?" I asked as I pulled down the machine gun's controls and turned on the screen. The screen flared white as I toggled to the camera's night vision feature.

"I don't know. Just crap streaking out of the snow."

He recoiled suddenly as something smashed the side mirror. I spotted it before it flipped away. An arrow.

I turned to Yoofi. "That ceremony to get us to the Cree realm—you closed the opening again, right?"

"Closed it, Mr. Wolfe?"

Shit.

As the images on the screen took shape, I could see them—the warriors. White light shone from their eyes as they gave chase. When a warrior stopped to let an arrow fly, light flashed in the projectile's wake. The van lurched as the arrow struck a rear tire and took off what sounded like a chunk of polymer.

"Can you go any faster?" I asked.

"Going as fast as I can, boss."

Fortunately, I'd kept the belt of salt rounds in the machine gun. I sighted on the nearest warrior and depressed the thumb paddles. Nothing happened. I checked the controls and tried again.

"Oh shit, boss," Rusty said. "The firing controls are system dependent."

Beam had mentioned being able to take control of certain weapons. Swearing, I shoved the controls back into the ceiling and slotted a mag of fresh salt rounds into my MP88.

"I'm going out," I said. "Keep driving. I'll catch up with you soon."

Before anyone could answer, I opened the side door and jumped. I landed in the soft snow and ran with the momentum for several meters to keep my footing. Arrows streaked past. One nicked my arm, sending up a spray of sparks. I brought the MP88 around and unleashed a burst of automatic fire. In flashes of light, the warriors darted behind cover. It wasn't until I felt my arm healing that I noticed the gash in my protective suit where the arrow had struck.

Damn things can tear through Kevlar?

I moved behind a large tree and hissed out a curse. By using the Cree realm as a stopover to get to Dabu's realm, we'd left a hole. I could blame Yoofi all I wanted, but the oversight was ultimately on me. Between the El Rosario mission and conversations with Prof Croft, I'd known the risk of moving between planes. I'd just been so damned fixated on recovering the staff and getting to the Wendigo's lair that I had overlooked it.

The truth was, I hadn't been myself for a lot of this mission. Neglecting to call for backup at Berglund's cabin, ordering the system workaround, hunting with Nadie—the list went on.

When I got back to the van, I knew what I'd have to do. *If* I got back to the van.

The warriors were picking up their attack again. Arrows streaked past me and blew chunks from my tree. I switched triggers and fired a volley of grenades in their direction. As the rounds began to detonate, I went back to the rifle and moved out to pick my attackers off.

I was sighting on one young warrior when something massive plowed into me. We hit the ground hard. Nadie's masked face snarled down at me.

"What are you doing?" I demanded.

"Saving your life," she said, pushing herself off me. "Stay down."

"Wait!" I shouted.

But before I could grab her, she was running toward the warriors. They hung back in the trees, watching her with gleaming eyes, bows in firing positions. I raised my own weapon, hoping to hell Nadie knew what she was doing.

As she neared them, she slowed and spoke in what must have been Algonquin. Her voice was strong and steady, without fear. Soon, she was standing in the warriors' midst.

She turned toward me at one point and I watched the painted faces of the warriors follow before returning their attention to her. The warriors were silent, respectful. As I watched, I noticed the similarity between their face paint and Nadie's markings. The painted patterns were meant to mimic the Masked Wolf People. After another minute, the warriors began to retreat.

I'll be damned.

"What did you say to them?" I asked when Nadie returned.

"Those are spirit guardians," she explained. "I told them you're not a threat."

Sounded like she'd said a lot more than that, but I let it go.

"There's an opening to their realm," I pointed out.

"Yes, but it's closing. They'll return before it's sealed."

That would be one less thing to worry about, anyway. "Thanks for your help," I said, my voice gentler than the last time we'd parted. As much as it killed the wolf in me, I turned again from her intense gold eyes and beautiful markings and set off in pursuit of the van.

"They only agreed to allow you to remain in their lands on the condition I watch over you," she called.

I slowed to a stop.

Oh, you're good, I said through the collective.

Those were the terms. She watched me through the falling snow.

She had me, dammit. I blew out my breath and jerked my head for her to come.

She did eagerly and we raced side by side, following the tracks of the van. After a couple miles, I could see its taillights. Rusty spotted me and braked. When the side door opened, Nadie jumped inside and lay across the back seats. She looked at me as if daring me to change my mind. I climbed in after her, took a seat beside Yoofi, and closed the door.

"Is everything all right?" Yoofi asked sheepishly.

I clapped his knee. "It is now."

"I am very sorry."

"No, I was leading," I told him, which reminded me of the decision I'd come to while facing the warriors. "Listen up, everyone. We're about thirty minutes out from our target. Mission execution has been uneven to this point, and that's on me. I haven't always been in control." I felt the wolf in me resisting what I was about to say, but I spoke over him. "I'm turning over command to Takara."

Yoofi made a noise of surprise.

"Uh, don't you think that's being a little drastic, boss?" Rusty asked.

From the passenger seat, Takara remained staring straight ahead.

"I'll provide any support she needs, but she'll be calling the shots. That all right with you, Takara?"

"I'm ready," she said.

Five miles later, we slowed on the approach to where we'd be disembarking. Rusty steered the van around a corner, and a vehicle, half buried in snow, glowed into view.

"Were we expecting company?" Rusty asked.

"It's Austin's," I said, recognizing the body and studded tires from earlier that day.

"Keep going," Takara ordered. "We want to be out of sight in case he comes back."

We ground past it, continuing until the road turned again. As Rusty pulled off to the side, Takara took the survey map from the dashboard and spread it out on the seat between me and Yoofi. Rusty turned in the driver's seat. Nadie came forward so she could see it too.

"We're here," Takara said, pointing out our position on the map. "We'll approach the target by this valley. Wolfe and Nadie will take lead." *Smart,* I thought. *Using our enhanced senses to scout the terrain ahead.* "Yoofi and Rusty will flank. No more than five meters separation due to conditions. I'll take the rear. Commo is still down, so watch and listen for signals." She went on to outline our approach to Cavern Lake, the recovery of Sarah and Ms. Welch, and then our retreat. She turned to me. "Check out Austin's truck. Nadie, go with him."

Though the wolf in me stiffened at the direct order, I liked the way she was taking control. I nodded and climbed out. As Nadie jumped out after me, I heard Takara going over equipment with the others.

Nadie's and my footsteps swished through the snow. She didn't say anything, but I could feel the question in our collective: Why had I given up command? The question triggered her father's assertion that Nadie and our offspring would never survive with me leading them.

Because it was the only way I could take back control, I snapped.

Nadie looked over at me but remained silent.

When we reached the truck, I swiped the snow from the driver door and opened it. A riot of smells hit me: grease, metal, something tar-like. I sniffed across a floor littered with drink cans and old clothing and then opened the glove compartment. I was searching for the missing pages from the Cree notebook, but that particular blend of paper and ink wasn't in here.

Sliding open the window between the cab and covered bed, I stuck my muzzle through. The bed was empty except for the remains of hauled firewood and some camping gear. Underneath that layer, I picked up the metallic scent of old blood. Human blood, and not from just one person.

With a grunt, I got out of the truck and closed the door.

Nadie claimed this version of the Wendigo was indestructible, even in human form, but as the faces of the victims scrolled through my mind's eye, I'd never wanted to take someone down more.

"I'm not smelling him," I said when we returned to Takara and the others, "but there's traces of human blood in the bed. I'm picking up a tar-like scent going off that way. Those depressions look like old tracks."

Takara shifted her gaze to Nadie as if debating whether to have her follow the trail. "We'll stick to the plan," she decided.

We moved off in formation. Before long we were entering the valley Takara had indicated on the map. I kept vigil on the terrain ahead, periodically checking in to see if Nadie was picking up anything.

With Takara in command, I focused on balancing against my wolf—not pushing too hard, but not yielding too much, either. After the first mile, I found the two entering into a kind of equilibrium, one side no longer struggling against the other for control. That's what I'd hoped would happen, but having to give up command smarted like hell. I reminded myself that it was temporary. I would be ready to lead the next mission. *Had* to be ready.

But for this one, I'd made the right call.

We arrived at the opening to Cavern Lake without incident.

Nadie and I scouted ahead, passing through what looked like a narrow doorway in the rock wall. Within a few steps, we were out of the snow. After several more, we were stepping into a humid enclosure with a high ceiling. I could smell the lake ahead. The Wendigo's hunger seemed to echo through the space, but it was just that—an echo. I couldn't sense its presence.

I looked over at Nadie, who indicated the cavern was clear.

I signaled back to the others. Rusty, Yoofi, and Takara entered while Nadie returned through the opening to keep watch outside. My team and I crossed the cavern together. Near the lake, we passed a large circle of stones. Old blood stained its center, and I smelled traces of human remains. They matched the scents from Austin's truck bed.

Yoofi moved to the front of the formation and stood at the water's edge. The rest of the team took up defensive positions, flamethrowers ready.

Raising his staff, Yoofi began to chant.

Dabu better keep his end of the deal, I thought.

I didn't have to worry. In the next moment, a dark orange light, like the color of the sky in Dabu's realm, pulsed out. I felt it as a warm breeze. The surface of the lake rippled. A second force emerged behind the first, this one reaching toward the edge of the lake and ... peeling it back.

Where there had once been water, crude steps descended into a subterranean chamber.

Yoofi waved for us to hurry. I could see by his straining face he wouldn't be able to hold the spell for long. I moved to the lake's edge and peered down the sights of my MP88. The smells emerging from the lair were dark and rank with death. If the

Wendigo was down there, I wasn't picking him up. But I wasn't picking up anything else, either.

C'mon, Sarah, I thought. *Be okay.*

I signaled to my teammates. Takara took lead, Rusty hesitating before he started down after her. I fell in behind them, and the three of us descended into the Wendigo's lair.

24

The steps deposited us into a large cavern. I couldn't tell when we'd passed into the realm between our world and the Cree's, but when I glanced up, the underside of the lake's surface glimmered overhead. I straightened my gaze and peered around. The smell of death had only thickened with our descent, and I noticed scattered remains of the Wendigo's victims.

Through the stench slipped a familiar scent.

I got Takara's attention and signaled to a smaller cave across the cavern. She had me take lead while she and Rusty moved in behind me. When we reached the opening, I peered inside. Sarah was sitting against the far wall of the chamber, alive. She was tending to someone on the floor beside her. A moment later, I picked up Ms. Welch's scent too.

While Rusty hung back to guard the opening, Takara and I rushed over to them.

Sarah's head turned slowly. Her hairline was matted with blood where she'd been injured from the Wendigo's attack. When she flinched away, I realized she couldn't see a thing in the darkness.

"Sarah," Takara whispered. "It's your teammates."

She blinked, and then her eyes did something I'd never seen. They glimmered with moisture. She nodded quickly and looked down at Ms. Welch, whom she'd wrapped in a foil blanket. The woman was younger than she appeared in the photo. Mussed blond hair hung over a dirty face.

"She's not doing well," Sarah whispered. "I've been trying to get her to drink water, but she's in and out. Knows who she is, but otherwise she's incoherent."

Dehydrated and in shock, I thought. "I've got her."

While I knelt and lifted her into my left arm, Takara asked Sarah, "Can you walk?"

"Yes." She used the wall to pull herself up. I noticed she'd lost her weapons and helmet and that her pack was hanging on by a single strap. Wasting no time, Takara guided one of Sarah's hands to her shoulder to lead her. She then signaled that we were heading out.

I led the way from the cave, one arm cradling Ms. Welch, the other sweeping my sixty-pound MP88 across the cavern. I half expected to see a hoard of nightmare creatures, like what we'd encountered in the Chagrath's realm, but this domain was exclusive to the Wendigo. Like Megha had said, a place to hide its victims from the two worlds it inhabited.

We reached the steps and began to climb. Above us, the opening in the lake trembled. I could see Yoofi beyond, his bared teeth shining white, sweat pouring down the sides of his face.

How's it looking outside? I asked Nadie.

Still clear, she replied through our collective.

We'll be there shortly, I told her.

I emerged beside Yoofi, set Ms. Welch down, then returned for Sarah.

"I've got you," I whispered, and took her into my arm. Sarah clung to my neck as I bounded up the steps. I wondered how much the experience reminded her of hiding from the zombies as a child.

I emerged again and stood over Ms. Welch. Rusty had just cleared the final step when Yoofi gasped and staggered back. The edge of the lake closed with a slap, throwing up a wave that caught Rusty in the back. Rusty swore under his breath and shook the water from his right sleeve.

I positioned Sarah behind Takara, then lifted Ms. Welch again. When I looked over at Yoofi, I found him stooped forward with his hand and staff on his knees, breathing heavily. I got his attention and gave him a thumbs up, then waved him into motion. Time to get the hell out of there.

He staggered into position, and we moved toward the cavern entrance in formation.

Someone's coming, Nadie called through our connection.

I signaled the information to Takara, and she motioned for us to take positions in the recesses on either side of the entrance. I found a place to prop Ms. Welch while Takara guided Sarah to a crevice in the opposite wall, maybe the same one Nadie had hidden inside earlier.

Can you see who? I asked her.

It's the young man whose truck we searched. I can smell the tar. He's coming toward us.

Austin, I thought. *Or should I say, the Wendigo.*

With Sarah blind and unarmed and Ms. Welch unconscious, we were in a piss-poor position to fend off Austin if he transformed. I signaled to Takara. After a moment, she signaled back. She wanted us to remain out of sight. When Austin passed us—presumably to go to his lair—we were to exit. Yoofi, Rusty, and I would take Sarah and Ms. Welch back to the van.

Takara's next signal surprised me. She would stay behind to engage him. I didn't like the idea of her facing the creature alone, but she was in charge. Besides that, it was the right call. Whether or not we *could* destroy the host, we needed to take a shot.

Is he armed? I asked Nadie.

He's carrying some sort of stick.

I wondered what he was doing with a stick.

Don't let him see you, I told Nadie. *We're going to let him through.*

Though everyone went still, the breaths of my teammates sounded too loud in my lupine hearing. I hoped Austin's hearing wasn't acute in his human form. After several long minutes, I heard his footfalls transitioning from the snow outside to the rock-strewn floor of the entrance. My nostrils flared. Yeah, same tar-like scent that we'd picked up in his truck.

His footsteps stopped. My finger moved over the trigger for the flamethrower.

In the next moment, a flashlight beam shot through the opening. *The hell is he doing with a flashlight?*

Across from me, Takara and Rusty had drawn back until they were behind a stone protrusion. Our own concealment wasn't as complete, but Austin would have to turn most of the way around after entering to see me, Yoofi, and Ms. Welch. The flashlight beam wavered as Austin resumed walking.

At that moment, Ms. Welch jerked and let out an unconscious murmur.

Shit.

I got Yoofi's attention and turned up a hand in question.

Yoofi nodded wearily. Holding the trembling staff over Ms. Welch, he mouthed a silent incantation. Smoke dribbled from the staff and fell over the woman's blood-knotted hair. It didn't look like much, but her next murmur was an exhalation of breath as she seemed to relax into a deeper sleep.

Whether Austin had heard her, I couldn't tell. He was still coming. In a few more steps, he limped into my field of vision. I didn't recognize him at first. He'd smeared something black over his face and much of his winter hunting clothes. Though a rifle was strapped across the top of his backpack, he was wielding the stick Nadie had mentioned. Faces had been carved into the length of wood, some human, some animal.

Austin's flashlight, which had been playing out ahead of him, shot to either side. Fortunately, he was already past our position. The beam hit the walls a good ten feet from us before steadying ahead again.

When he was halfway to the lake, Takara motioned for me and Yoofi to move. Carefully, I scooped up Ms. Welch and followed Yoofi from our concealment into the narrow tunnel that led outside. Rusty came in behind us, leading Sarah. Takara took up the rear.

With every step, I listened back, but Austin didn't seem to have heard us.

One by one, we emerged outside. The whooshing wind covered our hustle toward the trees. In the snow's dull glow, Sarah no longer needed someone to guide her. I handed her my sidearm and peered back to find Takara framed in the entrance to Cavern Lake. She had swapped the flamethrower for her M4 and already had it to her shoulder. She motioned at us to keep going. She would give us enough time to get clear before taking her shot.

We moved in a line toward the distant van. Despite her head wound, Sarah was kicking through the knee-high snow with surprising strength. Rusty appeared to be laboring to match her pace, but Yoofi was struggling. The effort to open the portal had exhausted him. Only one hundred meters out, and he was already falling behind. I was about to offer to carry him when Nadie appeared at his side.

"Climb on," she said.

Yoofi nodded wearily and threw a leg over her hunkered back. He wrapped his hands in her thick hair as she stood. We picked up our pace, Nadie and I taking the lead, Sarah in the middle, and Rusty watching our six.

That was the Cannibal? Nadie asked.

Yeah, I replied, but doubt was gnawing at me. Why had he appeared in human form? And what was that stick he'd been carrying?

It was a totem stick, Nadie said, picking up the thought. *Used by the old Cree medicine people.*

What about the black stuff on his face, giving off the strong odor?

"Ikwe sap," she replied.

I stopped as the name lined up with something I'd read in the Cree notebook. "Can you carry one more?" I asked, already setting Ms. Welch on Nadie's back. "Hold on to her," I told Yoofi.

I wheeled toward Rusty. "You're in charge of getting the group back to base. Don't wait for me."

"Wh-where are you going?" he stammered.

"To stop another innocent from being killed."

I fell to my hands and raced back the way we'd come. While searching through Mrs. Grimes's notebook earlier, I'd stopped on a page when I'd spotted the word "Wendigo." But the notes only described a substance that, rubbed over the body, was believed to disguise a person's scent from various mythical creatures, including the Wendigo.

That substance was Ikwe sap.

Austin wasn't the creature. Far from it.

When the cavern entrance came into view, I boomed, "Takara, no!"

She was where I'd last seen her, head poised behind the sights of her weapon. She stiffened slightly at the sound of my voice.

"Hold fire!" I shouted.

When she didn't respond, I bounded into the entrance and pulled her down by the back of her vest. She twisted around and landed on top of me, one arm braced against my throat.

"What the fuck are you doing?" she hissed.

"It's not him."

Before I could explain further, shots cracked and caromed off the stone above us. Austin had heard the commotion and was firing blindly.

"Stay down," I whispered.

I crawled forward until I could see the young man. He was almost to the lake, his flashlight hand supporting the rifle barrel. At his distance, though, the light couldn't illuminate me, and he had stopped firing. By his wide eyes I could tell he was listening for movement.

When I was sure Takara was safely out of his line of fire, I called, "Austin, it's Captain Wolfe."

He adjusted his aim slightly.

"Hold your fire," I said, my voice reverberating off the stone. "I think we're hunting the same thing."

"Oh yeah?" he challenged. "And what's that?"

"A Wendigo."

Though he continued to hold his rifle on me, a change came over his face. I approached his light cautiously. I was in my full suit and body armor, but I didn't want to absorb a round if I didn't have to.

"It killed Connor," I said. "Your friend."

During my race to keep Takara from wasting Austin, I'd been working to unpackage why he would be hunting the creature, and why he hadn't told anyone what he was doing. The revenge motive took care of the first question but not necessarily the second—unless he was worried he'd be laughed at.

But as I stepped into his light, Austin shook his head.

"No, man. You've got it wrong."

"How so?"

"The Wendigo didn't kill Connor," he said. "The Wendigo *is* Connor. But I know how to stop him."

25

"Connor?" I repeated. "But they recovered his remains."

"That's what I'm saying. When the blue light hit Connor, it shredded his body to shit, but his soul became that thing." He jerked his rifle toward Takara as she arrived from the darkness to his left.

"It's all right," I said. "She's a teammate."

Takara had gripped his barrel. Now she released it as he lowered it again, his eyes dancing crazily between us.

"Tell us everything that happened," she said.

"I grew up with Connor," he began with a sigh, as if relieved to be getting the story off his chest. "We were best friends, always hunting or fishing out on the bay. The day we turned eighteen, we enlisted together. They took him, but not me. Failed the vision part. Connor did two tours in Waristan. On the second, his convoy ran over an IED. The force slammed him into the roof of his vehicle. His body healed, but up here?" Austin tapped his temple and shook his head. "It was like he was six years old again. I just wanted to help him."

"By doing the Wendigo ceremony," I said.

"My mom had this notebook on the Cree. I was really into it growing up. She always said the mysticism stuff wasn't real, but for Connor's sake, I felt like I had to try. I started with the healing ceremonies. Nothing took. I then got the idea to try the Wendigo ceremony. But it was supposed to make Connor superhuman—not turn him into a freaking man-eater."

"Whose flesh did he eat?" Takara asked. "For the ceremony?"

"Mine," Austin said. "I took some of the shit my dad's been dealing so I could carve a chunk from my left hip. Drugs or not, it was about as godawful as it sounds. I prepared the meat in a dehydrator. When it came time for Connor to eat it, I told him it was jerky."

That explained Austin's limp.

"We did the ceremony over there." He pointed to the arrangement of stones by the lakeside. "Lasted a couple hours. All the time I felt these strange energies circling us. Connor went into a kind of trance. Then I did the last step, and boom. A bolt of blue light shot down and hit Connor. He started screaming." Austin shook his head. "Worst sound I've ever heard. The next thing I know this thing is bursting out of his body, shedding him like he's its second skin or something." I could see him reliving the episode in his mind.

"What did the Wendigo do then?" I asked to keep him talking.

"It came at me with its mouth open like it was going to eat me right there. My rifle was over by my pack, but even if I'd been holding it, I don't think I could have fired it. My body had locked up. I'd never seen anything so horrible in my life. The thing stopped and sniffed me over. Then it took off from the cavern. When I saw what was left of Connor, I panicked. We camped here a lot. If they found his remains ... I don't know. I got it in my head that people would think I'd killed him. So I gathered up what was left of him and scattered the remains near a deer stand. Somewhere I knew they'd be found."

"Did you do that with the other victims?" I asked, remembering the smell in his truck bed.

He nodded. "For the last couple months, I've been hunting the Wendigo, trying to kill it. But I can't seem to get close. And it keeps grabbing people, taking them here, I guess. Thing is, I don't find the victims till they're dead. The Wendigo leaves some of their remains in the circle where we did the ceremony." He pointed to the arrangement of stones. "And yeah, I do the same thing with them, take what's left and dump them in places I know they'll be found."

"To support the bear story?" Takara asked.

"'Cause it seemed like the right thing to do," he shot back. "Didn't want their families left wondering."

"Is that why you came tonight?" I asked. "To see if the Wendigo had killed again?"

"I came to end the damned thing. There was nothing in my mom's notes on how to do that, but she'd written down the name of the man who'd given her the info—a Cree name—and where he lived. If he knew how to call a Wendigo up, I figured he'd also know how to kill it.

"So a couple days ago, I drove out there. I remembered my mom telling me he'd been really old when she'd interviewed him, but I thought maybe he had family, someone he'd passed his knowledge down to. I don't know what the place was like when my mom went out there, but it's a shithole now. Old trailers, mangy dogs, trash blowing everywhere. I asked around, and come to find out, this dude is still alive. I found him in a trailer on the edge of the res. The door was busted and kicking back and forth. Past it, I could see the old man sitting in a recliner, like he was waiting for me. He was practically a skeleton. Arms and legs thin as sticks, a few wisps of hair left on his head. His body was shaking all over, like an idling motor. And the place smelled freaking awful, like death. I almost took off right there, but he smiled with these rotten gums and called me the 'Wendigo Caller.' He knew why I'd come."

"And he told you how to stop it," I said, bracing against the hope rising inside me.

"At first he wanted me to describe the ceremony. Then he had me tell him about the Wendigo's victims. I swear to God, his eyes were shining the whole time, like he was getting off on what I was saying."

I remembered the old man's parting words to Austin's mother. This was what he'd wanted.

"When I finished, he just looked at me for a long time," Austin continued. "It freaked the hell out of me. 'Now you want to know how to put a stop to it,' he finally said. I nodded. He grinned like he was thinking about it, then he shrugged and said something about the debt being repaid. He asked if I knew why the Wendigo left parts of its victims behind. Told him I didn't have a fucking clue. They're offerings, he told me, to the man whose flesh had given it life. He said the Wendigo avoided me because it 'feared and revered me'—those were his words. As its creator, I was the only one who could *discreate* it. And the Wendigo knew that."

I had never heard of a being leaving offerings to a mortal, but it made a certain sense. "The offerings were its way of appeasing you," I said.

"I guess. The old man said Wendigo summonings were almost always done from a place of greed. Someone murdered someone else and ate their flesh. But because I offered my own flesh, that gave me power over it."

"How do we destroy it?" Takara asked impatiently.

"The old man had me fetch this from a closet." Austin held up the totem stick. "He did this weird chant over it. When he finished, he handed it back, said I needed to meet the Wendigo in the same sacred space where I'd called it and touch this end to its stomach."

"And that will destroy it?" Takara pressed.

"According to the old man, yeah. Send it back to the stars."

My nostrils flared. Beneath the tar-like smell, I could just make out the sharp scent of bloody meat in Austin's pack. "So your plan was to cover yourself in that sap so the Wendigo wouldn't smell you, then bait the circle with—what is that, hog meat?—hoping to attract it."

"Yeah, hog meat sprinkled with this." He reached into a jacket pocket and pulled out an old Nalgene bottle. Something dark shifted inside, but it wasn't a liquid. "The old man gave it to me.

Some sort of ash. It's supposed to make the hog meat smell like human flesh." His face turned grim as he glanced at the circle.

"What?" I asked.

"I'm the only one who can kill it." He looked back at us. "Which means if it kills *me*, there'll be no way to stop it."

"Then we need to keep that from happening," I said.

I looked over at Takara to make sure we were on the same page.

"Do you have any more of that sap?" she asked Austin.

Reeking of tar, Takara and I took up positions in recesses along the cavern wall opposite the casting circle. Austin had already dumped the hog meat from his pack into the circle, and now he sprinkled the ashes over it. The scent hit me in a potent wave. When Austin finished, he peered over with a look that said *this is it* and clicked off his flashlight. Needing to be in range of the Wendigo when it entered the circle, he moved back several paces and crouched with the totem stick.

Kid's got balls, I'll give him that.

Takara kept vigil on the entrance while I did the same on the lake. There was no telling where the Wendigo would appear from. With full tanks on our flamethrowers, all we could do now was wait.

We were approaching the one-hour mark, when Takara got my attention with a hand motion. She pointed. Something was filling the cavern entrance. I hadn't heard the massive creature arrive, but it was here.

Hunger warped the air around the Wendigo as it straightened to its full height. When it tilted its horned head, I imagined its nostrils pulling in the scent of ash-enhanced meat. I checked again to ensure our own scents were covered. We'd slathered the Ikwe sap on thick and applied another layer to Austin. It was going to take a week to scrub the smell off us, but we were concealed.

With hungry noises, the Wendigo made a dash for the meat.

That's right, I thought, watching it close the distance to the circle. *Go feed your face.*

But when it reached the circle's edge, the Wendigo stopped suddenly. Its ribs heaved as it leaned forward and sniffed again. Drool fell from its deadly mouth. It paced around the circle, knuckles scraping the ground. I flicked my gaze over to Austin, who hunkered twenty feet away. With his flashlight off, he was blind. His cue to move in would be the sound of the Wendigo feeding. But the Wendigo wasn't stepping over the damned stones.

Did it sense a trap? Did it know it would be vulnerable inside the circle?

When Takara waved at me, I realized I was panting. I clamped my muzzle shut, but my wolf nature was responding to the mind-rending strain of the Wendigo's urge to feed—life's most basic need. The Wendigo paced around the circle again and released a horrid shriek. It wasn't the circle the creature was wary of, I realized, but the meal. Taking it down would only grow its appetite, making its hunger that much more agonizing.

In that moment, in that cry, I grasped the curse of the Wendigo.

Blood bubbled from the meat as it continued to react with the ash. The Wendigo could no longer resist. It plunged into the circle and fed greedily. We all moved—Takara between the creature and the cavern entrance, me between it and the lake. Austin stole forward, the wet sounds of the Wendigo's feeding his guide.

When he was feet away, he snapped his flashlight on. The beam hit the hunched-over creature in the low back where thick vertebrae stood out like tombstones. With his totem stick extended, Austin ran the final few steps.

The Wendigo cocked its head suddenly and twisted around. Even as Austin lunged for the creature's exposed stomach, I saw he wasn't going to make it.

The Wendigo slashed a taloned hand around, knocking the stick from Austin's grasp and Austin through the air. The young man landed hard, blood already leaking through his shredded hunting jacket. The Wendigo released an ungodly shriek that sounded like one part fury, two parts betrayal.

It rushed Austin, but I was there to meet it with a blazing jet of napalm. The Wendigo staggered back, the fire that engulfed it reflecting brilliantly over the lake. I kept the trigger depressed and moved forward until I was between the creature and Austin. I noticed the totem stick off to my right. I was tempted to grab it, but according to the Shaking Man, the Wendigo's creator had to wield the stick for it to work. And Austin was still down.

With another shriek, the Wendigo turned from me and fled toward the cavern exit. Takara's flamethrower burst to life, hitting the Wendigo square in the chest. The creature spun from the surprising assault.

"Austin!" I called, trying to stir him.

The young man jerked and pawed a hand around as if

attempting to recover the stick, but his head had hit hard when he landed, and he was semi-conscious at best. When the Wendigo doubled back toward me, I met it with more napalm. Together, Takara and I steered it toward the circle.

"Austin!" I tried again.

With a furious sound, the Wendigo lowered its head and ran straight at Takara's stream of fire. Takara set her legs, but the creature wasn't slowing. Flames broke around its massive horns.

At the last moment, Takara threw her flamethrower aside. With a pair of sharp scrapes, blades popped from the forearms of her suit. She drove the right one into the Wendigo's gut, skewering it. When the creature doubled over, she brought the other blade through its neck. Fluid and tissue flew from the savage strike before twisting into black smoke.

The Wendigo should have been decapitated. Instead, it reared its head back and released an ear-splitting cry.

I hit it with more napalm from my side, but the hunger that enveloped it was squelching the flames as fast as they were lighting it up. Takara grunted into her next attack: three slashes intended to drive the creature into the circle.

The Wendigo swung back this time, and Takara narrowly leapt out of the path of its descending fist. Sensing an opening, the creature stretched past her, toward the exit. I pursued.

Within strides, the Wendigo was pulling away.

No, goddammit. We had you. We fucking had you.

The Wendigo disappeared through the corridor leading out. I anticipated another chase through the snow, one the Wendigo would win. But a moment later, it was stumbling back into view, forearms to its face.

What the...?

Shards of light were exploding into the creature, blowing chunks of sinewy flesh from its body.

The Cree warriors! I realized.

Their portal had yet to close, and they were still patrolling their lands for intruders. They'd sure as hell found one. The warriors climbed through the entrance after the Wendigo, their painted faces bold and unafraid.

Though the creature was regenerating from the attack, it seemed to understand it would find no shelter in our world. With another shriek, it turned and sprinted toward the lake—its lair.

Takara, who had been swapping out the tank on her flamethrower, was too late getting the fresh one installed before the Wendigo was past her. I was out of position as well, but I launched into a run to head it off.

With a ripple, the lake peeled back from the shore, revealing the steps we had descended a short time ago. If the Wendigo reached them, it would be in its own domain. From there it could continue to the Cree realm. The Wendigo would come back eventually—its inexorable need to feed dictated that—but how many more victims would it claim before we'd have this kind of chance again? If we'd even *get* another chance. Because there was no way Beam and Centurion were sending us back up here without a profit motive.

It was now or never.

With arrows lancing off the creature's back, I clamped my MP88 to my suit, charged in low, and took out the Wendigo's legs. The massive creature fell, its emaciated limbs lashing around as its momentum threw it into a roll. As the Wendigo scrambled to get up, I landed on its back. Thighs squeezing its ribs, I began hammering the back of the creature's head with my fists.

Just need to subdue the damned thing long enough for Austin to recover.

I could hear Takara beside the young man, trying to revive him.

The Wendigo reached around and seized me in one hand. With fingers almost long enough to encompass my thick torso, it jerked me to its front and brought its other hand around me. Pain speared my sternum as it bore down with both thumbs. The preternaturally sharp talons cracked my chest plates and threatened to pierce my vest and suit.

But the pressure alone...

Teeth gritting, I lashed with my free hand. My claws severed the bundle of tendons on its right forearm. Before the tissue could regenerate, the hand spasmed. I did the same to the left.

Its grip slackened and I thrashed free. When the Wendigo lunged its horned head toward me, I drove my fist into the twin septum where a nose would have been. The blow opened a crack that ran up between its eyes before fusing again. The Wendigo flinched, but now the pits of its eyes were twisting. In the next instant, a dull fog enveloped my mind.

Trying to steal my will, my consciousness, I realized, *like it did Nadie's.*

I forced my gaze away, but everything was already a blur.

I felt my knees thud to the ground.

26

A shriek brought me back, but it hadn't come from the Wendigo. I blinked my eyes open. The entire cavern appeared to be crackling with fire, and there was a creature overhead, brilliant red-orange flames ripping and rippling around its feathered form.

I squinted from the heat. "Takara?" I rasped.

I hadn't seen her dragon form since El Rosario. As I took in the massive winged creature, I remembered how majestic she looked—and yet how utterly terrifying. Her beaked mouth opened and released what sounded like a war cry. The Wendigo, who had snapped its head around, tried to shrink away. Takara swooped down and seized it around the waist with a pair of clawed feet. Her head tilted toward me, malevolent eyes wreathed in flames.

"Get back," she warned.

With a searing flap of her wings, she rose into the air, the Wendigo thrashing in her grip. At the high dome of the cavern, flames spewed from Takara's dragon form and blazed in the lake's reflection. The Wendigo screamed and slashed at her, but its blows only passed through fire.

Soon, the Wendigo became lost in the roaring storm.

The Cree warriors stopped shooting. They wandered forward, bows at their sides, staring at the spectacle. About twenty meters from me, firelight glistened from Austin's face. But though he was peering up, he was still lying on the ground, one side of his jacket soaked with blood.

"Your stick!" I called to him, jabbing a finger toward it.

I sensed Takara's plan—to exhaust the Wendigo so that when we got it back into the circle, the creature would be too weak to fend off Austin's next attempt. But Austin only looked over at the totem stick, then back at me, too rattled to comprehend the situation.

Breaking into a sprint, I recovered the stick and moved toward Austin. Above, Takara's dragon form swelled as her assault grew more intense. Black smoke billowed from where the Wendigo continued to shriek. My ears ached with the pressure of a building energy that seemed to be coming from Takara.

When the pressure spiked, I threw myself over Austin. The energy detonated like a bomb. Fire ripped throughout the cavern and raked across my back. I used my body to shield Austin, grinding my teeth against the scorching pain. When the heat relented, I chanced a look.

Takara's dragon form cruised through curtains of steam rising from the lake. In her clutches was the Wendigo—or what remained of it. The giant creature was arced back, its mouth gaping wide, arms and legs stiff and still, like a charred corpse's.

I knew better. Already, wisps of black smoke were snaking back toward the Wendigo. Whether it took seconds or minutes, the creature would reconstitute itself. So what in the hell was Takara doing? Her dragon form swooped around the high cavern again, as if taking a victory lap.

"The circle!" I shouted. "Get it into the circle!"

The dragon angled her head and dove toward me. She released the Wendigo, and the creature crash-landed into the circle of stones.

"C'mon," I said to Austin, lifting him by the back of his jacket and pressing the totem stick against his chest. "Let's move." Austin was still in bad shape, but if it took holding the stick in his hand while I carried him to the Wendigo, so be it. We wouldn't get a better shot.

In a gust of fire, the dragon landed between us and the circle.

"Takara," I said, shielding Austin from her heat. "The Wendigo."

But the dragon only stared down at me. A minute earlier, I could see a hint of Takara in those eyes. Now they were furnaces of malevolence. The terrible creature loomed over me.

"How dare you give me orders," she said in a piercing voice.

I tried to move around her, but she cut in front of me. Fire crackled from her wings.

"I could incinerate you right here," she said.

"Listen to me, Takara—"

"I am *not* Takara."

Takara had never opened up about her dragon nature, so I'd never understood what it was exactly. But like with the Blue Wolf—or even the Wendigo—it seemed to be another being entirely. Challenge shone in her hawk-like eyes. I could feel the weight of my MP88 where I'd clipped it to my back, could feel the wolf in me wanting to meet her challenge with force.

But I talked it down.

"Remember your training," I said in a soft voice. "Remember your meditative practices."

"Who are you talking to?" she demanded.

Beyond the dragon's fiery form, the Wendigo was regaining its strength. There was no time for this, but it was the only way. I wasn't going to fight her. The dragon puffed out her chest in a display of power. Sparks flew from her batting wings. But did red crescents just glimmer around her eyes?

"I see you, Takara," I said. "I see you fighting."

The dragon released a ferocious shriek and shook her wings again.

"Keep it up, Takara. You can do this. You're strong enough. It's why I put you in command."

Without warning, the dragon lunged toward me. I'd been holding Austin behind me, but now I set him on the ground and threw my arms out. In a final burst of flames, the dragon's feathers vanished, and Takara wilted into my embrace. Smoke plumed from her leathers as I held her against me. I could smell the heat of her scarred skin, but she was herself again. She let out a small moan.

"It's okay," I whispered. "I've got you."

Her moan became words. "Finish ... the mission..."

Beyond the dissipation of smoke, the Wendigo was stirring.

I set Takara down, out of harm's way. "You ready, soldier?" I said, turning to Austin, but he wasn't there. He'd gained his feet and, stick in hand, was staggering toward the casting circle. Fires lingered in several nooks and crannies around the cavern, serving as small pyres. In their light, the Wendigo rose to a knee.

The Cree warriors resumed firing at it, but this time the creature ignored the flashing arrows. It rounded on Austin, who looked like he was moving in slow motion, one elbow pinned to his bleeding side.

"I'm so sorry, Connor," Austin grunted. "Was just trying to help you."

He looked up at the Wendigo's face. But unlike Takara's dragon, there was no humanity in the creature. Not even a glimmer. With a roar, it drew back a clawed hand. But while it had been fixating on Austin's voice, I had been moving in from behind. In one quick motion, I seized it around the neck and slammed it onto its back. The Wendigo let out a terrible screech.

"Now!" I shouted.

Austin lunged in and thrust the stick at the Wendigo's exposed stomach.

"Love you, brother," he said.

The totem stick hit home with a detonation of light. I heard a rapid chant, as if the totem faces were speaking at once, and then a blue beam shot down from the cavern ceiling and into the circle. One second I was holding the Wendigo, and in the next, I was being blown backwards. I tumbled for several feet and came to a rest as the blue light faded from the space.

I peered toward the circle. Where the Wendigo had been lay a scattering of gray dust. I spotted Austin ten meters away. He had been blown off, too, and was lying flat on his back. The totem stick was nowhere in sight.

I let out my breath. It was done.

I was looking for Takara when I felt the pressure of her hand on my shoulder. A glance at her pale face told me she was still suffering from her transformation, but she was standing. She watched me as I rose.

"I'm returning command to you," she managed.

Before I could respond, she winced and shifted her gaze to Austin. She leaned against me, and we approached him together.

"Hey, man," I said, kneeling beside him. "You all right?"

Austin struggled onto his elbows and blinked his vision straight. "Is it gone?"

Besides the evidence in the circle, I couldn't feel the Wendigo's hunger anymore. The being was truly banished.

"Yeah."

Austin lay his head back and started to cry. Relief, exhaustion, the horror of the last two months—it was all coming out. I turned in time to see the Cree warriors filing quietly from the cavern, returning to their realm. The final one stopped, brought a fist to his chest, and closed his other hand around it. His eyes gleamed at me. I mirrored the gesture, and he disappeared.

Austin caught my side of the exchange. "Cree warrior salute," he said.

"Then you merit one too. What you just did took serious bravery."

His eyes danced through his tears. "Or serious insanity."

"Let's take a look at your side." I lifted his layers of clothes from the wound. Blood leaked freely, but the damage from the Wendigo didn't go deeper than the muscle. He'd be all right.

I pulled a pressure bandage from my pack to stop the bleeding.

"The Wendigo ceremony was missing from your mother's notebook," I said when I'd finished and pulled his jacket back down.

With a nod, Austin reached into a pocket and produced a dirty sheaf of folded-up paper. As I accepted it, I considered Austin's role in the killings. *He was a pawn*, I reminded myself. *An agent in the Shaking Man's hunger for revenge. He thought he was helping a friend.*

But would he attempt more conjurings?

"Burn it," Austin said of the notes. "That doesn't need to be out in the world."

I did the honors, hitting the sheaf of pages with a blast from a flamethrower. As the pages disintegrated to ash, I wondered if we should check on the Shaking Man next, gauge his level of threat. But that would be straying way outside the mission parameters, and I had no idea what we'd be walking into.

"Do you have the keys to your truck?" I asked Austin.

He patted a pants pocket, producing a rustle of metal.

"Then let's clear out," I said.

27

Everyone who had left Cavern Lake ahead of us had made it back to the lodge safely. I found Sarah tending to Ms. Welch, who was already improving. Yoofi snored in his bedroom, while Rusty hammered on a keyboard in the command-and-control center, checking configurations on our restored system.

I'd called ahead with the news of mission accomplished, but we were all too spent to celebrate. For now, a few weary smiles and claps on the shoulders sufficed. Through the mission's peaks and valleys, we'd all had a role in its success. Like the celebration, I would worry about the particulars later.

I found a bed for Austin and helped Takara to hers. She made a face, but I was back in command and wanted her to start what would be a lengthy recovery. I then sent a SITREP to Beam and called Olaf with an update. During the same call, I spoke to Mayor Grimes to inform him the threat had ended and his son was safe. I left out the details. How much he found out would be up to Austin.

Grimes didn't thank me, but I could hear his relief. The roads around the lake were socked in, he said, but he would have them plowed in the morning so Olaf could return to us and Austin to them.

"So, we're good then?" he asked in a lowered voice, referring to his side business.

"Not my jurisdiction," I replied. "But maybe you should start thinking about the price of discretion. You lost several people, insisting this thing was a bear attack. And it could have been a lot worse. Was it worth it?"

His end fell quiet.

"If there's a next time, call us," I said.

"I will. Right now, though, I have wolf issues. A pack got to my dogs last night."

I found Sarah as she was finishing up with Austin's wounds. "I can keep an eye on him and Ms. Welch," I said, "make sure they're doing all right. Why don't you get some sleep?"

"What about you?"

"Full of energy," I lied. "I can sleep on the flight back."

Sarah gave me a sidelong look as she stripped off her latex gloves. I thought about the skunk database, the one she hadn't told me about. Right before she stepped from the room, I stopped her.

"Hey, what happened to Nadie?"

"The she-wolf? She followed us back here and then left."

"Left? Did she say where she was going?"

"No. Why?"

I felt a vague disappointment, like a howl echoing off into the distance.

"Just wanted to thank her for her help with the mission," I said. "That's all."

Sarah looked at me for another moment before leaving.

By morning, the storm had ended and the rising sun gleamed over the virgin snow. The plow arrived, circled the drive, then headed back toward town. Olaf returned and Austin prepared to depart.

"Be good," I told him on his way out.

"After what happened? Don't worry."

We clasped hands and he was off, healed and limping less than he'd been the night before. Yoofi had recovered enough by sunrise to apply some magic to him. He'd done the same for Ms. Welch, who was sitting up and talking. According to Sarah, she remembered being attacked at the cabin but almost nothing else, which was just as well. While Sarah made arrangements to have her transferred to a Centurion medical facility, I stuck my helmeted head into her room.

"Hey, how are you feeling?" I asked.

"Like I need a shower," she said with a self-conscious smile. Something about her spoke to expensive tastes—probably why she'd ended up with Berglund—but there was a sincerity to her as well.

"Shouldn't be much longer," I said. "I'm Captain Wolfe, by the way."

"I guessed as much. Thank you for what you did out there."

"I'm just glad you're safe."

"I understand Karl contracted you?" When I nodded, she made a face. "I hope he wasn't a problem to work with. He can be ... a little overzealous sometimes."

A little? I thought.

"He'll be happy to see you," I said.

About thirty minutes later, Berglund arrived with the Centurion team. Their vehicles had barely pulled in front of the lodge when he jumped out and hustled up the front porch steps. A bandage covered his forehead. When I saw the cast on his wrist, I remembered smashing away his sidearm. I opened the door so he wouldn't run into it. Even though our last exchange had involved me cracking a rifle butt against his head, Berglund hardly glanced my way as he hurried past.

"Caitlyn?" he shouted. "Caitlyn, baby, are you in here?"

"Back here," she called.

Their reunion was tearful, mostly on his end, and filled with *Oh my God*s and *I can't believe it*s. The rest of us gave them their space, but after ten minutes of the same, the Centurion team announced it was time to move out.

As they loaded Ms. Welch onto a plinth and carried her to a medical van, Berglund bounded around them like a large dog. From a window, I watched him offer loud opinions on how his girlfriend should be carried and loaded—which the team wisely ignored.

When the leader climbed into the front vehicle, I caught a look of exasperation on his face. *Oh, he's just getting started,* I thought, ready for Berglund to be someone else's problem.

"Oh, hey, can you hold on a sec?" Berglund called to the team.

I groaned as I watched him make his way back up the steps. I'd spoken too damned soon. I met him on the front porch to spare my teammates.

"Forget something?" I asked.

"Yeah." He threw his arms around me and pressed his head to my chest. "You were right," he said in a voice that verged on sobbing. "You told me you'd get the job done, and you goddamned got it done. I don't know what to tell you, man. I should've listened. I know I should've listened. Here's what I'm gonna do," he said, standing back and wiping his eyes. "I'm gonna give you and your teammates a nice bonus for your trouble. Off the books. How's that sound?"

"We didn't recover her for you," I said.

"I know, but you recovered her. That's all that matters."

I was about to blow him off when an idea hit me. "Then how about paying it forward? These missions aren't cheap, and most of the world can't afford them. If you're serious, how about getting together with Centurion and setting up a fund for cases where the client is cash-strapped."

Berglund stared up at my visor as if his head were filling with an epiphany. "A hardship fund. That's a great idea. I'm gonna do that. I'm really gonna do that. And I'll put it in Caitlyn's name."

"I have one request, though," I said.

"What's that?"

"You have no say in where and how that money's disbursed." While such a fund was desperately needed, the last thing I wanted was for the man to be involved in future missions.

I watched Berglund's face harden with resistance—a reflex probably, because it quickly softened. "Heh. You got yourself a deal, Captain Wolfe. Seriously, I can't thank you enough for getting her back to me. And I'm sorry about the collateral damage." He was referring to the hunters who had attacked Nadie and me. "I'm gonna make that right too."

When he came in for another hug, I figured *what the hell* and let him.

"I don't know if you've met your Caitlyn yet," he said when he stood back, "but you'll know it when you do. They're one in a billion."

Already have, I thought, but didn't say it.

I watched him climb into the front of the medical van. The vehicles pulled out in a line. I checked my watch. We were due to fly out in about an hour, which meant packing time. I was turning to head back inside when something caught my eye off to my right.

At the side of the lodge, three large spruce trees grew close enough together that the ground beneath them was free of snow. That's where Nadie stood now. She was in her human form, dressed in the hunter's clothes from the day before. Her dark hair hung in a single braid over one shoulder.

I descended the steps and walked toward her.

"I didn't expect to see you," I said.

"I came to say goodbye," she replied when I arrived in front of her.

"I noticed you closed our connection."

She smiled sadly. "Though it didn't last long, our collective mind showed me all I could have wanted in a mate. Your strength, your leadership, your sense of justice. I also felt your love." She looked away. "But it wasn't for me. It's for the woman awaiting your return."

I nodded. "Her name's Daniela."

When Nadie didn't say anything, I removed my helmet and brought her chin around so our eyes met.

"I wasn't born like this," I said. "I won't be staying this way."

"I know."

"Your pack will be glad to have you back. They thought you'd passed to the other side." I remembered the lonely howls as the pack disappeared into last night's snowstorm.

But Nadie was shaking her head. "I can't live under Aranck's rule. Not anymore. Not after..." She glanced up at me and then away as her voice trailed off.

"So what will you do?"

"Become a lone wolf. Explore the territories Aranck forbade us from entering. There are whole worlds out there I know nothing about." She chuckled and smoothed my furrowed brow with her hand. "Don't worry for me, Captain Wolfe. Our kind are survivors."

"Be careful," I said.

"You too." She rose onto her tiptoes and kissed my cheek. Her dark eyes lingered on mine before she turned and walked away. I watched her until she disappeared behind a tree. Moments later the air crackled, as if from a burst of static electricity. She reappeared in her wolf form just long enough to blend into the snow-covered landscape.

I didn't know if it was my wolf instincts, but I glimpsed a future where she was running with a fellow shifter. I could even see their offspring, three or four shifter pups. She'd find her pack.

Eyes flashed gold—a final look back—and she was gone.

I released a farewell howl and rejoined my team.

28

I gave Rusty his promised time off. He flew out the morning after our return to spend a week with his wife and kids. Mostly his kids.

Though the others had the option to travel, none seemed interested in going anywhere. Yoofi was still recovering from his efforts to get us into the Wendigo's lair. He'd also caught a chill. He spent most of the day in bed, Sugar Nice thumping on the stereo and a hot water bottle at his feet. He didn't say anything more about the invitation to Dabu's feast, and I didn't bring it up. Like Yoofi, I was in no hurry to return to his underworld.

Takara remained at the compound too. Though I could tell she was still in pain, she didn't talk about her transformation. She barely talked at all, in fact. So I was surprised when she knocked on my door one evening and offered to begin teaching me to control my wolf.

We sat across from one another on the floor of my living room, eyes closed, her voice guiding me through the exercise. She had me imagine myself growing around my wolf. Afterwards, I felt mentally sturdier, more in control. We would continue the next night, she told me in a tone that sounded like an order. But I sensed a level of respect that hadn't been there pre mission. Whether that came from me handing her command or talking her down from her dragon state, I wasn't sure. Either way, I interpreted the meditative training as her peace offering—one I accepted.

For his part, Olaf spent his days lumbering around the compound. I had put my concerns for him on hold during the mission, but with that behind us, I was back to watching for any signs of humanity. On the third morning, I spotted him walking along the perimeter fencing like a caged animal.

"Olaf," I called, catching up to him.

He stopped and turned his dull gaze toward me.

"Just wanted a brief word," I said. "We can keep walking."

With a grunt, he heaved himself back into motion. We walked in silence while I worked out what I was going to say. For a minute we were just a zombie and a wolfman out on a morning stroll.

"You're a damn good soldier," I said at last, "and I'm glad to have you on the team. You've been vital to the success of the last two missions. Problem is, I don't know what's going on inside your head." When I turned, I was eye level with the network of old scars that criss-crossed his lumpy skull. "So I want you to listen to what I'm about to tell you. I want you to remember it. If there ever comes a point where you want out, Olaf, you need to tell me. You're not a prisoner here."

He continued to plod beside me, his breathing and scent unchanged.

"Do you understand what I'm saying?"

Olaf nodded once, but was it a reflex, or was there a part of him actually processing what I was telling him? Sarah was right to the extent that we couldn't keep going around and around with this. If a person was trapped inside there, I had to hope I'd thrown him a lifeline. Beyond that, I needed to let it go.

I had a team to command.

I walked with Olaf for several more minutes to see if he'd say anything. He didn't. When we cleared the back of the barracks, I noticed Sarah sitting out front. I gave Olaf's thick shoulder a squeeze, said, "Consider what I told you an order," and separated from him.

Other than the debriefing, Sarah and I hadn't talked about her ordeal in the Wendigo's lair. She'd been spending a lot of time working in her office, maybe so she wouldn't have to relive what had happened.

"How goes it, Program Manager?" I asked.

"Captain," she said.

I took a seat in the end chair, still angled from our conversation the week before. "Anything new from corporate?"

"They're monitoring some patterns around the globe, but they haven't told me anything specific. Our last client, Berglund, has been in touch with them, apparently. He wants to set up some kind of hardship fund to help with future mission costs. That should expand our reach."

I snorted in surprise. The son of a bitch had actually followed through. I'd had my doubts.

"Other than that, nothing really."

"I talked to Professor Croft this morning," I said. "He apologized for not getting back sooner, something about being stuck in the faerie realm. Anyway, he can't believe we took down a Wendigo, much less a primal one. He was seriously impressed. Sends his kudos. I told him about the Shaking Man. He said he'd alert his superiors. They'll check him out when they're up there."

Sarah nodded.

"How about you?" I asked.

She blinked behind her glasses. "What about me?"

"How are you doing after the encounter?"

Her fingers went to the faint scar line where her head wound had been. She must have understood what I was getting at. "I'm an adult now, Jason. And a soldier. I was prepared for what happened. In fact, being captured might have been the best thing that could have happened from a mission perspective. It allowed me to give Ms. Welch early medical attention. I don't know how much longer she would have lasted in the state I found her."

Sarah had a point, but her scent hadn't lied. She had been petrified when we'd reached her. Regardless, she didn't want to talk about it. I peered around the compound, empty except for us misfits who couldn't, or didn't want to, leave. Maybe now was the time to have our other talk.

"How long have you known about the skunk database?" I asked.

When she turned toward me, a part of me was sure she was going to backpedal or outright lie, setting off a serious leadership problem. But she replied, "Shortly after joining Legion."

"Why didn't you ever mention it?"

"Because it holds suspect data. It's quarantined so as not to contaminate our queries. As Prod 1s are verified, they're transferred over. The database is a placeholder. Nothing more."

I thought about how she had known Yoofi would need to cast a reveal spell.

"But you queried it," I said. "That's how you knew we were facing a Wendigo."

As she watched me watching her, I braced again for the possibility of a lie. "I had some suspicions," she admitted.

"But you kept them to yourself."

"I didn't want to contaminate—"

"All right, listen," I interrupted. "We're not computers. In the future, we'll query the skunk database when the results from the main database don't square with what we're seeing or we hit a dead end. And you'll share your suspicions. Agreed? If we're going to co-manage this team, we can't keep info from each other."

"Like you did with the she-wolf?"

"What are you talking about? You knew about Nadie."

"But not what she wanted."

I felt my face grow warm. "It was irrelevant."

"It had a compromising effect on you. That's why you transferred command to Takara."

I wanted to argue the point; instead, I cycled through my practice with Takara from the night before. "You're right," I said. "The environment had an effect, but her presence made my wolf more dominant. To the point, at times, that I couldn't entirely control him. I should have told you."

"I'll share from now on," she said.

"Yeah, so will I."

She squinted past me. "I think I understand your concern for him."

I followed her gaze to the distant fencing, where Olaf was little more than a dot now.

"You need for him to be sentient. Because if he isn't, you're worried the same thing could happen to you."

I gave a neutral grunt. The woman was more astute than I'd given her credit for.

My ringing phone saved me from having to answer her. I pulled it out and checked the display.

"Mr. Purdy," I said when I answered.

"I wanted to call and congratulate you on your second successful mission. I can think of worse forming habits," he said with a chuckle. "Yes, I know it was a team effort, but you were my pick to lead, and you're making that decision look better and better all the time."

"Even to Beam?" I asked. Following the mission, the Director and I hadn't communicated except through electronic reporting. That none of us had been reprimanded for the subnet hack told me he was keeping up his end of the deal. But that didn't mean things were kosher between us.

"He got his payment and then some," Purdy responded. "He's fine."

I stood and paced from the barracks. "Yeah, until the next mission."

"Let *me* worry about that. The larger picture, remember?"

"As long as you're handling things."

I still didn't know what was happening on his side of the curtain, and a part of me didn't want to. I'd be done in ten months. But I bristled at the idea that he could be using me and my teammates as pawns, no more significant to him than Austin or his mother had been to the Shaking Man.

"There's another reason for my call," Purdy said.

"And what's that?" I grunted.

"Are you sitting down?"

29

Four days later

I rolled onto my side and squinted up at the light falling through a pair of airy white curtains. I was on a soft, clean-smelling bed. A ceiling fan rotated slowly overhead. For a moment I had no idea where I was.

A slender arm slipped around my waist.

"I could stay in here all day," Daniela murmured, her tumble of hair tickling my bare back.

With a smile, I let my head rest back on the pillow. I then lifted Daniela's arm and pressed my lips against the soft flesh of her palm.

"Nothing stopping us," I replied.

As dreamlike as it felt, this was real. Purdy's news was that Biogen had made a breakthrough, a drug that could restore me for days instead of hours. The change to my human form had been excruciating, a process that involved a combo of IV gene therapy, submersion into a special suspension, and electric shocks. But it worked. After twenty-four hours of monitoring, Biogen cleared me to travel, to come home. And here I was, arrived late last night.

When I gave Daniela's hand a playful nibble, she giggled and withdrew her arm.

"I'm surprised you have anything left after last night."

"Hey, we have eight months apart to make up for." I rolled until I was over her and gazing down on her beautiful, sleepy face. We kissed.

By the time we separated, her expression had turned serious. She reached up and ran a thumb over my bristly cheek. When I realized she was circling the scar that marked me as the Blue Wolf, I took her hand and held it.

"I was really worried this time," she said.

I kissed her hand again and looked into her concerned eyes, remembering the dream she'd shared. But I was also remembering my hunt with Nadie and how close I'd come to allowing that part to overwhelm the rest of me, including my devotion to this incredible woman.

"What is it?" Daniela asked, watching me.

"I think it's time you knew what happened to me in Waristan."

"Really?"

I told her over breakfast and while we walked her dogs in the neighborhood. I described what I could about the bombing that had led to the old woman marking me. I spoke of changes coming over me. I told her the real reason I had left the military and taken my current position—for a cure. I explained why I had kept her in the dark, how I hadn't wanted her to worry for me.

Daniela mostly listened, the clinician in her knowing I needed to talk.

By the time I finished, we were hanging up the leashes while her dogs panted contentedly on the kitchen's tile floor. Daniela led me to the living room, where we took a seat on the sofa.

"How are you now?"

"Getting there," I replied carefully.

"These 'changes' you keep referring to..."

Her words lingered like a question. I could see in her face that she knew I was leaving out an important piece. And I was. I'd told her a lot—probably too much—but I hadn't been able to tell her about my physical transformation into a seven-foot, four-hundred-pound creature covered in hair.

I still couldn't bring the Blue Wolf into our relationship.

I tapped my head. "They're up here mostly," I replied, which wasn't a complete lie. "But listen to me. I wouldn't have come here if I thought I was putting you in danger. I can tell when I'm in control and when I'm not, and the short-term fix is working. I'm in control. We're getting closer to a cure."

Daniela kissed my temple firmly, then guided me until I was on my side, head resting on her lap. She began running her fingertips through my hair. It felt more wonderful than anything I'd felt with Nadie.

"Whatever happens," she said, "I'm not going anywhere."

"Just ten more months and I'll be back for good," I murmured.

"How can I help you?"

"Marry me."

She snorted a surprised laugh. "You already popped the question? I said *yes,* remember?" She showed me her left hand and wriggled the diamond engagement ring with her thumb.

"No, I mean this visit." I sat up. "Today."

She tilted her head, trying to read my face. "You're really serious."

"I'm not leaving again without making that commitment to you."

"But what about all the … the planning?"

"What planning? We already have the rings. Your parents are in town. The courthouse is open. We'll have our reception in the spring, when I get back. Yes, I'm completely serious."

Daniela looked around in a kind of dazed wonderment.

I took her hands and held them to the center of my chest, where my heart was pounding.

"What do you say?"

She looked at me for a long moment. Then, eyes glimmering, she kissed me and nodded her forehead against mine.

"Let's get married," she whispered.

Acknowledgments

The Blue Wolf Dream Team returned for the third installment, almost to the person. A big thanks to my beta and advanced readers, with special thanks to Beverly Collie and Mark Denman for their helpful feedback; to Ivan Sevic for yet another inspired cover design; to Aaron Sikes for his solid editing; and to Sharlene Magnarella for final proofing.

I also want to thank James Patrick Cronin for his excellent narration of the Prof Croft series and now the Blue Wolf audiobooks.

As always, many thanks to my readers for exploring this universe with me.

About the Author

Brad Magnarella is an author of science fiction and fantasy. His books include the popular Prof Croft novels and his newest urban fantasy series, Blue Wolf. Raised in Gainesville, Florida, he now calls various cities home. He currently lives and writes in Washington, D.C.

www.bradmagnarella.com

BOOKS IN THE CROFTVERSE

THE BLUE WOLF SERIES
Blue Curse

Blue Shadow

Blue Howl

Blue Venom

* More to Come *

THE PROF CROFT SERIES
Book of Souls

Demon Moon

Blood Deal

Purge City

Death Mage

Black Luck

Power Game

Made in the USA
Middletown, DE
07 May 2019